TENNIS SHOES
ADVENTURE SERIES
THE LOST
SCROLLS

TENNIS SHOES
ADVENTURE SERIES
THE LOST SCROLLS

a novel

CHRIS HEIMERDINGER

Covenant Communications, Inc.

Covenant®

Cover illustration by Joe Flores.

Published by Covenant Communications, Inc.
American Fork, Utah

Copyright 1998 by Chris Heimerdinger

Printed in the United States of America
First Printing: November 1998

20 19 18 17 16 15 14   17 16 15 14 13 12 11

ISBN 1-57734-418-9

For my son, Ammon,
the liveliest jewel in my crown

Special thanks to Daniel Rona, Mike Agrelius,
and all the wonderful people at *Israel Revealed Tours*
for the memories of a lifetime
and the testimonies of eternity.

Also to John Gee for his wonderful Greek translations.

PROLOGUE

There was one story in the scriptures that I never understood.

It's a story in the Book of Mormon—that final scene in the last chapter of Ether. My dad read it to Melody, Steffanie, and me once as part of regular scripture study. You know the scene. There are these two armies—one commanded by Shiz, the other by Coriantumr. Millions of people have already been killed. Coriantumr and Shiz write letters to each other trying to negotiate peace, but the people won't hear of it. They still want to fight. Neither side is going to be satisfied until the other is totally wiped off the map.

The battle continues to rage until there are only twenty or thirty warriors remaining on both sides. *Twenty or thirty*—out of *millions!* You'd think by now somebody would get a clue, right? "Hey, almost everyone's dead! Let's just call it a draw and go home!"

Nope. They just kept right on fighting. They fought until there were only two guys left—just Coriantumr and Shiz. Finally Coriantumr slays Shiz, and the whole thing is over. Coriantumr wanders the earth alone for the next several moons, and finally dies of old age among the people of Mulek. End of story.

Can you believe it? It's almost too much to accept! I mean, who would be crazy enough to watch millions of their own people get slaughtered and not try to put a stop to it. It's almost like the people were possessed. They were so full of hatred and bitterness and resentment that they could no longer control their own actions. The whole thing seemed ludicrous. *No one* could feel that much hate. No one could become so blind that they'd actually bring about their own destruction, right? Eventually *someone* would recognize what was happening and let common sense win out, wouldn't they?

When my dad first read it, I remember I shook my head. I even wondered if the story was somehow inaccurate. Maybe when it was condensed down to fifteen chapters, it got simplified to make it more readable. As it was, it just seemed so far-fetched. Almost laughable.

I wasn't laughing now.

I wish I could somehow tear from my mind all the things I've seen. I wish I could keep them from haunting my dreams. After all, no one should have to carry those kinds of images in their head, especially at fifteen years old.

But even before I saw these things, I was no stranger to tragedy. When I was only ten, I witnessed one of the greatest natural disasters in the history of the world. I watched as thunder and fire and wind and lava rained down upon the land of the Nephites, entirely obliterating a wicked city called Jacobugath. And yet the things I'd seen on the opposite side of the world could hardly compare to this.

The disaster in Jacobugath was terrible. But the people, though guilty of horrible sins, had no idea it was coming. Some didn't even know what had hit them. There was nothing they could have done.

The disaster I witnessed in Judea was of a different kind. To start with, it was anything but natural. The people knew exactly what was going to hit them. They could have done everything in the world to prevent it. Instead, they'd actually egged it on. They'd encouraged it until everything was gone—their beautiful city, their way of life, and God's holy temple.

From the very outset, their cause had no chance for success. To everyone else, this was obvious. But not to them. Common sense no longer ruled in the people's hearts. They fought among themselves as much as they fought the enemy. Like the people of Ether, they were consumed with hatred. I think they were even drunk with it. So drunk they couldn't see straight.

And yet, it still seems incredible that up to the very end—to the very last minute—the people still believed that God would save them. They knew with absolute certainty that He would come down from heaven and rain fire on the invaders, rescuing them from their horrible fate. But the fires of heaven never came. It must have seemed as if God had forgotten them.

But He hadn't forgotten. He'd already come. He'd been there just thirty-six years before. And in their midst He was crucified.

Yes, God had already saved them. He'd even warned them of the fate that awaited their nation. But only a few had been able to hear.

Still, despite all that I saw—the smoke and fire, the suffering and death—I recall that the scriptures spoke of another day. A day that's just beginning to dawn. A day when this nation and this people will rise again. And this time, they will know Him.

That's the day I yearn to see. I'll do everything I can to try to bring it about. After all, it's the day and time that I'm from. So I *will* see it. I know I will. There's only one problem. Just one thing I have to do first.

I have to get home.

CHAPTER ONE

This is for posterity, right?

Tell me this is for posterity, 'cause if it ain't, I don't see any reason for going through all this junk all over again by talking about it. It was hard enough the first time. Reliving it won't do anybody any good unless it somehow benefits countless unborn generations of lost and wandering souls who just might find strength and solace by reading my words and saying to themselves, "Just look what my great-great-great-grandmother Meagan went through umpteen years ago. Now see? Stop whining! Life's not as bad as I think!"

I guess I shouldn't be so testy. There were some good things that happened, too. Some really wonderful things. But I've spent the last fifteen years of my life (which includes all of them) developing a reputation as a brooding sourpuss, and I'd hate to kill all those hard-earned perceptions overnight by getting sappy all of a sudden, so let's ignore all that and get down to business.

I suppose I should introduce myself. My name is Meagan Sorenson. I was born in Oregon City, Oregon, and moved to Salt Lake City, Utah, with my mother when I was five. I should also give you an update as to what's happened so far. I know that Harry, in his typical shoeshine-boy fashion, has already given the nitty-gritty details. I'll just give a quick summary and go on from where the story starts to get really interesting. That is, from the point where it's mostly about me.

I suppose it all started when I was nine or ten years old. That's when my mom met this really bizarre but sorta sweet guy named Jim Hawkins. They dated on and off for about five years and then—wallah!—the two of them are suddenly en"gagged" to be married. That was a Pepto Bismol moment, I gotta tell ya. I should have seen it coming from a mile away, but you might say I was a little preoccupied.

The preoccupation was with Jim's son, Harry. He was the youngest of the Hawkins tribe, which included his older sisters Steffanie and Melody. The boy was exactly my age and just dumb enough to be cute and cute enough to be dumb. I know, I know. It seems rather beneath me to confess that I actually had a crush on a male of the human species, but when you see a fairly gnarly-looking guy practically every day of your life because his dad is dating your mom, your mind starts doing weird things, so I can't take full responsibility for the lapse in sanity.

Needless to say, I was just a bit peeved to think that my secret crush might become my real-life brother. If I'd wanted a brother in this life, I'd have bought a cardboard cut-out and stood it up in my closet. Fortunately, Harry was too dense to realize I had a crush on him. But I was afraid that his sisters had noticed and dropped a hint. Any way you looked at it, it was a terribly awkward and depressing situation. In my heart I prayed that something might happen to foil the wedding plans forever.

To my deepest regret, my prayer was answered that very night, and in a way I never wanted or expected. My mom received a phone call telling her that Harry had been in a motorcycle accident with his sister, Melody. His sister was still in the hospital. At first it didn't seem like anything was seriously wrong, but then the pain in Melody's stomach wouldn't go away. A few days later she was diagnosed with ovarian cancer.

The Hawkins family was devastated. It was the same disease that had taken the life of Harry's mother when he was eight. Now they were terrified of losing a sister as well.

Shortly after the operation, my mother and I joined the Hawkins family at the hospital. Melody was in the recovery room, delirious with painkillers. That night she said something very strange. She asked her father, "Is Marcos with you?"

The question seemed to come out of nowhere. I'd never heard the name of Marcos in all the years I'd known Melody. The mere mention of the name made everybody in the Hawkins family very nervous. When I asked Harry who Marcos was, he became very defensive and told me to mind my own business.

Something weird was going on. I could feel it in my bones. From that moment on, I watched Harry like a hawk.

The next morning I spied him trying to skip school by hiding out in a clubhouse across the street from my house. Later, he snuck out again and made his way home. Of course, I felt a moral obligation to find out what he was up to. When I crept into his garage, I found that he'd packed up a whole bunch of camping gear and tied it to the back of his rickety Honda motorcycle.

He almost flipped out when he saw me. Still, he refused to tell me what was going on. He screeched off on his motorcycle and left me standing there in his driveway. Well, I wasn't about to be brushed off so easily. I ran home and hopped on my own motorcycle—a much superior Yamaha 200—and followed him at a safe distance up Parley's Canyon. Along the way Harry's chariot threw a rod in the middle of I-80, forcing him to sputter off to the side of the road. Naturally I offered him the hand of rescue, which he took grudgingly. He agreed to let me drive him to his destination— though only on the condition that once we arrived, I would drop him off, turn my bike around, and mosey on home. Yeah, right. I'm gonna make a drive like that without getting some answers? I don't think so! I agreed to his terms, though he might have missed the fingers crossed behind my back. Or was it my toes?

Eight hours later we arrived at the foot of a mountain near Cody, Wyoming. I followed Harry all the way up the mountain, *ignoring his pleas and protests to go home, until we finally reached a deep, dark, dusty cavern.*

This was the first time I really wondered if Harry was off his rocker. He kept tight-lipped about everything, hoping, I think, that I'd just give up, get scared, and go home. But this only riled me all the more. If Harry was going inside that cave, so was I.

An hour later, as we stood on a narrow shelf overlooking a bottomless pit, I grabbed his collar and demanded an explanation. He tried to give me this goofy story about how these tunnels were a secret passageway to Book of Mormon times. Did he think I was an idiot? I felt like beating him against the wall like a car mat. But Harry wouldn't budge. He said he'd already told me where we were going, and if I wasn't willing to accept it, he had nothing else to say.

I almost went back, but my pride wouldn't let me. I still believed the answer to this mystery would start to reveal itself at any second. That second didn't arrive until we reached a room deep in the cavern that glittered like the lights of Las Vegas. Harry called it the Rainbow Room and promised me that our journey was almost at an end. Actually, this was where the whole discombobulated adventure began.

We heard moaning in the caverns and discovered this he-man, warrior dude lying injured in the tunnel. Harry actually knew the guy! His name was Gidgiddonihah, or some such thing. Harry said he'd met him during an adventure among the Nephites four years before. The man was delirious and asked Harry if he'd seen Marcos. Apparently the man was traveling with Marcos through the cavern when they were attacked by a band of men called Pochteca. Harry seemed to know what he was talking about, but I didn't have a clue.

Harry took off to get the guy a drink of water so there I was, left alone with Conan the Nephite, when suddenly the tunnels were swarming with all these Arab guys holding nasty-looking knives. They dragged Gidgiddonihah off, and then one of them came after me. I beaned the jerk with a rock, knocking him cold just long enough for Harry to find me. Harry, like the typical brainless male that he is, insisted that we go after Gid. Soon we found ourselves in the midst of a room more glorious and beautiful than anything I ever could have imagined—an enormous room filled with swirling bands of colored energy all rotating around a massive, glowing ball like a miniature galaxy!

About now I'm this blithering, freaked-out zombie—though I did have the presence of mind to scream when the man I had beaned with the rock rushed us from behind. Five or six more goons appeared from an opening in the wall ahead. We were trapped!

Harry and I tried to run, but the thin floor fell out from under us, and we were sucked into an underground river. My lungs filled with water, and that's the last thing I remember. When I woke up again we were outside—but not in Wyoming. Instead it was a desolate, lifeless valley that might as well have been Mars. Harry didn't seem to know if it was the land of the Nephites or Timbuktu.

I solved the mystery a short time later when we arrived at an enormous blue lake whose water was the vilest, saltiest, bitterest stuff I'd ever tasted. That's when I remembered the posters at my mother's beauty salon—the ones advertising facial packs from the Dead Sea. It was the Dead Sea! Somehow that cavern had transported us to the land of Jerusalem in 70 A.D.!

I figured out the year, too. We met two fugitives from Jerusalem in the ruins of Qumran—a Jew named Barsabas and his nine-year-old grandson, Jesse. Barsabas was a Christian. He'd just rescued eleven scrolls from a secret library in Jerusalem that he claimed were written by the apostles of Jesus Christ. He said Jerusalem was under siege. Apparently the Romans wanted to turn the place into a parking lot. Barsabas was being chased by a group of bizarre, religious fruitcakes who called themselves the Sons of the Elect. They were looking for a particular scroll called the Scroll of Knowledge, and they thought Barsabas had it. Supposedly it was a record of the secret teachings of Jesus after His resurrection.

Barsabas had actually left this scroll in Jerusalem. But this didn't stop the Sons of the Elect from shooting him with an arrow. In his dying breath, Barsabas begged Harry and me to take the sacred scrolls and get them into the hands of an apostle. Unfortunately, the Sons of the Elect arrived and stripped the scrolls out of our hands. In their frustration at not finding the Scroll of Knowledge, they burned the sacred testimonies one by one. In the end, with the help of Jesse, we were only able to save a single one. Later we discovered that it was the only existing copy of "The Gospel According to Matthew"!

The Sons of the Elect were certain that if we'd gone to the trouble to save it, it must be their precious Scroll of Knowledge. So now we had a bunch of bald-headed nutcases on our tail as we escaped and began our journey toward a city called Pella. This was where all the Christians from Judea had supposedly settled to wait out the war.

On the way we got cornered by the leader of the Sons of the Elect, Simon Magus. His wardrobe suggested that he was trying to imitate the Savior Jesus Christ, but his face looked like a cross between Rip Van Winkle and a zombie from Night of the Living Dead. *He demanded that we give him the scroll or his archer would kill us all.*

Again, with God's help, we managed to escape. For the next three days we traveled through the war-ravaged land until we finally arrived at Pella. We did not, however, receive the kind of welcome we might have expected.

The Christians at Pella didn't want anything to do with us. It was their belief that Jesus had come to save the Jews alone. Fortunately the Bishop, a man named Symeon, was a little more tolerant. He was an actual nephew of Joseph and Mary. A cousin of Jesus! He invited us into his home where we met his daughter, Mary, and his wife, Anna, who was gravely ill. We showed him the gospel of Matthew. I thought we'd almost convinced him of the errors of his people's ways when his house was suddenly stormed by the Elders of Pella, who demanded that Symeon burn the scroll on the fire.

At the last minute Symeon gave it to an old prophet named Agabus. Agabus urged us to take the Book of Matthew to the region of the Seven Churches in Asia Minor and give it to the Apostle John. These Seven Churches, he explained, were the last strongholds of truth and authority in all the land.

The next morning the Sons of the Elect attacked. Jesse and I were taken captive while Harry was left with an impossible mission—find the Scroll of Knowledge and bring it to a mountain called Gerizim. He had only ten days to do it, or Jesse and I would be sacrificed.

That's where we left off. Jesse and I had become the prisoners of a band of religious wackos whose entire existence was consumed by getting their hands on the Scroll of Knowledge. As to what had happened to Harry, Jesse and I had no clue. I might have hoped he was on his way to Jerusalem to find the Scroll of Knowledge, but I didn't have the courage to believe it. Jerusalem was a city surrounded by tens of thousands of blood-thirsty Romans. Even if Harry got there, the chances of getting inside seemed out of the question. And even if he did, the chances that he might ever get out again seemed astronomical. Most tragically for Harry, the entire purpose for which he had come on this journey—to find Marcos and bring him back to his sister—appeared to have failed.

I felt I knew only one thing for sure. If I was to survive beyond the next ten days, I couldn't count on anyone to save me. If I was to survive, it would have to be by my own wits. My own tenacity and perseverance. So that, my friends, was exactly what I intended to do.

Only two things threatened to stop me. First, my fear. I was nearly catatonic with terror. Second—and this was probably more life-threatening than the first—my uncanny ability to get on people's nerves. Though I must confess, if I had to die anyway, nothing was going to give me greater pleasure than to think I might, in the process, drive my captors absolutely crazy.

CHAPTER TWO

Marcos was gone.

As I watched the gold and crimson sun sink behind the Samaritan hills, I thought of my friend and how much I envied him. It had been a very short reunion. Less than half a day. And yet as I recalled the marvelous events that had made it possible for me to send Marcos home to be with my sister, my heart soared with gratitude.

After Simon Magus had kidnapped Meagan and Jesse, I'd thought all my hopes of ever finding Marcos and Gidgiddonihah, or even of ever going home, had been completely shattered. It wasn't ten hours later that I found them both in an obscure village called Salim. They were among the prisoners slated to fight to the death with professional gladiators.

Marcos defeated both of his hulking opponents. When the crowd demanded that he be torn to shreds by a five-hundred-pound lion, I set the lion free, scattering everyone in the square. In the confusion, Marcos, Gidgiddonihah, and I fled into the hills.

Marcos was deeply grieved when I told him about Melody, and he made up his mind to set out for the modern century. Gidgiddonihah, to my ultimate relief, agreed to go with me to Jerusalem to try to save Meagan and Jesse.

It was hard to believe it had all happened only the day before yesterday. Marcos had left us yesterday morning, as promised. I wasn't sure if he would ever reach my sister or not. But at least I had found him. As I watched the western sky deepen into darker shades of red, I tried to comfort myself that I had succeeded in my original mission.

Comfort didn't come easy. I'd have given anything to have gone home with Marcos that morning. Fate had other plans. I stiffened my jaw for the task that lay ahead. I could do it, I told myself. I could save Meagan and Jesse. My heart was listening. My brain, however, was another matter. Even with Gidgiddonihah, I just couldn't see how I could possibly reach Jerusalem, find the Scroll of Knowledge, and take it Mount Gerizim in time. I didn't even know where Mount Gerizim was.

Gidgiddonihah sat by the fire constructing a makeshift sheath for the Roman sword he'd taken from the gladiator trainer named Problius during our escape from Salim. His intention was to wrap it in an old piece of tent canvas that we'd found along the trail and hang it behind his shoulder, much like the obsidian-edged swords from his homeland.

"You know," I said to him, "Romans like to hang those things at their belts."

Gid scoffed. "Only a short sword can be hung at the belt. On my hip I could never draw it as quickly."

I realized this was probably true. Still, that edge wasn't dull. I'd have been worried that by drawing it too quickly, I'd cut off my own head. The sword was a beautiful weapon. I wondered if Problius had won it by crushing some gladiator superstar back in his younger days. The ball of the hilt had no less than seven jewels—six emeralds and one ruby. Problius' name was engraved on the handgrip. At least, I think it was his name. The letters were in Latin. No doubt the old buzzard would have been eager to get it back if we ever ran into him again.

I stared at Gidgiddonihah in awe. I still couldn't believe he was here. Just his presence buoyed up my spirits. And yet Gid knew less about this land than I did. I certainly couldn't count on him to act as a guide. Earlier that day we'd interrupted several farmers to ask if this road would eventually lead to Jerusalem. They looked at us like we were nuts for choosing such a destination, but confirmed that it would indeed connect up with the main highway to the capital a few leagues farther on.

It wasn't Gid's savvy as a guide that I was counting on. It was his skill as a fighter, as well as his knowledge of how to survive in an ancient world.

No, it was more than that. There was something mystical about Gidgiddonihah. I couldn't have explained it. It was sort of like Ammon from the Book of Mormon. Or better yet, like one of the stripling warriors of Helaman. I almost believed he was invincible. No matter how intense things got, Gid's presence made me feel like everything would come out all right. Maybe it was just a touch of hero worship. I had to remind myself that he was just a mere mortal, like the rest of us.

Our camp was on the summit of a small hill, just high enough to give us a clear view of the surrounding fields in case someone tried to sneak up on us. A cool breeze was blowing out of the west, fanning the tall, dry grass. To the south the light of the sunset almost made it look like the fields were on fire. The thought gave me a chill. In that direction lay Jerusalem.

I moved closer to the fire and took off my sandals. Then I massaged my aching and blistered feet. Man, I missed my Nikes. Two days ago I'd had to trade them in Salim. The unique treads made my trail too easy to follow. I was sure that was how Simon and the Sons of the Elect had found us at the River Jordan. These sandals had much thinner soles than my sneakers. I felt every pebble. It might take a while before my feet became properly calloused. Unfortunately, I didn't have a while. After today, there were only seven days left to complete my mission. My feet would just have to hold out.

Gid had a thoughtful look on his face. For the last two days he'd been satisfied with only brief explanations of what we had to do. Our destination was looming closer. He decided it was time to demand a few more details.

"So this Scroll of Knowledge," he began. "You say it's in a secret hiding place inside the ruins of a house once owned by Jesus Christ?"

"By His brother," I corrected. "I mean, His *half*-brother. His name was James. Apparently after James was killed, somebody burned his house. But the sacred books were protected inside some sort of vault."

"Do you know where in Jerusalem this house is to be found?"

I shook my head. I'd been so worried about just getting *inside* the city that I hadn't given a whole lot of thought as to how to find the burned-out house. "We'll have to ask someone when we get there."

Gid stared at me. I felt like an idiot. Surely Jerusalem covered several square miles. After so many months of being bombarded by the Romans, there might be *hundreds* of burned-out houses. I felt certain there were no Christians inside the city. The Christians had all fled to places like Pella until the Savior's prophecy of the destruction of Jerusalem and the temple was fulfilled. It seemed unlikely that there was anybody living there who even *remembered* a man like James.

"Are you sure the scroll is still there?" asked Gid.

"That's what I was told. I have to believe it's true."

"What does this scroll say?"

I swallowed. This was the one subject I wished I could have avoided. Yet I had to tell Gid everything I knew. "Jesse's grandfather, Barsabas, told us it was the sayings of Jesus after His resurrection. He believed that for forty days Jesus taught His apostles the secrets and mysteries of the universe."

Gid looked skeptical. "And this Barsabas was a good man? A righteous man?"

"Yes," I said. "At least I think so. He'd fallen away from the Church for a few years, but he was trying to make things right again by rescuing the testimonies of the apostles."

"But his efforts failed."

"It wasn't his fault," I defended. "And he *did* save the Book of Matthew." I indicated my shoulder sack where the fragile parchment scroll was still protected inside two tube socks.

"Why didn't he try to save the Scroll of Knowledge?" asked Gid.

"He *did* try. But then the Romans surrounded the city. He said he had to leave other scrolls behind, too."

"And this scroll is to be used as a ransom?"

"Yes," I said, shifting nervously. "It's the only way the Sons of the Elect will ever set Meagan and Jesse free."

Gid sighed deeply. He looked very doubtful. "Perhaps we should forget this scroll and just find this mountain called Gerizim. We could ambush them when they arrive and force them to tell us where they're hiding your companions. They might even bring your companions with them. We could stage a rescue—"

I shook my head anxiously. "Simon Magus is too smart for that. He doesn't trust me as it is. I feel certain if we don't come to Mount Gerizim with the scroll in hand, Meagan and Jesse will be killed."

Gid leaned forward and said bluntly, "Who's to say if you give him the scroll that he won't try to kill them anyway? You say this man is a sorcerer? A servant of evil? Who's to say he won't try to kill us *all*?"

I just sat there. I didn't know what to reply.

"Forgive me, Harry, son of Jimhawkins," said Gid. "I will do all I can to protect you and save your companions. But it will serve neither you nor your friends if we both rush headlong into the jaws of death. Nor will it serve anyone if I help you to offend God by recovering a sacred book only to give it into the hands of the devil!"

He'd expressed the irony so well that I'd almost forgotten the true reason I was going through with it. "It's what the Lord told me to do," I said firmly. "I don't know why or what's going to happen, but I know I'm supposed to go to Jerusalem. I realize it doesn't make any sense. And if you ask me what we're supposed to do once we find the scroll, I couldn't give you an answer. All I know is that this is what I've got to do—alone if I have to."

Gidgiddonihah let my words hang in the air. The guy had a way of making you shake in your boots even if he *agreed* with you. Nevertheless, I didn't break eye contact.

"All right Harry," he said finally. "We will go to Jerusalem. We will find this scroll. And we will leave the rest in the hands of the Lord. You're not a boy anymore, son of Jimhawkins. I'll never treat you like one again."

That was that. Gid never questioned the prudence of what we were doing again. As night settled in, we ate a meal of barley gruel and fig cakes and contemplated the day ahead. The weight of responsibility on my shoulders felt heavier than ever. I thought back again on my prayer three days before on the banks of the Jordan River as my mind was reeling in panic over Meagan and Jesse's abduction. Had I really been inspired to go to Jerusalem?

Yes. There was no reason to doubt. I knew what I was doing.

Before I fell asleep in the tall grass, I thought again of Gid's promise not to treat me like a boy, and I felt a pang of regret. A part of me desperately wanted to remain a boy forever. I guess I couldn't stop the hands of time. In two days we'd be at the walls of Jerusalem. Jerusalem was no place for a boy. Like it or not, tomorrow I would have to become a man.

CHAPTER THREE

When my eyelids fluttered open, I was engulfed by total dark-ness. I was sure I'd gone blind. Whatever drug they'd forced me to take had stolen my eyesight! My muscles felt as weak as a baby's. I could hardly move. Simon Magus and his wackos had left me both crippled and blind!

"Help!" I cried hoarsely, trying to sit up.

I heard a voice in the blackness. "Meagan?"

"Jesse!" I replied. "Jesse, where are you?"

I felt his fingers touching my elbow. The fingers slid down my arm until they could grasp my hand.

"Jesse, I can't see!"

"I can't see either," said Jesse.

"What did they do? Are we blind?"

"No," said Jesse. "It's just where they put us."

"Where are we?"

"I'm not sure. Some kind of cave. I remember seeing the light of their torches when they laid us here. Then they left."

I could feel the strength start returning to my muscles. I touched Jesse's warm face. I wrapped my arms around his nine-year-old shoulders. "Have they sealed us in? Why isn't there any light? Where's the entrance?"

"I don't remember," said Jesse. "I was too groggy."

The chamber smelled moldy. The ground was damp and cold. I started shivering. "We have to get out of here. I can't take this. I'll go crazy!"

"Don't worry," said Jesse bravely. "I'll search around. Maybe there's a way out."

He started to crawl away.

"Wait!" I screeched, digging my nails into his wrist. "Don't leave me alone!"

"All right," he said. "We'll search together. Don't be frightened."

I felt embarrassed. A nine-year-old kid was telling me not to be frightened. I should have been comforting him.

"Keep a hold of my hand," I insisted.

I started to feel confident that I wasn't blind. Not that I could see my hand in front of my face any better. But somehow, maybe by instinct, I perceived that there was depth out there. Cautiously, weakly, I rose to my feet. Jesse stayed with me. I used my free arm to feel around in all directions. I'd never felt so vulnerable. So insecure. I could easily have stepped over a cliff or stuck my hand into a nest of scorpions. What was this place? Why did they bring us here? Would we be stuck in here the entire time, with no food or water?

My hand jammed into a hard stone wall. It was covered with a gross, moldy film. I swallowed hard to keep from heaving. Oh, this was disgusting! What was this place!

I finally felt secure enough to let go of Jesse's hand, allowing me to use both arms to search for obstacles. "Stay close," I ordered Jesse. "And keep talking."

I felt along the greasy, filmy wall an inch at a time, sliding my feet to keep from tripping. Jesse had moved away from me about a yard.

"There's another wall over here!" he announced.

It was a corridor of some sort. But where did it lead? As I continued to feel along the stones, I came to a gap where a block was missing, leaving a space about two feet square. I did not want to reach my hand into that gap. But I had no choice. It might be a passageway, like an air duct or something. My fingers were tangled up in spider webs immediately. My body went as rigid as a corpse. Then my hand ran into a back wall. The gap only went in about two feet. My arm also knocked something over. It sounded like a clay pot. I latched onto it and rolled it in my hands. It was some sort of bowl with three legs. I felt inside the lid. The contents were very fine and ashy. Oh, no, I cried inwardly. Don't tell me it's an urn and I've just stuck my hand into a dead person's ashes!

Reluctantly, I smelled it. It was sort of a mentholatum smell, but milder. Inside the shelf I also felt melted wax. Apparently it was some sort of place for burning candles and incense.

"There's a stairway here!" said Jesse. He sounded about ten or twelve feet down the wall.

"Going up or down?" I asked.

"Up," he said.

Up was good. I could live with up. Down was another story. I couldn't imagine anything good going down.

"Wait for me." I moved hastily to catch up. Suddenly my foot slipped. I shrieked and dug my nails into the greasy wall. My foot landed on a step below.

"I thought you said it went up! The stairs go down!"

"Down?" said Jesse, baffled. "Not over here. Over here they go up."

Great, I muttered under my breath. The stairway divided in the middle, like a split-level house. One side went up and the other down.

"I found the middle," Jesse announced. "We can go either way."

"We'll go up!" I insisted. I reached out. "Where are you?"

He found my hand and pulled me over to his side. I pressed against the wall, practically hugging the thing.

"This way," said Jesse. He held my hand tightly, this time determined not to let go.

We started climbing. After ten steps, Jesse declared, "The wall ends. There's a room."

"A room?"

This was getting more complex with every step. The place was a *labyrinth! We could get so lost that not even Simon and his cronies would be able to find us.*

"Should we go in?" asked Jesse.

"Do we have any choice?"

I knew two steps sideways would send us plunging into the other stairwell. Jesse led the way into the room. After a few more steps, he said, "Wait. There's something . . ."

He moved to the right. I continued forward. My knees collided with a low stone shelf. I reached out with my left hand and felt a bundle of cloth—very old and deteriorated.

"Don't touch it!" said Jesse urgently.

It was too late. My fingers penetrated the cloth and grasped a thin, brittle object, like a stick. No one needed to tell me it was a piece of bone. No one needed to tell me it was human.

I jerked away, my flesh crawling. This place was a crypt! A tomb! Simon had imprisoned us inside a catacomb!

"Get me out of here!" I yelled. "I have to get out of here!"

I turned around, prepared to bolt. Fortunately, Jesse caught me. He led me back out onto the stairway. I'd lost my sense of direction. Any second I expected to run smack into a hanging skeleton or a half-decomposed body. As we reached the stairway, Jesse determined that it continued going up. Groping in the dark, he led me to the topmost step.

"Bend down," he warned. I bumped my forehead anyway.

The passage forced us to arch our backs. Then the channel started winding to the left, and the ceiling steadily sloped up until we could stand again.

I saw a sliver of light. What a glorious sight! And yet it was so thin, the corridor wasn't illuminated by it at all. The passage was a dead end. Or maybe it was an exit that had been blocked by a large stone.

"Push!" I said. "Help me! Push!"

We pushed with all our might. The stone wouldn't budge; it was wedged into place like a cork. I wasn't sure if the sliver of light at the upper edge came from the sun or from the light of a torch in a tunnel beyond.

I started to feel claustrophobic.

"Hey!" I screamed. "Is anyone out there! Hey!"

I pounded my fist on the stone, producing no sound at all. I found a broken piece of mortar on the floor and crashed it against the stone.

"Hey! Please! We can't breathe! Get us out of here! Please!"

Jesse joined in the yelling. "Help! Anyone! We're trapped!"

In the midst of all our ranting, the corridor suddenly filled with firelight.

I spun around in dread, certain that some corpse had come back from the dead to feed on the living. For an instant, the face that met our eyes did nothing to convince me otherwise. Then I recognized the shrunken skull painted with only the thinnest layer of skin and the deep yellow eyewells with the coal-black pupils. It was the cancer-eaten mug of Simon Magus. Behind him stood two of his most devoted stooges—the broad-shouldered, shrill-voiced Menander, with the protruding Adam's apple, and the grizzle-bearded Saturninus, with the hair growing out his nose and ears. Menander and Saturninus both carried torches. The fire reflected off their bald heads. Simon appeared to be the only one in this outfit who had the privilege of growing hair, though it was as thin as spider webs and as white as ash. He was still wearing the white robe that I swore was meant to mock Jesus Christ.

"Awake, I see," Simon observed in his wheezing voice. "Good. Very good."

I shaded my eyes from the sudden light. Jesse covered his eyes, too, his forehead scrunched up in an angry scowl.

"How did you get in here?" I demanded, trying to sound defiant.

"That's not important," said Simon. "Still trying to play the stubborn maiden, I see. Perhaps a few more days in here will make you a bit more agreeable."

"I doubt it, you piece of slime. When this is over, you're gonna kill us anyway. So what does it matter?"

"Oh, ye of little faith," he replied. "Don't you trust your friend Harry to bring me what I want? If he fails, I've sadly underestimated his attachment to you."

"I hope he brings your scroll and puts a torch to it right in front of your eyes."

Menander stepped forward as if to strike me.

"No, Menander," Simon ordered.

Menander reluctantly obeyed. "I can no longer tolerate her blasphemy, your Holiness. She should be beaten until she shows proper respect!"

"Some fillies are best left unbroken," said Simon. "You might squelch their fire, make them far less attractive. This one might serve us better if her fire is allowed to burn." He addressed me again. "Still, I find it hard to believe that you would rather remain here, among the souls of the damned when you could be basking in the lap of luxury with the immortal blessed."

"Better here than anyplace where I'd have to smell you all day," I retorted.

Menander seethed. Simon only chuckled. He'd read me well. He knew how disgusting I found this place. I knew his offer had conditions. I cringed to imagine what they might be.

"What do you want from me?" I asked.

"Good," said Simon. "Right to the point. No mincing words. My demands are simple. We still have the unfinished business of your 'toys.'"

Toys. He was referring to all the modern-day gadgets and gizmos he'd stolen from Harry: duct tape, pliers, pocketknife, cassette player—he probably had the flashlight now, too, and anything else Harry had brought. Back near Jericho he'd wanted us to tell him the name of the blacksmith who'd forged such tools so he could learn their "secrets." Simon was no fool. He knew an opportunity when he saw it. *Knowledge was power. Nothing thrilled these goons more than knowing secrets that nobody else know. No doubt they considered Harry and me a remarkable pair—maybe even a threat.*

Simon continued. *"If you will reveal all the secrets of these objects, I will give you opportunities for knowledge and power beyond your wildest dreams."*

"Oh, is that so?" I said tiredly. *"Listen, bucko. I have more knowledge and power in my little finger than you've got in your whole worm-eaten body."*

Simon leaned in, his eyes wild with confirmation. *"You have read the scroll! I knew it! You have gleaned its powers!"*

I drew in my chin. What was he talking about? Suddenly it hit me. Of course! He thought we'd gotten our "toys" and any other strange talents we possessed from reading the Scroll of Knowledge. Little did he know, we hadn't even seen the thing.

It occurred to me, I really did have more knowledge than he could ever dream. A wicked little idea began percolating in my brain. Oh, this was too choice! Too exquisite. The possibilities were endless! Merlin, Gandalf, and Nostradamus, eat your heart out! Make way for Meagan the Magnificent!

"The Scroll of Knowledge is nothing," I declared. *"The things I know—the powers I possess—could knock all you guys out of your shorts. I'll be the one who makes the deals around here. You get us out of this place, give us a warm bath, some clean clothes, hot food, and a pair of comfortable beds, and I might consider showing you all an evening you'll never forget."*

I gazed right into Simon's beady little eyes. For an instant—just an instant—I thought I might have seen intimidation. Saturninus made no effort to hide the mesmerized look on his face. In Menander I saw only contempt.

Simon smiled. *Intimidated? The whole idea suddenly evaporated. The malevolence in his eyes sent a chill up my spine. I swallowed. Had I forgotten? I'd seen this guy walk through a pack of blood-thirsty hyenas. I'd seen him snap Jesse's javelin in half when Jesse was standing fifty yards away from him. I feared I'd thrown down the gauntlet in a very dangerous game.*

The urge to pray came over me. This was almost a surprise. I'd never been all that religious before. I'd thought more about God in the last week than I had in my entire life. I realized if I was going to take on Simon Magus, I needed an ally. I needed to talk to God. Little did I know, Simon was about to give me just such an opportunity.

"I think," he began, "another night in these corridors might make you somewhat more willing to 'knock us out of our shorts' without so many conditions."

He turned on his heel. Menander smirked and followed. Saturninus hesitated. His eyes seemed to ask, "Why are you being such a fool?" Then he, too, turned and departed. My heart wilted. I'd pushed too hard. Why couldn't I just be sweet and nice once in a while? I was about to call out, "Wait! I take it back! I'll do anything you ask! Just get us out of here!"

Pride made me bite my tongue. Savage, stubborn pride. I wasn't gonna let them beat me. I still had the upper hand, even if they didn't know it.

"Don't count on it, scabhead!" I yelled. "You'll be lucky if I teach you how to tie your own shoelaces! You hear me?"

Jesse was nearly beside himself. "Why must you provoke them? You'll get us killed!"

The light from their torches was fading fast.

"Come on!" I said. "We have to follow them!"

Within seconds we were bustling through the corridor and back down the stone stairway. Simon and his men were already descending the second stairway that curved underneath. We rushed past the vault containing the skeleton, still following the torchglow. At the bottom of the second stairway loomed another passage with more tombs and skeletons. The torchlight was disappearing! We entered a wide tunnel with dripping water. I heard a deep grinding echo, as if some heavy stone was sliding back into place. The light snuffed out. We were again engulfed by darkness. We hadn't moved fast enough. We hadn't seen the way out! Another night in this dungeon looked inevitable.

"Jesse!" I cried. "Jesse, where are you!"

He touched my arm. I grabbed his hand.

"I'm sorry," I said. "I'm sorry I couldn't get us out of here."

"Don't provoke them anymore," he begged, "or we'll starve in here."

"We're not going to starve," I assured him. "They're afraid of me, Jesse. Can't you feel it? That's why they're doing this. You have to trust me. Soon I'll have every one of them wrapped around my finger."

"Are you sure?" he asked.

His faith sounded strained. Jesse had once called me a prophetess. He'd drawn the conclusion when I told him that Titus, the Roman general, would one day become Emperor. I knew he wanted to believe every word I said. But was it misleading to let him think I was certain about anything?

And yet Simon's interest had been piqued. I was sure of it. He wanted desperately to know what I knew. It was like an itch the guy couldn't scratch. From here on out I'd play my cards very carefully. But I would not give in or change my tactics.

Tomorrow would be a very interesting day. I could feel it in my bones. I just had to get through one more miserable night of darkness without losing my mind.

CHAPTER FOUR

The next morning Gidgiddonihah and I were up with the sun. As we made our way southward, all the grim signs of war began to appear again, just as they had in the Jordan Valley. The farther we walked, the worse it seemed to get—towns reduced to rubble, women mourning over freshly dug graves, children along the roadside latching onto our cloaks to beg for food. So much misery and suffering. I wished I could save all of them, carry them all home to the modern world, make all their dreams come true. It was just too much to hope.

The farther south we ventured, the fewer trees studded the hillsides. They'd all been hacked down. Finally we crossed a boundary where there were no trees left at all. Just mile after mile of severed stumps, as if God had mowed down all the forests with a cosmic lawnmower. I felt sure that the landscape of Judea had once been teeming with forests and groves. Now all of them were gone. We spotted a caravan of wagons loaded down with timber; it was headed south with a garrison of heavily armed Roman soldiers. The siege at Jerusalem must have required every ounce of available wood in the countryside.

"What do you think all the trees are for?" I asked Gid.

"Fortifications," he replied. "When I was young I helped my uncle, Gidgiddoni, fell trees for the fortifications of Zarahemla to defend against the Gadiantons. But I've never seen devastation quite like this. At least not by the hand of man."

We tried to steer clear of Roman soldiers whenever we saw them, but it was becoming harder and harder to avoid them. If they weren't marching from place to place in formations of a hundred or more, they were guarding mule-drawn wagons filled with food and supplies. Once we saw what looked like a caravan of coffins heading north. It looked like the Romans shipped bodies all the way back to Italy to be buried by loved ones. Finally we abandoned the road altogether and took to the foothills. The last thing I wanted to do was get into a scrape with some overly curious soldiers.

Around mid-afternoon, we reached a ragged-looking village with empty streets and hollow buildings. Now and then we'd catch a glimpse of some inhabitant behind a window or around a corner, mostly the very old or the very young. They didn't much like the look of strangers—especially strangers with a sword the size of Gidgiddonihah's. I had a feeling the only people around here with swords were soldiers or bandits, neither of whom were very popular. They'd probably both had a turn at ransacking the place.

We located a spring near the center of the village, enclosed by a barrier of old, weathered stones. Several mangy dogs growled at our approach. We scattered them with stones. Afterwards, I took the pleasure of burying my sweaty face in cool water. It tasted wonderful and felt good on my sunburn. I sure missed my sunscreen. Like everything else, it had been stolen by Simon Magus.

After I refilled my water pouch, we stood and found ourselves face to face with a dark-haired woman in a threadworn dress. She had a long scar that ran down her forehead and across the bridge of her nose. In the background I could see two small children—both girls—peering over the top of a low stone wall.

"Please," the woman begged. "My children are starving. Can you spare a few coins? Perhaps a little food?"

My heart ached for them. It was the same question we'd been asked a hundred times already.

"We don't have enough even for ourselves," I tried to say sympathetically.

The woman smiled sorrowfully and started to walk back toward her children.

"Wait," called Gidgiddonihah.

She turned back. Gid reached over his shoulder and pulled the sword out of its hide sheath. The woman raised her arm in fear. The children also looked terrified.

"No, no," Gid reassured her. He turned the blade down. "I mean you no harm."

The woman lowered her arm, still apprehensive.

"May I see your knife?" Gid asked.

There was a knife with a bone handle in her sash. It looked more like an eating utensil. She gave it to him cautiously. Gid laid his sword down on the wall and used the knife to pry two of the jeweled stones out of their setting. After they popped out, he held them toward her.

"Here," he said. "These will feed your children."

The woman didn't know what to say. Finally she worked up the nerve to snatch them out of Gid's palm. She was about to dash off, afraid, I guess, that Gid might change his mind. At the last second she paused.

"Thank you," she said, her eyes looking down. Then she retreated hastily. Her small daughters scurried after her, enthusiastically asking if they might have a peek.

Gid replaced the sword in its wrapping. He realized I was staring at him.

"Are you ready?" he asked. "Let's go."

As we left the village, I said, "That was really cool, Gid."

"Cool?"

"Yeah. Nice. By her reaction, I'd say you just fed her family for a very long time."

"Unfortunately, we can't do it very often," said Gid. "We might need some of these jewels just to feed ourselves."

"If I didn't know better, I'd swear you knew that lady from before."

"Oh? How come?"

"I don't know. The way you looked at her."

"Maybe I'm just a softhearted old man," he said wryly. His face suddenly went somber. "She reminded me of someone."

"Someone special?" I asked.

It occurred to me just how little I knew about Gid. I vaguely recalled that he'd been married once, but I didn't think he had any children. He was pretty much a loner in this world. That might have been just as well. I feared the disturbance Meagan and I had created in the Galaxy Room had caused thirty-six years to jump by in the world of the Nephites, just as it had jumped by here. Most everyone Gid had known was likely dead.

"Actually," Gid replied, "it was someone I hated. Someone I wronged very deeply."

I found that hard to believe, but my curiosity was piqued. "Who?"

With difficulty, he said, "The midwife who helped to deliver my son."

I felt sorry I'd brought it up.

Gid continued. "It was the scar." He absently drew a line across the bridge of his nose. "She had a scar very much like that. An injury from her childhood. She hadn't been practicing her profession for very long, but there was no one else available. No one else. . ." His voice trailed off.

"Did . . . did your son die?"

"No." He sighed longingly. "No, the boy lived. For a year anyway. It was my wife, Rebah, who died that day."

After a pause, I said, "I'm sorry."

"I blamed the midwife," Gid continued. "I cursed her and threw her out of my house. Since I was a leader in the army, she feared she might be banned from her profession. So she left Zarahemla. I did nothing to stop her."

"Was it her fault?"

Gid shook his head. "It was no one's fault. No one could have saved my Rebah. It was just her time. A year later I traveled to Gideon to find the woman, to beg her forgiveness. I found only a grave marker. She'd died from the same fever that took the life of my infant son."

I felt a knot in my chest. "I didn't know."

Gid shrugged. "It happened a long time ago."

"You must have loved them a great deal."

Gid looked straight ahead, lost in the memory. "Yes," he said simply.

We continued our journey southward through the treeless hills. I remembered that my dad had once said everybody in this world had hidden pains, so we should never judge too harshly. I'd seen a side of Gidgiddonihah that I hadn't known. Somehow, I liked him even better.

* * *

Late in the afternoon we heard a faint cry.

We stopped in our tracks and looked around. We were in a canyon very near the main road. The sound seemed to echo so I couldn't pinpoint the source. The more experienced ears of Gidgiddonihah honed in on it immediately.

"Over there," he said, indicating a thin trail that went around a rocky bluff.

His radar was confirmed as we heard another sound—the whinny of a horse or mule. The animal was in some sort of distress.

"Stay low," Gid whispered.

We crept up the trail and around the bluff. Gid motioned for me to get down on my hands and knees. We crawled the last ten yards until we could see just over the hill and down into a narrow ravine.

Interpreting the situation took less than a second. Four scrubby-looking men wearing rough cloaks and dark turbans, and armed to the teeth had accosted two travelers on the road and had dragged them into the ravine. One of the victims was an old man, his hands tied behind his back. The other, I gathered from the cries, was a girl. I couldn't see her very well. Two of the bandits stood over her. The last two were trying to rummage through the travel bags strapped to a mule. The mule was kicking up a storm.

My heart started pounding. It was a highway robbery. No doubt these men were the kind of parasites who crawled out of the slime in every war.

"What are we gonna do?" I whispered.

"Shhh," said Gid, still appraising the situation.

The girl's hands were tied as well. She was pleading with her captors. Bile rose in my throat. I could see that the bandits had the vilest intentions. They laughed as the girl struggled, one goading the other to hurry things along.

"Please!" I heard the old man beg. "Please don't do this!"

I crinkled my brow. The voice sounded familiar. I caught my breath. *Oh, my gosh!* I *knew* that man! I knew them both! It was Symeon, the Bishop of Pella! And the girl—oh, the girl!—it was his sixteen-year-old daughter, Mary!

Indignation boiled in my blood like liquid fire. These people were relatives of *Jesus!* A blinding rage took over. I don't even remember rising off my feet. I have only a vague recollection of Gidgiddonihah whispering harshly, *"Harry, wait! Not yet!"*

I started bounding down the slope of the ravine, each step booming in my ears like thunder. My focus riveted on the two men standing over Mary. I had no weapon. I must have thought rage alone would sustain me. I'd tear them apart with my bare hands. I felt prompted to reach down and grab a thick, knotted stick. Then I continued my undeviating course, the bandits bouncing up and down in my vision.

Mary's cries and the mule's kicks kept them unaware of my approach until I was almost on top of them. The two slimeballs fighting with the mule noticed me first, but they looked so surprised by my appearance that they didn't know how to react. I kept right on marching toward the bandit whose back was toward me. He was leaning over Mary, grabbing at her cloak.

His partner turned his head, looking just as baffled.

"Hey," he growled.

The man with his back toward me turned around. He got a chunk of knotted wood right in his teeth. The blow lifted him off his feet. His companion reached inside his tunic, and I saw the flash of a dagger. He lunged at my heart. A blur of color appeared between us. It was Gidgiddonihah, his sword striking downward. The bandit cried out and collapsed.

The man I'd smashed in the face was lying on the ground. He pulled himself to his knees, spitting blood. He made a feeble strike at Gidgiddonihah with his own dagger, but Gid cut short the effort with a single thrust. Both men lay face down in the dirt.

We turned our attention to the last two men. Like the vermin they were, they scrambled up the opposite side of the ravine as fast as their legs would carry them and disappeared over the other side. The mule, overwhelmed by the excitement, bolted back toward the main road.

I went swiftly to Mary. She was lying against the side of the hill, cowering and shivering. Her dress had been torn. Her long black hair was tangled with dirt and twigs. I untied her hands.

"It's all right, Mary," I said soothingly. "Do you remember me? It's Harry. We met in Pella. Remember?"

Mary looked up in surprise. Gid looked equally surprised to hear me speak her name. She stared at my face, gathering up the torn parts of her cloak. Suddenly she recognized me. My heart soared. Symeon, his eye swollen and his nose bleeding from the bandits' blows, also recognized me.

"Harry of Germania?" he exclaimed in disbelief.

"Yes, Bishop," I replied. "This is Gidgiddonihah. He's a friend. Everything is going to be all right."

* * *

As soon as we climbed out of the ravine, I used my water bag to wash the blood off Symeon's nose and face. Gidgiddonihah went to apprehend their mule.

"I shouldn't have brought her," Symeon mourned. "I knew these highways were dangerous. No place for a young girl. I'm a very stupid man."

"It wasn't your decision," Mary responded. "If you had tried to leave me in Pella, I would have followed you."

"Why are you here?" I asked, still mystified. "Where are you going?"

Symeon's face lit up with gratitude. "We're here because of you, Harry of Germania."

I raised my eyebrows. "Because of me?"

"It was you who awakened my conscience," said Symeon. "Now you've saved our lives. They would have killed us. They told us so. I'd be dead now, but they kept me alive for their own sport to see what they would do to my daughter. Oh, Harry! I'm so glad to see you. It's a sign from God."

The hair prickled on my neck. He sounded like old Barsabas. Barsabas had thought our arrival in Qumran was a sign that we would help him save the scrolls. I didn't want to be responsible for any more signs from God.

"I still don't get it," I said. "Why did you leave Pella? What about your wife?"

Grief filled Symeon's eyes. "Anna has gone home. She died in my arms the very night that you and your friends departed. We buried her before sunrise and took the road to Bethshan. A part of me believes she died of shame. Shame for her husband—"

"No, Father," Mary objected.

"Yes, it's true," Symeon insisted. "I'd become a puppet. A jackal to a council of men who no longer listened to God's Holy Spirit. Before my wife died, I whispered an oath in her ear. I promised I would end the charade and fight to make right all that I had helped to make wrong. But I need the holy words. Words like those that are written in the sacred scroll of Matthew. I promised I would go to Jerusalem, find the library of Bishop James, and bring the sacred scriptures back to my people."

"You're going to Jerusalem?" I asked incredulously.

"Yes. For the first time in years, I feel I'm back on the path of right."

Gid returned, leading the bishop's mule by the reins. He'd overheard our conversation and listened eagerly. I could hardly believe it. Symeon had the same objective as we did!

"What about the Romans?" I asked. "How were you going to get inside the city? How were you gonna get out again?"

"If it is God's will that I save his Holy Word, a way will be opened," Symeon declared. "I know a man among the Romans who did much business with my estate in Cana. His name is Joseph ben Matthias. Three years ago he was commander of all the Jewish troops in Galilee. After he was captured by Vespasian, the Romans made him a negotiator for peace. I have heard he serves in the camp of Prince Titus."

"This man was a commander and now serves his enemy?" asked Gid suspiciously.

"He's one of the brightest young men I've ever met," said Symeon. "And he's always been very respectful to Nazarenes. If it becomes necessary, I think we may find him a very sympathetic ally."

Nothing like having friends in high places, I thought. Maybe this *was* a sign. How could it be anything else? Gid and I didn't have the first clue about how we might get inside the city. Even if we had, we might have searched for that old burned-out house of James until kingdom come. Symeon could lead us right to it.

"Where are Meagan and Jesse?" Mary finally asked.

I told them the sad tale of what had happened after we left Pella. I also revealed that we both had the same mission—to find the secret library of Bishop James. Symeon's belief that our reunion was part of a divine plan became even more entrenched.

I had to tell him the truth. "I'm afraid most of the testimonies of Jesus that were written by the apostles have already been destroyed. They were burned by the same men who kidnapped Meagan and Jesse. I still have the Book of Matthew, but I don't know if there's anything else in that vault even worth saving."

"There *must* be more," Symeon insisted. "If I can't find more testimonies, I'll never be able to convince the people at Pella that Thebuthis and the elders have corrupted God's word."

"Barsabas told us there were more," I said, "including the scroll we're seeking. But I don't know what any of the scrolls will say."

"They will say the truth," said Symeon. "They *must*. Or else all the souls at Pella will be lost."

His face was determined, but his logic seemed off. I knew without revelation—prophets and apostles—scripture alone might not be enough. The Bible had been around for fifteen hundred years. People could make it mean whatever they wanted. Still, I wasn't gonna burst his bubble. If God's purpose for bringing us together was only to save Meagan and Jesse, that was enough for me.

Gid wasn't comfortable bringing Mary. "A battleground is no place for a young woman. We'd only face more incidents like today."

Mary held the torn shoulder of her cloak. "I won't leave my father. He's not as strong as he thinks. He needs me to look after him."

"It's impossible," said Gid. "Her presence puts us *all* at greater risk. We could be challenged by every band of ruffians we meet."

Symeon approached his daughter. "He's right. You should have stayed in Pella."

"Father, I *couldn't* have stayed," said Mary. "As soon as the elders found out that you had abandoned the community, I'd have been shunned like a leper."

"So where can we take her?" I asked.

Mary bristled. She didn't want her destiny decided by anyone but her. Symeon paced about. He didn't have an answer. I had the feeling he didn't have many friends left in this world. At least not in Judea.

"What if I were a boy?" Mary blurted out.

"What?" I asked.

"You're *not* a boy," said Gid.

"But if I was, I'd be at no more risk than any of you. Right?"

"This is pointless," said Gid impatiently. "We need to make a decision—"

"I could cut my hair," said Mary. "I could wear a boy's tunic. I could even wear a hood."

I saw what she was getting at now. Shades of *Swiss Family Robinson* or *Yentl.* It was a silly idea. Even when I was a little kid I knew that girl in *Swiss Family Robinson* was a girl from the beginning. Nobody fooled me. I shook my head. "It'll never work."

"Why not?"

"Because you're too . . . well, you're too. . ." I could feel myself blushing. "Because you look too much like a girl."

"I don't see what other choice we have," said Mary, "except maybe to leave me in the hills while the rest of you go into Jerusalem and—"

"No," said Symeon firmly. "These hills are full of bandits."

"Then this is our only option. Let me try."

"It *won't work!*" I said with more emphasis. "It's not just the way you look. It's *everything!*"

"Oh? Like what?"

"The way you talk—"

"I could keep silent."

"The way you *move*—"

"How do I move?" she asked innocently.

My face must have been as red as a pomegranate. I let out a nervous laugh and continued shaking my head.

"*You're* a boy," she observed keenly. "You could *show* me how to move."

Gidgiddonihah scrutinized Mary more closely. "I'd have to see the end result."

"So you will," said Mary. "I'll cut my hair tonight."

Symeon didn't like anything about it. "It's not right," he said, almost as if the disguise was a sin.

"Father," Mary pleaded, "if you have another solution, I will hear it. Otherwise I must try."

Symeon wandered away several steps, still shaking his head. Again he mumbled, "Not right."

We made our camp on another hill overlooking the terrain. I was sure I could smell smoke. We must have been getting close to our destination. Something else strange was in the air as well. Or perhaps I should say in the *earth*. I heard it, or felt it, only after we'd settled in. Every few seconds there was an odd vibration in the ground. It was like clockwork. It reminded me of that scene in *Jurassic Park* where a shock wave rippled the surface of a puddle. I was half tempted to look around and see if T-rex was stomping toward us.

"What *is* that?" I asked.

Gid concentrated on the sound. It baffled him, too.

"It almost sounds like somebody firing off a cannon," I said.

No one responded. Nobody else knew what a cannon was.

Symeon listened for several seconds, then concluded, "The ram."

"The what?"

"The battering ram," said Symeon. "The Romans are trying to breach the wall of Solomon. As Jesus foretold, the city is about to fall."

We looked at each other, wondering what this might mean for our mission. Nothing good, I was sure. If the Romans were already inside the city when we got there, we'd never get near it. They'd cut us down as soon as we tried to enter. We were definitely better off if the Romans were still being kept at bay. Suddenly this seemed a strange thought: if the *Romans* couldn't get inside, how did *we* expect to?

Gid had taken the weapons from the slain bandits. In addition to his sword, he now wore a long knife, a dagger, and a leather sling. He was starting to look like the Gid I remembered—that "mess-with-me-and-you're-dog-meat" kind of look. He gave me one of the daggers, plus the blade of another dagger that had been broken off.

"Find a place for this," said Gid, referring to the three-inch piece of steel. "A hidden blade could save your life."

He tried to give the last knife to Mary. She shook her head.

Gid insisted. "You will carry a weapon. If you were a boy, you would have a weapon."

She took it reluctantly. As the sun started setting, she found a very practical purpose for the tool—to give herself a haircut.

As each silky strand dropped to the earth, it felt like a needle in my heart. Such perfect hair. It was a crime against nature. She had no mirror. After every cut she reached up and felt the progress with dissatisfaction. She noticed me staring. I blushed and tried to pretend I'd been looking past her.

"I'm not cutting very evenly," she said to me. "Can you help?"

I hesitated. How could I be a party to such actions? She held the dagger handle toward me. I took it. She turned and flipped all of her remaining hair behind her head to make it lay down her back.

"I want it as short as yours," she said.

I set the blade against the first lock, then I stopped.

"What's the matter?" she asked. "Go ahead and cut."

"It's just . . . so beautiful."

I sounded like a moron. But I wasn't flirting. It was just a fact. She looked back at me, as if seeing me for the first time.

"It doesn't matter," she said. "I've already ruined it. Cut!"

I did so, and it was almost like lopping off a limb.

She spoke again, her voice mellow. "I wanted to thank you for what you did today."

"Gid did most of it."

"All I saw was you. You were very brave."

"Gid thinks I was pretty stupid. He's right. If they'd seen me coming sooner, we wouldn't be having this conversation."

"Maybe it was foolish," she said. "Just the same, I'll never forget it."

I continued to cut, unsure what to say next. I'd never been at a loss for words around a girl before. I didn't like it. Maybe it was just who she was. Who her *family* was. I wasn't sure how to act. We were both silent for the next several minutes as I continued to cut, letting each strand fall gently to the earth.

Finally, Mary said, "You must be very worried right now."

"Worried?"

"About Jesse and Meagan."

"Yes," I said.

"She's very pretty."

"Who?"

"Meagan."

"I suppose she is."

"Are you betrothed?"

"With Meagan? Oh, no. Meagan is going to be my *sister*. My father is marrying her mother. No, we're not betrothed. Not even close."

"I see."

"What about you? Are you . . . ?"

"Betrothed? No."

"Oh." I left it at that.

"There was a suitor when I was thirteen," she continued, "but with the war coming—"

"Thirteen? Really?"

"Is there something wrong?"

"Well it . . . just seems awfully young."

"My sisters were married at that age."

"Wow," I said. "I haven't even been out on a—" I stopped myself, suddenly not wanting to confess my inexperience. Not that she'd have known what a "date" was.

Mary went on. "When I was fourteen, my mother got ill. I needed to take care of her so. . ." Her voice trailed off.

"You must have loved your mother very much."

She nodded. The feelings were still tender. After all, it had only been three days. She'd hardly had time to mourn her mother's death. Now this terrible attack. I knelt in front of her as she wiped a tear. I showed her the last lock of her hair.

"Finished."

She felt her scalp. I'd made it an even two inches all the way around. Well, fairly even.

"How do I look?" she asked.

I saw her father shut his eyes and turn away. The transformation was overwhelming. But did I think she'd pass for a boy?

No way. Not unless the world had gone blind.

Gidgiddonihah came over. He took one look and sighed, obviously not all that convinced.

"Maybe we could dirty up her cheeks," I suggested.

"Why?" she asked.

"Well, like maybe you got some peach fuzz."

"Peach fuzz?"

"Like a beard coming in."

"Oh."

She immediately set to rubbing in some dirt. When she was done, she looked like a girl with dirty cheeks.

"We'll keep her in the background," said Gid, turning away. "And her tunic should have a hood."

In the distance glowed the lamps of a nearby village. In the morning we'd look for a market to buy what we needed.

It was hard to fall asleep. I lay awake a long time. But it wasn't just the anxiety of knowing that tomorrow we would reach Jerusalem. The rumbling in the earth—the echo of the battering ram—sounded without interruption through every hour of the night.

CHAPTER FIVE

*"Okay, Jesse," I called into the darkness. "You start us out. Ready?"
It was his turn to do the "wah-ooo's." And so he did.*

"Wah-ooo, wah-ooo, wah-ooo, wah-ooo. . ."

I accompanied him with the lyrics.

"When criminals in this world appear,
To break the laws we all hold dear,
Then people come from far and near,
To shout the cries for all to hear for
UNDERDOG!"

Jesse said the second one: "UNDERDOG!"

"UNDERDOG!"

Back to Jesse: "UNDERDOG!"

We sang together on the chorus:

"Speed of lightning!
Roar of thunder!

Fighting those who rob and plunder!
Underdog. Ah-ah-ah-AH! Underdog.
UNDERDOG!"

"Perfect!" I cried.

The kid had a great voice. We'd been singing now for hours. I could tell that both of our voices were feeling the strain. But the songs made the darkness and the stench and the hunger a little more bearable. Thirst wasn't really a problem. There was a nice steady drip coming from the ceiling. We took turns standing under it in the dark, avoiding the deep puddle in the corner where it drained. I thought it would taste rancid, considering all the tombs and skeletons it might have seeped through in the chambers above us. But the drink tasted like heaven—perfectly pure and cold.

Jesse also taught me a couple of his songs—a sad one about a young soldier who comes home to find he's lost everybody he's ever loved. The tune reminded me a little of "Greensleeves." It fit the life of little Jesse so well that my heart went out to him.

He also sang a song I didn't much appreciate about a sailor who gets drunk and keeps stumbling into the wrong house. He said it was an Egyptian beer-drinking song. I don't think I'll repeat any of the lyrics. I tried to top him by singing the love song from Titanic, *but let's face it, I was no Celine Dion.*

I must admit, I'd pegged ole' Simon Magus pretty well. Jesse and I were only entombed in that crypt another nine or ten hours before I heard a stone grinding in a nearby tunnel. Soon the light of several torches again illuminated the chamber. Into the passageway stepped Saturninus and Menander, along with two more cueball-heads who I remembered from our encounter with the Sons of the Elect back at Qumran. Their names were Reuben and Cleobius, though I preferred to call them Ren and Stimpy. One was short and tubby, the other skinny and tall, and they were both mindless buffoons.

"Your presence is requested by the Standing One of God," said Menander grumpily.

"'Bout time," I said, rising and taking a good long stretch.

"You are to be fed and bathed before we bring you to his palace," said Saturninus.

"Now we're talkin'," I responded. *"Can I also get a back massage? This stone is brutal."*

Menander thinned his eyes. *"You'll receive no more than we have been instructed to give you."*

"I'm sure if it had been up to you, we'd got a lot less, eh, handsome?" I tapped Menander on the cheek.

He reeled backwards. *"Do not touch me, you husk of corruption!"*

I crinkled my nose. *"Husk of corruption? That's a new one. Is that an insult or a flashback of what you ate for lunch?"*

His eyes were flaming. This guy hated me but good. I remained determined to taunt them as much as I could. It was the best way I could cope. They had to know they hadn't beaten me. They could never *beat me.*

"Bind their hands!" Menander barked at Ren and Stimpy. *"Put the hood over their eyes. And if this one says another word, gag her."*

I smiled at Menander and pantomimed that I had zipped my lips. My hands were yanked behind me and tied. Just before they dropped a black cloth over my head, I gave Menander a wink, which he also didn't appreciate.

They treated Jesse with the same rudeness. Then one of the henchmen, I think it was Stimpy, took me by the arm and led me through the corridor. I heard the rock slide back into place behind us. I wondered if this might mean that the stone could be moved by one or two people. But then I became aware of other footsteps. We'd been joined by other thugs en route. For all I knew, that stone had been moved by five or six men.

I had no idea where we were going, but I climbed up and down a lot of steps. Minutes later I sensed that we had stepped out into the *open air. I might have expected to feel the warmth of the sun, or to detect sunlight through the black hood. I sensed neither, so I guessed it was after dark.*

After walking for another five or ten minutes down a steep trail where the grass scratched at my legs, I arrived at a flight of wide stone steps. I climbed them, then I was led through a narrow passage where our footsteps echoed. Finally, we reached a room with a smooth tiled floor.

Along about here, Jesse and I were placed in the able hands of others.

"Bathe them, but do not speak to them," I heard Menander say. "They are both possessed by witchcraft. If you speak to them, the devil's spell will leap upon you as well."

Some female voices whispered. This cheered my heart. Women could never be as callous as men, could they?

Jesse and I were separated. The women led me into a warm, humid room with the sound of running water. My hands were untied and the hood was removed. I sucked in a deep breath and took in my surroundings. It was a sauna of sorts. Steam seeped into the room from vents in the floor, escaping through a small hole cut in the roof. What a deal. A warm bath! This place was like a resort.

There were three women with me, all of them armed with towels and scrub brushes. They wore starkly white, one-piece dresses, tied with a bright red sash. Unlike their male counterparts, they all had full heads of hair, though it was cut to a very uniform length just above the shoulders. The women looked at me with a hint of apprehension. After all, they'd just been told I was possessed. Their eyes darted from my cloak, to my face, to each other. I gathered that they were trying to figure out how to tell me to disrobe. To ask directly would be a violation of Menander's command. I wasn't about to make it easy.

"What?" I said, as if I couldn't figure out what they were trying to say.

One of them grabbed the hem of her dress and made the motion of slipping it off over her head. I made the same motion as if it was some kind of ballerina step.

"You want me to dance?" I asked.

One of the women, a tough-looking broad with an underbite, wasn't fooled. She grabbed a thin stick off a nearby counter. It looked like a switch. She snapped it against a pillar without taking her eyes off mine.

"All right, all right," I said. "I'm taking it off."

I wondered why they hadn't just taken it off for me, but they seemed reluctant to touch me. As Menander had so poetically stated, to them I was a husk of corruption. I had cooties from one end to the other. Even when I handed one of the women my cloak, she took it in two fingers like a dead reptile.

"Come on, ladies," I said. "Lighten up. Whatever I have, it ain't contagious, I promise you."

Suddenly my head was doused by a bucket of water—ice cold!

"Holy heaven-to-betsy gosh darn rotten—!"

The ladies hesitated, maybe thinking I was reciting some kind of evil spell. I'd thought this was going to be a warm *bath! I swear that bucket was filled with liquid nitrogen. The water was also mixed with some kind of horrible green soap that made my skin itch from head to foot. The women set to work with their four-foot scrub brushes, attacking my skin with the stiff bristles. I sank down to my knees and did the best I could to protect my face. They splashed another bucket over my head, just as cold as the first. My will to fight was floundering. I started to sob. I'd had it. What was the point of resisting? My snotty, tough-as-nails attitude was only making things worse.*

"Please, Father," I said aloud. "Please, please help me."

My "groomers" kept grooming. Finally, I'd had enough. I came to my feet and grabbed one of the scrub brushes out of a woman's hand just as she was about to sandpaper my face.

"Back off!" I growled. "All of you! Get away from me!"

I moved toward the wall that emitted steam. Along the edge were some other buckets that I felt sure were filled with warm water. Helga the Horrible grabbed up her switch.

"Try that on me," I seethed, "and I'll stick it down your throat."

Helga hesitated, then she stuck out her jaw, determined to take me on.

I had another inspiration. "Or better yet, I'll put a curse on you that by morning you'll all die an unimaginably horrible death!"

"We don't fear your curses, witch," said Helga, breaking Menander's rule of silence.

"Oh, you'd better, sister," I said. "You think Simon invited me here because I'm an amateur? Now back off! *"*

They gaped at each other, torn between their fear of me and their fear of failing in their responsibility to clean me up. I grabbed one of the pots of warm water and dumped it over my head. Then I dumped another, and another. The women kept their distance, I guess figuring that since I was finishing the job myself, nobody would be the worse.

My body still itched horribly even after I'd rinsed it off. When I was done, one of the women—the youngest one (she couldn't have been much older than me)—brought me a towel. After I'd toweled off, she handed me a flask containing some sort of lotion.

"What's this?" I asked.

The girl pretended to rub the lotion all over her body. Then she smiled slightly, which took me by surprise. I frowned at her. I refused to believe that anyone was actually being kind. The smile disappeared and she backed away. I went into a corner and rubbed the lotion everywhere. The stuff worked pretty well and the itching disappeared.

The women fetched me some new clothes—the same kind of nurse-white robes that they were wearing, but the sash they gave me was black. I was sure the color had a negative connotation. But with the white cloak, the black belt made me think of a karate gi, so

I put it on thinking, "Anybody messes with me, I'll give 'em a karate chop right between the eyes."

I was relieved beyond words when they reunited me with Jesse in a large room with a banquet table. The table was laden with bread and dates and strips of fish pickled in some kind of pink sauce. The room overlooked an enclosed courtyard filled with all sorts of flowers and plants. The light from the lanterns reflected off the surface of a small pool beyond the flowers. It looked like a cistern for catching rainwater. I could hear the trickle of a stream. The villa was situated at the base of an ancient-looking ridge. I wondered how Simon had managed to occupy such nice digs. It was like an old Greek castle. I was surprised the Romans hadn't confiscated it when they invaded. Obviously Simon had some bucks. Maybe he'd pooled all his followers' money and purchased this estate as a kind of commune.

Jesse and I were left to ourselves, though Ren and Stimpy and a few other watchdogs were posted at various entrances.

I embraced Jesse happily. "Are you all right?"

Jesse nodded. "I can't say that I appreciate their baths."

"Rough, eh?"

"I haven't taken a bath since Passover. And that was only because my grandfather made me."

"Then I guess you were due," I said, trying to smile. "That soap was like lye! What was that stuff?"

"It was for lice," said Jesse.

"Lice! I don't have lice! I've never—!"

Then I thought about where I'd been and felt itchy again.

Jesse lowered his voice. "Meagan, listen to me. If they put us back in that place, I might have figured out a way to—"

He stopped. Saturninus had entered the room. What timing! What had Jesse been trying to say? Saturninus approached hastily. He had Harry's backpack with all of its toys and goodies. He placed it gently on the table, as if everything inside was something fragile and precious.

"The Standing One has asked me to bring you these," said Saturninus. "He has many questions that he will expect you to answer."

Saturninus had an unnerving squeak to his voice. Still, he was the only one who spoke to me with any kind of respect. I wasn't sure what to think of it. Did he feel guilty for how I was being treated? I suspected he believed I really did have some sort of power, though he wasn't sure what it was. My instincts told me if I was going to try to manipulate anyone in this outfit, it was Saturninus.

"Do I at least get to finish my dinner," I said, swallowing.

"Of course. We will wait here until he comes."

"You plan to wait here with us?"

"I have been commanded not to let these items out of my presence."

I scrutinized him, then I nodded. "Good. That's good. I'd rather have this stuff in your hands than in the hands of that other creep. What's his name?"

"I'm sure Menander would be just as capable," said Saturninus. "Menander is the First Elect of God."

"So what's that make you?" I asked.

"The Second Elect."

"Ah. That makes sense. How'd he get ahead of you?"

"Our station is chosen by the Aeons of the Third Heaven," said Saturninus calmly. "It is foreordained by our ancestry and sanctioned by the Unknown God. In Menander flows the blood of David, Solomon, Jeroboam, and the great kings of Israel's past. When Simon is taken back to heaven, Menander will be the Standing One."

"Hmm," I said. "That's a shame. He doesn't quite seem to have what it takes. Know what I mean?"

Saturninus shook his head.

"He's not exactly a people person, now is he?"

"Menander sings with the tongues of angels," Saturninus defended. "Only the most purified have this capability."

I was tempted to laugh, but I restrained myself. I felt sure his defense of Menander was for my benefit alone. I still remembered how these two men had behaved toward each other back at Qumran. No matter what Saturninus said, these guys did not *like each other.*

"Haven't you ever *sung with the tongue of an angel, Saturninus?" I asked.*

"Well, yes," he said hesitantly, "but not with the same—"

"Oh, don't sell yourself so short. Something tells me in your bloodline runs a pretty impressive nobility as well."

Saturninus considered me with great interest. "Oh?"

"Like maybe the blood of Melchizedek and Moses and other great prophets."

Saturninus looked mildly stunned. He leaned in. "Who told you this?"

Bingo. I'd hit pay dirt. I wasn't sure exactly what I'd said, but something had struck a chord. I had to keep cool. Besides, Jesse looked nervous enough for both of us.

"No one told me," I replied. "I can see it in your eyes. Didn't you know?"

He kept his eyes glued to mine for several more seconds. Finally, he tried to shrug it off. "You're only a child. And a woman. How could you know such things?"

"Don't underestimate me," I said with lethal seriousness. "Melchizedek was the greatest king and prophet this world has ever known. And his blood runs in yours. Why, compared to you, the blood running in Menander's veins is like dishwater."

I'd definitely roused his interest. He continued to look at me with a strange mystical curiosity, but then he pointed a sharp finger at my nose. "Don't try to flatter me, young lady. I know what you're trying to do."

I smiled warmly. "I wouldn't dream of trying to flatter you, Saturninus. I may indeed have selfish reasons for telling you these things, but I cannot lie about what I see. I am bound by the oaths I've made to my own Aeons."

"What Aeons are those?" he asked.

He would have to ask. I hesitated, then said the first names that came into my head. "James T. Kirk and Jean-Luc Picard."

Saturninus scoffed, "I have never heard of these Aeons. There are no such beings."

"Oh, they're real," I assured him, "and they're powerful. They have both visited strange new worlds, sought out new life and new civilizations, and boldly gone where no Aeon has gone before. They have whispered in my ear, and they have much to say about you. You have a very bright future, Saturninus. Don't blow it by hitching your camel to the wrong star. Know what I mean?"

He was eating it up. He seemed frustrated that he wasn't sure how to interpret all this. Jesse, on the other hand, looked at me more queerly than he'd ever looked at me before. Who could blame him? I was sounding like a mad sorceress. I wanted to shake him and say, "Can't you tell I'm bluffing?" But I couldn't stop now. I was on a roll.

"You are a mystery to me, Meagan," said Saturninus. "I cannot say if you are a prophetess or a demon. But Simon will know. Nothing can escape his all-seeing eye."

"Oh yeah? What if I can prove to you that he doesn't see as much as he thinks?"

Saturninus looked offended. "Simon is the Standing One of God. He has brought the words of life to a misguided world. You are a daughter of the flesh, so I cannot condemn your disbelief, but I will not hear any more of your disrespect and blasphemy!"

"Calm down," I said. "Don't get your pantyhose in a tangle."

"My what?"

"I'm not saying your boss isn't a powerful guy. I'm just saying he's a bit past his peak. I mean, look at him! He's a poster boy for skin cancer! You don't honestly believe a guy could look like that and still be immortal, do you?"

"You don't know what you're talking about. You have no under-standing of—"

"I understand more than you think. And tonight I intend to prove it. Simon somehow believes if he can get his hands on the Scroll of Knowledge, he'll suddenly have all the secrets of the universe. I'm here to tell you that I have all of those secrets already. I have them in here." I pointed to my brain. Saturninus looked confused. Then I remembered that ancient people believed knowl-edge came from the heart, not the brain. I pointed to my heart. "And in here. But I'll only share all of my secrets with the one who is most worthy to possess them. Right now Kirk and Picard are telling me that person is you."

Saturninus looked tempted. Oh, he looked tempted. But at the last minute he shook his head. "You are a vain and foolish girl. I'll make a prophecy of my own. After tonight you shall both know the true meaning of power and righteousness on this earth and who wields it. It is in the hands of the Elect of God!"

"Well spoken," resounded a wheezing voice from behind.

We turned to face the doorway exactly opposite the courtyard where Simon Magus was sitting in a sedan chair held by four of his followers. Menander and several other thugs had also gathered. I'd heard them arriving as Saturninus was speaking. I had the impression that much of what Saturninus had said at the end was for their benefit.

I noticed a young man at Simon's side that I hadn't seen before. He was in his early twenties, with a lean physique and a smooth face. In fact, it was too smooth, like a wax statue. To my surprise, he had a full head of greasy blonde hair; I think he'd stiffened it with some kind of oil. His cloak was plain, like his compadres, but he wore a kind of fancy leather boots that came all the way up his leg, the tops hidden by his skirt. He narrowed his eyes and smiled back. It was a leering kind of smile that chilled me to the bone. I looked away.

The porters set Simon's sedan chair at the head of the table. The room felt crowded. Jesse and I were on display.

Simon continued where Saturninus had left off. "Righteousness is indeed in the hands of God's elect. And ever will be until darkness is defeated by light. Tell me, Meagan, now that you have experienced darkness in its grimmest form, how much more do you appreciate the light? Even the light of the moon and stars?"

"Oh, I don't know," I said. "It wasn't so bad down there. We were having a pretty good time, weren't we, Jesse? Singing songs, telling jokes—"

Simon snickered. "Yes. I'd have been disappointed if you hadn't answered with your usual sarcasm." He indicated the young man. "I want you to meet the son of my spirit, Cerinthus the Divine. He is descended from the highest heaven through the cosmic spheres to be conceived by the Earth-mother, Helena, my eternal companion."

Oh, brother, *I thought.*

"Although Helena has since returned to the Invisible God, Cerinthus is heir to all her spiritual gifts. Tonight you will give us a demonstration of the 'toys' in your travel bag and tomorrow you will give Cerinthus a private lesson on their particular functions. From now on he is to be your pupil and your master."

Again Cerinthus gave me a greasy, leering smile. I wanted to smash the plate of fish into his face. My master? A private lesson? The squirming in my stomach almost made me vomit. There was no way I was gonna be left alone with this wax-faced punk.

Saturninus proceeded to take each item out of the pack and place it in front of me. For most of the people in the room, this was the first time they'd seen the various articles. I heard a lot of whispering and speculation. I realized most of the stuff had been tampered with. The flashlight, for instance, didn't come out in one piece. It came out as six batteries, a separated canister, and even an unscrewed lightbulb. Somebody had unwound about ten feet of the duct tape and tried to wind it back onto the roll, making it look like a total mess. One of the cassette tapes—Enya's Memory of Trees*—had been completely pulled off the cassette. The tape was* now meticulously rewound on a wooden spool while the plastic cassette was empty. The metal jack had also been broken off the earphones. The thing was useless!

I picked up the spool and the earphones. "Who's the bozo who did this?"

Cerinthus frowned. That figures, I thought. My pupil and master had tried to figure it out on his own.

"Is there something wrong?" asked Simon.

"It's ruined," I said. "I can't make this play now. I'm not sure if the flashlight works anymore either. What a mess! I'm surprised you didn't smash the pocketknife with a rock to see how all the little blades worked."

Simon looked at Cerinthus the Divine, who shifted nervously.

"I thought she claimed to be a powerful magician," Cerinthus said defensively. "She should be able to undo any damage I've inflicted quite easily."

Everyone turned back to me. I could feel the pressure. I decided to make the best of it, though I wasn't about to give any truly useful information.

"You wanna know what these things are for? All right. I'll tell you. Listen carefully." I picked up the duct tape. "We use this stuff on cats."

"Cats?" said Menander.

"Yeah. You know. Kitty cats. It's a great way to forecast the weather. What you do is tear off a little piece like this, then tape the ends together like this. Then you stick it on the bottom of a cat's paw and watch them jump around trying to shake it off. Whichever foot the tape comes off first tells you if it's going to rain or snow or be sunny."

The audience stared at me strangely.

"Is that its only use?" asked Menander.

I gave him a sharp glare. "Or I could use it to seal the mouth of whoever asks stupid questions and interrupts my demonstration."

He frowned and closed his mouth.

"Thank you," I said coolly. I picked up the package of size 8 fishhooks. "Now these are for medicinal purposes. They work kinda like earrings. Whenever you have a headache, you just jab one of these things through your earlobes, and I promise you'll forget all about your headache." I grabbed the pliers. "This we use for pulling nose hairs. Works great. Try it before you leave."

I picked up the little bottle of Salon Selectives shampoo. "Ah, now this—this is a special elixir that makes you irresistible to women. Just drink the whole bottle and wallah!—you'll be mobbed by cute babes. Definitely worth the effort. You guys could use all the help you can get."

I picked up the tube of Colgate Tartar-Control Toothpaste. "Oh, and this—this stuff is priceless." I grabbed a piece of bread off Jesse's plate. "We use this stuff like honey." I took off the cap and squirted a few mint-flavored stripes across the bread. "You've never tasted anything like it. Here. Try a bite."

I handed the bread to Menander. He sniffed it. Then he looked back at me suspiciously.

"Go on, Menander," said Simon. "No poisons can hurt you here."

Hesitantly, Menander took a bite with a big glob of toothpaste and started chewing. After a few seconds, he tilted his head as if to say, "Not bad," and took another bite.

"It also cures baldness," I added. "A couple bites of this and that ole' scalp will grow back as fast as crabgrass."

Menander spit out the second bite and glowered at me.

"Sorry," I said. "I forgot how you folks feel about hair."

"Hair is a symbol of vanity," said Saturninus. "Only the divine can withstand the temptations of the vanities."

Of course. Why didn't I think of that? Now I knew why Simon and Cerinthus had hair. They were divine. This made me wonder why Cerinthus hadn't been slated to take over the Sons of the Elect after Simon was—ahem—taken back to heaven. The more I learned about these people, the weirder they got.

The only thing left to demonstrate was the flashlight. "Now this," I explained, holding the various pieces, "is what we call a light saber. The evil Darth Vader once used this to try to kill the righteous Aeon Obi-Wan Kenobi. However—" I screwed the lightbulb and the top back into place, but I left the batteries on the table "—your spirit son has unfortunately discombobulated it. If you intend to put us back in that cozy dungeon, perhaps you could leave it with me, and I'll see what I can do."

"Perhaps not," said Simon. He gestured for Saturninus to bring it to him. The batteries remained on the table. "A better plan, I think, would be for you to reassemble it tomorrow in the presence of Cerinthus. A thing of light obviously does not belong in a place of darkness."

"Obviously," I said, deflated.

"You will also reassemble your audio destructor." He indicated the cassette player. "Audio destructor" was the name Harry'd given it back at the boulder near Jericho. "I must confess," Simon continued, "I was somewhat disappointed when it didn't cause deafness, as Harry had promised. I would have easily cured such a malady by my faith. Frankly, his lies have caused me to suspect the truth of all your descriptions here tonight. Tomorrow I will expect you to verify them in the presence of Cerinthus."

"I'd be happy to verify them," I declared. "But only to Saturninus." Cerinthus looked put out.

"Oh?" said Simon. "Why do you favor God's Second Elect?"

"Because he's the only one with true understanding."

Cerinthus became defensive. "Saturninus is only a mortal. His understanding will always be limited by the flesh. I have the gifts of prophecy and seership, tongues and healing. You will reveal your secrets to me."

"My, my," I said. "Prophecy and seership, tongues and healing, eh? That's a lot of gifts. So why don't you dazzle me, Mr. Cerinthus? If you can tell me more about the future than I already know, perhaps I could be persuaded to teach you some secrets." I glared as if I could see right into his soul.

"It is a wicked and adulterous generation that seeks after a sign," said Cerinthus handily. "I will not cast my pearls before swine."

"I can certainly understand," I replied, "since you have so few pearls to spare."

It was all Cerinthus could do to keep his composure. Everyone in the room was squirming. Only Simon seemed calm and entertained.

"Let me tell you what I see for the future," I said. "Particularly with regards to your silly religion. I can promise you that in the centuries to come, the Sons of the Elect will be entirely forgotten."

"That's a lie," said Cerinthus. "You see nothing of the future."

"Oh, yeah? Then tell me this. Who will be the next Emperor of Rome?"

Cerinthus looked nervously at Simon. At last he gathered his wits and replied, "Titus, son of Vespasian."

I nodded. "Very good. Not bad at all. An obvious guess, however. Who will be Emperor after that?"

Cerinthus straightened up and declared, "There will be no Emperor after Titus. After Titus, the Roman empire will fall. The world will come to an end. The spirits who are saved will be gathered into the oneness of eternity while the works of the false creator will be annihilated."

"Wrong!" I blustered. "Wrong, wrong, wrong! After Titus, the Emperor will be his brother, Domitian. After that it will be Nerva. And after that—" I had to think a second "—Trajan. And as far as the Roman empire, it'll be around for a good three hundred and fifty more years, so don't sell the farm just yet. Let me ask you this— how long will Vespasian be Emperor?"

"This is all nonsense," said Cerinthus. "Why should we listen any longer to such—?"

"Nine years," I said. "Until A.D. 79. That is, 79 years after the birth of Jesus Christ. In that same year a volcano called Mount

Vesuvius is going to blow its top and completely bury the city of Pompeii with sixty feet of ash and lava. The exact date is August 24, in case anyone is taking notes."

"It seems quite convenient," said Menander, "to speak of events so far in the future—"

"You want something closer to home?" I asked. "All right. Tell me this. When will Titus retake Jerusalem? Anyone? Anyone at all?"

They stared at me with open mouths. I'd never had a more captive audience in my entire life. I was loving every minute.

Finally, Cerinthus scoffed, "Prophecy such as this is worthless. It does nothing to edify the soul or bring about salvation. It is the frivolity of the devil."

"Sounds like a cop-out to me. C'mon. Too tough for you? Let me make it easier. On what day will the Romans destroy the temple?"

They were mystified. No one dared to reply. At last Cerinthus boldly declared, "The temple of Judah will not be destroyed."

"Wrong again! Boy, when you're off, you're off. Want me to tell you?"

The room was so quiet you could hear a pin drop. I reached for a bowl of grapes and popped several into my mouth. As I chewed, I said, "August 30. The exact anniversary, by the way, of the destruction of the former temple by Nebuchadnezzar, king of Babylon."

"That's in three days!" declared Saturninus.

A tingle ran up my spine. I hadn't realized it was so close. I had them right where I wanted them. And then I wondered—what if Josephus had been wrong? Oh, please, *I cried inwardly,* don't screw up on me now, Josephus!

Menander slapped his hand on the table. "Now we will all see her for what she is—a false prophetess and a deceiver! The Emperor has already declared that he would let the temple of Judah stand as an ornament to the Empire. Deceivers must be stoned. In three days I say we pass sentence on this charlatan and—"

"Silence, Menander," said Simon tiredly. "You're letting passion override wisdom. Remember, she is the key to recovering the sacred

Scroll of Knowledge. And as for her prophecies, have you learned nothing? If she is wrong, she is merely an obnoxious prattler, harmless and benign." His eyes cemented on mine. *"However, if her visions are true, we may know of a surety that she is a witch of the darkest order. It is then that we must act quickly and ruthlessly."*

My heart pounded against the wall of my chest. Wait a second, I thought. This wasn't how it was supposed to go.

"For God's purposes, we cannot condemn her," said Simon. "The young boy, however, is more expendable. If her prophecy comes true, we will stone the boy here in the villa courtyard as a means of drawing from our young witch all the appropriate soul-purging confessions."

Jesse looked at me for some sign of assurance. I had none to give. I could scarcely draw air into my lungs.

"You can't do that!" I railed. "If my prophecy is true, you must regard me as a great prophetess or I'll curse everyone here with a curse so terrible that—"

"You see?" Simon said to Menander and Cerinthus, "a prophetess of God does not rain curses so casually on her hearers. I'm afraid the demons have a strong hold on her. Her works are darkness. That is all they will ever be. Light does not come from darkness. Light, my children, may only come from light."

Simon had the flashlight aimed right at me. Suddenly the beam shot straight into my eyes. The light was working! Working without batteries? It wasn't possible! I squinted and turned away. When I turned back, the light was off. No one else was reacting. Was it my illusion alone? Simon was smiling. He knew I'd prophesied correctly. I felt like the ultimate idiot. I'd challenged the powers of darkness. I'd done it alone. Without God. Without anyone. It was all being thrown back in my face.

"Bind them," commanded Simon. "Take the boy back to the catacombs. Take Meagan to Cerinthus' quarters. He may begin her rites of purification tonight if he so chooses."

My heart filled with horror. "No! I won't be separated from Jesse!" *I clenched my teeth.* "If you separate us, I swear I'll never reveal any secrets to anyone! Do you hear me?"

Simon considered my threat. "You would rather remain among the dead than in the presence of a god?"

"You're darn right I would."

Cerinthus grinned. "It's all right," *he said.* "There will plenty of time to perform the proper rites. She may rot in those tunnels as long as she likes."

Simon turned back to me. "And if I agree, will you vow to share the secrets of these articles with Cerinthus?"

"Yes," *I said meekly.* "But you have to agree to never separate Jesse and me. Not just tonight. For as long as we're here."

"I'll decide that tomorrow," *said Simon,* "when I see how cooperative you can become."

I trembled frantically. My hands were retied and the cloth hood was pulled back over my head. The last thing I saw was Simon's cancerous face, looking deeply pleased. I'd played right into his hands. In three days he was going to kill Jesse. What had I done? My career as a sorceress was over.

As they led us away into the night, one glimmer of hope hovered in my thoughts. It was Jesse's statement from earlier that evening. A statement that he hadn't finished: If they put us back in that place, I might have figured out a way that we can—

I repeated the statement in my mind all the way back to the catacombs. Each time I filled in my own word at the end.

The word was escape.

Please, God. It had to be escape.

CHAPTER SIX

It was sweltering. I'd never felt anything like it. A hundred and ten degrees in the shade. That is, if there'd been any shade.

We'd bought what we needed that morning in a village along the highway, including a boy's cloak with a hood for Mary. But it was too hot for the hood. She left it hanging behind her neck as she rode the mule. If she'd worn it, she might have drawn more attention to herself. What kind of weirdo would wear a hood in heat like this?

We walked those last few miles toward Jerusalem in silence. The air was still and lifeless—not a flicker of wind. The smoke hung thickly against the hills. The smell of death was like poison in my lungs. I didn't like to swallow, afraid it might make the nausea worse. Every step was like dragging a ball and chain on both legs. But it wasn't just the heat. Something inside me wasn't eager at all to reach our destination.

The eeriest thing about those last few miles was the terrible quiet. Nothing moved. No birds. No people. The only sound was the distant boom of the battering rams, growing increasingly louder. The booming had a hollow echo, as if it was coming from inside me, like the beating of my heart. Everything sounded hollow—our footsteps, the clatter of the mule's hooves. I know that the sky was miles above us, but today it felt like a thick wool blanket draped over my head, suffocating.

Everything in the distance shimmered with heat waves. As we stepped over the next rise, the view down into the valley looked melted and warped. And yet there was no mistaking it. Below us loomed the walls of Jerusalem.

There it is, I told myself. The setting of a thousand Sunday School lessons. The city of David and Solomon and Jeremiah. The place where Jesus was crucified, buried, and resurrected. A city of countless miracles. But not today. Today it was only a place of doom.

Our hillside was about a mile and a half north of what remained of the outermost wall. Symeon was dumbstruck. He just stood there, speechless, his eyes watering with tears. He'd heard many rumors and reports about what to expect, but I don't think anything had prepared him for what he saw.

"It's all gone," I heard him mumble. "The neighborhoods, the suburbs, the groves, the gardens . . . I don't know this place anymore."

Huge areas looked like they'd been plowed under by a bull-dozer. Like everyplace else for twelve miles around the city, there were few if any standing trees. Gullies and ditches had been filled in with dirt. Ridges had been skimmed off to make them level. Everything up to the last standing wall that encircled the only two undefeated sections of Jerusalem had been laid waste to make room for Rome's invading armies.

To the south I could see a massive sea of tents with red Roman banners. There were other army camps to the east and north. The red-caped soldiers moving about the hills looked like tiny fire ants. Now I understood where all those trees had gone. For every stone wall enclosing Jerusalem, the Romans had faced it up with a wall of their own made out of crossed timbers filled in with earth. They'd constructed gigantic wooden towers, like portable apartment buildings. Each one was four or five stories tall with eight wooden wheels at the base. It would have taken a hundred men just to push it around. At the top I could see lookouts peering down upon the rebels inside the city. It was from inside the base of these towers that the men sent the battering rams forward, crashing into the thick stone walls. The soldiers inside were invisible to us. The towers' fortified walls protected them from the stones and arrows of the Jews, allowing them to carry on their destructive labors, unmolested.

Only ragged segments of Jerusalem's outermost walls remained. The neighborhoods that had once been inside them had been flattened and demolished. Tent cities and catapult nests now stood in their places. The Romans had entirely surrounded the last two quarters of the city with a single wall constructed of rubble and high wooden spikes. It must have been four or five miles long. For the thousands of Jewish rebels still inside, there appeared to be no escape.

I caught my breath as I laid eyes on the last remaining structure that still revealed the glory that had once been Jerusalem. On the eastern end, sticking up through all the mayhem like a polished jewel, stood the Holy Temple of God. In the blistering heat, it shone like a snow-capped mountain with glistening golden plates. Beautiful porches and towers, also rimmed in gold, surrounded it on all sides. I shook my head with regret. This was a building whose days were numbered, a building whose fall Jesus Himself had prophesied. The tallest of the Romans' siege towers stood against the temple's outer wall, bashing it endlessly with the ram. The Romans were trying to smash a wide gap leading inside the temple at this very moment.

I continued gazing, almost hypnotized by the white walls and golden spires, when Mary gave out a small, piercing cry and burst into tears.

"God of Abraham!" I heard Symeon exclaim. "God of Jacob!"

It took a few more seconds before I saw what had upset them. When I did, my stomach turned to jelly. How could I have missed it? The immensity of the city walls and the glory of the temple had obscured the smaller details.

At the top of the timber embankments west and north of the city, hoisted upright by ropes and positioned in full sight of the city's battlements, stood hundreds and hundreds of crosses.

At first my mind refused to believe it. How could I be expected to comprehend such a sight? My blood became slivers of ice. I might have thought that that pit near Jericho—the mangled corpses and bones—would have prepared me, somehow numbed my senses. But I was not prepared. The scene was like something out of a twisted horror movie. Beyond imagination. Beyond understanding. *Human beings* had done this!

The bodies had been nailed in strange, contorted, unnatural positions. Still living. Still breathing. I turned away. I couldn't look anymore. How could people—*any* people—become so inhuman, so hard, so past feeling? I reeled in grief and anger. The world had gone insane!

I looked at Gid. He was a seasoned warrior. He'd seen death and destruction in so many different ways. And yet his face looked no less stricken than ours did. "I'd almost forgotten," he said, "how depraved men could become."

"Here the Messiah was betrayed," said Symeon in a low voice. "Here He was crucified. He came unto His own, and His own received Him not. Now they cry unto Him, and He does not hear." His face was streaming with tears.

I shut my eyes. The day was broiling like an oven, but my body was shivering. I tried to block the images from my mind. I *had* to block them out. It was the only way I could stay focused. The only way to stay sane. Our quest was too important. I had to find the will to go on.

Mary had slipped down from the mule. She knelt, pouring out her heart, praying for strength. I knelt with her. Gid and Symeon followed.

"Fortify our hearts, O God," Symeon prayed aloud. "Enlarge our spirits. Help us to conquer our fears, our grief, and revulsion, and accomplish what we came here to do. We relinquish our fate into Thy merciful hands."

As I arose heavily from my knees, I felt it. God's strength. Just a little. Enough to swallow my fears. I was ready to go on. Ready to turn everything over to the Lord.

Gidgiddonihah surveyed the landscape one final time. "If we're to get inside," he declared soberly, "we'll have to climb that spiked wall that goes all the way around. I expect it will be easier after dark. No doubt there are sentries marching around it at every hour. We'll have to hope there's a blind spot."

"What part of the city was James' house in?" I asked Symeon.

He pointed to a hill inside the oldest wall. "In the Upper City. It's the same house where Jesus first blessed the bread and wine of remembrance. The same house where He first appeared to His apostles after He appeared to my mother and His mother at the garden tomb."

I stared at the hill and tried to imagine such marvelous occurrences. I couldn't see it. There were too many other terrible sights. It was hard to envision any sacred event taking place here at all.

"Once we get over the siege wall, how do we get inside the city gates?" I asked.

"We request admittance," said Symeon. "No one of the blood of Abraham may be denied entrance to the holy city. It's the ancient law."

I looked at him strangely. Did he really expect them to still obey that law?

I could tell Gid had doubts, too. Still, he said, "They might let us in. After all, they might see us as reinforcements. We'll get a little closer. Then we'll find a place to hide until dark."

We made our way down the hill and started across the no-man's land that lay between us and Jerusalem's outermost wall.

My nerves were on edge. We stuck out like sore thumbs on that terrain. Any second I expected a troop of Romans to appear and demand to know what we were doing.

Mary continued to ride the mule. She tried to look brave, though her cheeks were still wet with tears. So far her disguise had been unnecessary. No one had stopped us to ask questions. But if we were going to be stopped, I knew it would be in the next few minutes.

We crossed field after field trampled by horses and men. We'd made it about halfway to what was left of the ruined third wall when Gid stopped in his tracks. He'd just stepped around an abandoned stone house, the roof charred black and partially fallen in. He looked back at us and waved for us to halt. The mule whinnied. Symeon tried to hold its head to keep it quiet. I crept closer to Gid and immediately saw the problem.

Across the field, near another shack, a Roman soldier was foraging through the rubble. He didn't look particularly big or burley. Gid could have taken him in a heartbeat. Nevertheless, his hand was on the hilt of his sword, as if he half-expected to find trouble. He picked up something that looked like a hair comb and started to polish it with his thumb. Finally, he thought better of it and tossed it away.

About twenty yards farther I could see his horse. It was grazing in a thin strip of meadow. Gid and I went back and joined Symeon and Mary. Mary slipped down from the mule.

"What do we do?" I asked.

"We wait," Gid replied, whispering.

Mary peered through a window in the stone wall. She had a perfect angle through the front doorway, offering her a clear view of the soldier.

She gasped. "He's coming."

We moved to the window. The soldier was walking right toward us. Obviously this was his next site to scrounge for souvenirs. Gid reached up slowly and slipped the sword out of its hide sheath.

If he found us, a fight seemed inevitable. *Please,* I prayed. *Just go back.* The soldier didn't look much older than me—eighteen or nineteen. He wouldn't have stood a chance against Gid. *Go back. No reason for anyone to die today.*

As he reached the doorway, Mary and I crouched below the window frame. She held my hand like a vise. Gid crouched as well, his sword ready to strike. Symeon continued to hold the head of the mule. If that mule let out even one soft whinny or kicked at the ground, our cover would be blown. I heard the soldier enter. I held my breath.

I heard a whinny. But it didn't come from our mule. It came from the soldier's horse out in the meadow. I heard rapid footsteps as the Roman rushed back out the way he'd come in.

"Stop!" I heard him shout.

I peeked over the window frame in time to see the cause of the commotion. Someone had commandeered his horse. The new rider was galloping fast back toward the city walls. It was a Jewish raider. Pretty gutsy fellow, I thought. But how did he expect to get back inside the city gates? Maybe he knew a secret way. The raider galloped into a thicket of scrub and disappeared.

We crept back to the edge of the abandoned farmhouse. The Roman soldier was running toward the meadow. He'd drawn his sword, but as he realized the chase was hopeless, he sputtered to a stop and threw it down in despair. He dropped to his knees and buried his face in his hands. I was perplexed. His anguish seemed too intense. After all, it was just a horse. He drew his dagger from a sheath at his waist. He gripped the blade in both hands. Then he turned it inward. Oh my gosh! He was going to kill himself!

"No!" Mary yelled.

The soldier leaped to his feet. We froze. Mary looked stunned. The word had just popped out. The soldier retrieved his sword.

"Come out!" he demanded. "How many are you?"

Calmly, Gid stepped out, followed by Mary and me, then by Symeon leading the mule.

"Who are you?" he barked. "Jews?"

"He's asking if we're Jewish," said Symeon, as if interpreting. No sense explaining that Gid and I already understood. Symeon had spoken in his native tongue. The soldier drew his own conclusions.

"So you *are* Jews," he said. "Deserters from the city?"

We didn't reply.

"Do you understand me? Are you deserters?"

We kept silent. The Roman approached cautiously. He indicated Gid's sword.

"Drop it. In the name of Caesar. You're my prisoners now. You hear me? Drop it!"

"Go back to your unit, soldier," said Gid. "We mean you no harm. Nor your people."

He drew closer. "So you *do* understand. Then understand this. I need that mule. I need to turn you over as my prisoners. Or my life isn't worth a pair of dice." His sword hand was shaking.

"They would execute you for losing your horse?" asked Gid.

He ran out of patience. "Drop your weapon or raise it!"

Mary and I backed away. Gid held his ground. The Roman lunged. Gid dodged it easily and tripped the man on his face. As he tried to recover, Gid smashed down on his hand. The soldier wailed and dropped the sword. Next Gid pressed the point of his own sword against the man's Adam's apple.

The Roman closed his eyes. "Do it! Do it quickly!"

"I have no wish to kill you, boy," said Gid.

"They'll kill me anyway!"

"That's not my affair."

We heard crashing sounds from the bushes beyond the meadow. The Jewish raider reappeared, still riding the soldier's horse. The thicket was suddenly swarming with Romans. Over twenty of them! Apparently they'd cut off the raider's escape. Two of the soldiers were on horseback. They were chasing the raider toward *us!*

Arrows were flying. One arrow had already struck the raider in the leg. I watched as a soldier at the edge of the thicket fired an arrow straight at its target. But it didn't hit the rider. It hit the *horse!*

The horse collapsed, crushing the rider beneath it. The raider tried to struggle free, but seconds later his attackers were on top of him. Both horse and rider were ruthlessly executed right before our eyes. I stood there in amazement. Mary and Symeon turned away. I snapped to my senses. We had to run! My eyes darted around. There was no place to hide!

Their attention now turned to us. Bows were loaded. Arrows were aimed.

"Let that man go!" one of the horsemen shouted at Gid. He reined in his beast a few yards in front of us and glared down with steely eyes. "Drop your weapon!"

The other horseman, a milder-looking man with ruddy cheeks, took up a position behind us. Gidgiddonihah hesitated, his sword still directed at the young soldier's throat.

"Gidgiddonihah," pleaded Symeon. "It's all right. Joseph ben Matthias will help us. Put down your sword."

Gid looked at Symeon and Mary, then at me. He sighed in disgust and removed the point from the soldier's neck. The soldier rolled away. Gid looked the horseman straight in the eye, then tossed his sword to the ground.

"Your other weapons," said the horseman.

Gid began removing his long knife and dagger. Mary and I tossed down our daggers as well.

"I see you understand Latin," the horseman observed. "Who are you?"

"A warrior like you," said Gid. "But this is not my war. My companions and I came in peace. This man attacked us, trying to take our mule."

"It's a lie!" proclaimed the young soldier. "These men were with the Jew who stole my horse. I was arresting them all when I was pulled off my mount. This man overpowered me while I was trying to—"

"Shut up, Cassius," said the horseman. "I don't believe a word of it. You'll answer for the life of that horse. Don't doubt it for a minute." He faced us again. "You're trespassing on restricted ground. What are you doing here?"

Symeon stepped forward, his knees shaking. "Please. My name is Symeon Cleophas. We are looking for Joseph Matthias. We have heard that he is an interpreter for his eminence, Prince Titus."

"Never heard of him," said the horseman.

The other horseman chimed in. "You mean Josephus the prophet?"

Even Symeon looked astonished to hear a Roman refer to a Jew as a prophet. "He was the commander of the Jews in Galilee," Symeon clarified.

Suddenly I wondered if I recognized the name as well. Wasn't Josephus the name of that historian dude Meagan had mentioned back at Qumran?

"Are you a relative?" asked the second horseman.

"No," said Symeon. "Just a friend. A business associate. I seek his help on an urgent personal matter. I have enlisted the help of these men to take me and my son—" he indicated Mary "—safely to his—"

"Tell it to the warden of the stockade," the first horseman blustered. "You're trespassers and you've attacked one of my men. I arrest you on suspicion of consorting with the enemy."

The foot soldiers swarmed on us. They seized my travel bag with the Book of Matthew! How could I have been so stupid as to carry it into a war zone? I should have hidden it in the hills. I should have done *anything* but bring it here.

One of the men retrieved Gid's sword. He rolled it over in his hands with great interest. Then he read the Latin name on the hilt. Suddenly, he looked at Gidgiddonihah with surprise, even a little fear.

We're dead meat, I thought. He knows about the incident at Salim. He knows the sword is stolen. The soldier took the sword to the first horseman. The two of them spoke in private. They scrutinized Gid for a long moment. Then the horseman repeated his command. "To the stockade!"

The soldier who'd taken my travel bag rifled through the contents. The scroll was in his hands! Hysteria gripped me. I was on the verge of screaming out for him to get his grubby hands off it.

I didn't have to. The steely-eyed horseman yelled at him, "Leave that alone! Keep their things together."

He glanced at Gid again and rode over to the other horseman with the ruddy cheeks. After another exchange of words, the second horseman rode off toward the city walls. Something funny was going on. I wanted Symeon to ask them what it was, but I kept my mouth shut. I reminded myself that so far I'd done everything I'd felt prompted to do. The Lord was in control. I had nothing to fear.

CHAPTER SEVEN

"What was it, Jesse? What did you figure out?"

The question burst from my lips as soon as Menander and his cronies had left us alone in the catacomb. The trouble was, no one had bothered to untie our hands. They'd just dumped us inside. The black hoods hadn't even been removed from our heads. Did they expect us to stay like this all night? It was the creepiest feeling I'd ever had. Rats could attack us and there was nothing we could do to defend ourselves. I could hear the slimy little buggers scurrying about even now.

"Figured out?" asked Jesse, his voice muffled by the hood.

"Yes!" I said desperately. "You said if they ever put us back in here—don't you remember? You were about to say something when Saturninus interrupted."

"Oh that," said Jesse unenthusiastically. "It was probably nothing."

If my hands had been free, I'd have throttled him. I'd vested all my hopes in that unfinished statement. I'd been praying he might have figured out a way to escape.

"What do you mean?! What were you going to say?"

"I was going to say that I thought I might have found a way to get out."

I knew it! "What? Tell me what it was!"

"It was just something I saw. Something when they first came to

get us. I shouldn't have gotten your hopes up."

"Tell me!"

"Well, you remember when they first brought in the torches? The light was so bright. It even frightened some rats along the wall. Remember how water was dripping from the ceiling? Well, all that water flowed into a puddle in the corner."

"I remember," I said. "I stuck my foot in it while I was getting a drink. So?"

"So when the rats saw the light, they jumped into it."

"The puddle?"

"Yes. They dove under the surface and disappeared. They didn't come back out. I know because I watched the whole time before they put the sack over my head."

"Where did they go?"

"I don't know. But I think it's more than just a puddle."

"An underwater tunnel?"

"It has to be."

"But you only saw rats! What makes you think it would be big enough for people? What makes you think it would lead anywhere at all?"

"I told you it was probably nothing."

I groaned inwardly. How could I have let myself get my hopes up? I'd really thought it was something important. Besides, we weren't even in the room with the dripping water anymore. They'd deposited us somewhere else. Somewhere closer to the entrance. It seemed to me that it would be a better idea to find the stone that was sealing us in. Maybe together Jesse and I could move it.

"Can you get your hands free?" I asked.

"No. Can you?"

I strained again at the ropes. They'd tied them with leather straps. There was no give. I'd tear my own flesh before I could slip out.

"Give me your hands," I said.

"What?"

"Turn around. Let me see if I can untie the knot."

We turned back to back. I felt the knots on Jesse's hands with my fingers. It seemed simple enough. But how could I untie them if I couldn't even see them?

"Let me try," said Jesse.

He felt the knots on my hands. He began picking at one with his fingernail.

"Can you get it?"

"I think so."

He kept at it for two or three minutes. I started losing patience. It wasn't going to work! But then he got a piece of it. The knot came loose. My hands were free!

I yanked the sack off my head. Not that it helped. The place was still as black as pitch. But at least I could breathe more easily. After massaging my wrists, I went to work on Jesse's knots. It didn't seem any easier than when I was facing backwards, except that I now had the advantage of using my teeth. A minute later I untied the first knot. His hands came loose. Now we were both free! Well, in a manner of speaking anyway. Actually, we were no better off now than we had been the day before.

"Let's find the place where the stone covers the entrance," I suggested.

"It's no use," said Jesse. "There are guards there. I heard them when they brought us back. I think they've been there the whole time."

I knew he was right. Simon wouldn't just leave us unguarded. I was too important to his scheme. I fought down a wave of panic.

"We have to get out of here, Jesse. In three days the temple is going to be destroyed."

"How do you know this?"

"Trust me. I know."

"Then you really are a prophetess."

"Not even close. Listen, I don't expect you to understand. You just have to believe me. If we don't find a way to escape, Simon will kill you. He'll do it just to tighten his control on me."

I couldn't see Jesse's face, but I knew my words had left him mystified. Why wouldn't they have? To him the only explanation would have been supernatural. And yet despite all that had happened—all the bizarre things he'd seen and heard—Jesse still believed in me. He decided to trust me.

"We have to find that room," he said. "The one with the water dripping. We have to find out where the rats disappeared."

I shrank at the notion. "But Jesse—"

"We just have to find out!"

Without hearing any arguments, he grabbed my hand and began leading me through the tunnels. We felt our way through the darkness for only a short distance before I began to hear the familiar sound of falling droplets. It was the same room. I'd have recognized that drip anywhere.

Jesse felt his way across the floor until he reached the place where the water gathered. I heard a splash as his foot sank in. It did sound deeper than I'd first thought. I heard Jesse shiver.

"What's the matter?"

"It's so cold!"

The water likely came from a spring deep in the earth and was kept doubly cool in this awful cave. Despite my lack of faith, Jesse was right that the water had to go somewhere. Still, I couldn't imagine the passage would be large enough for anything but rats.

Jesse continued splashing around. It sounded as if he'd gotten himself in pretty deep.

"What have you found?"

"There is a tunnel!" he said excitedly.

"There is? How big?"

"Not very. Just a little longer than my forearm. But it's perfectly square. And it's as high as my hip."

I wasn't even wet, but I shivered anyway. A part of me had hoped that Jesse was wrong. It would be a swim in total darkness. The water was like ice. No, it wasn't rational. That passage could go on forever. We'd drown for sure. How could we be certain it came out anywhere at all? Maybe it just went down into the ground. Then again, the rats had gone somewhere . . .

No! I couldn't do it. Ever since Harry and I had taken that water ride in Frost Cave, my fear of drowning had shot off the scale. Add to that the fact that I could see exactly nothing! Underwater tunnels were simply not an option.

"I'll swim in a ways and see how far it goes," said Jesse.

"Jesse, wait," I said sharply. "Let's . . . try to think of something else. We'll leave this as a last resort."

"This is our last resort, Meagan. What other resort do we have?"

I hated to admit it, but he was right. My breathing quickened, as if my lungs were already fighting for air.

"I'm going in," said Jesse. "Wait here."

Where else did he think I was gonna wait? "Jesse! Jesse!"

"Yes?"

I searched for something to say. I was stalling. Finally I said, "Be careful."

"I will."

I heard him draw a deep breath. Then I heard a ripple in the surface as he went under. My heart was pounding. This was ridiculous. The whole reason we were trying to escape was to save Jesse's life. What was the point if he drowned in that tunnel? Thirty seconds later, I heard another splash and a deep gasp of air. Jesse had returned.

"Oh, it's cold!"

I could hear the shivering in his voice.

"Well?" I asked anxiously. "What did you find?"

"I only went in a little ways. It comes to a turn and keeps going. I'll catch my breath and try again."

"No, Jesse," I said. "This is insane. It's too far. What if you black out and can't get back?"

"I'll get back. I have to find out how far it goes."

My body was quivering with panic. Just how long could those

small lungs of his go on without air? Two minutes at the most. Then he'd start to drown.

"*I can't take this, Jesse. We have to think of something else.*"

"*Don't worry,*" *he said.* "*I know what I'm doing.*"

Before I could say anything else, I heard him take another deep breath. There was another splash and then silence.

Immediately, I started counting, "*One one thousand, two one thousand, three one thousand . . .*"

What would I do if he didn't come back in two minutes? I doubted if I could hold my breath as long as Jesse.

"*. . . thirty-one one thousand, thirty-two one thousand . . .*"

Why did it have to be so dark? If there had just been a little light, I would have felt so much better, so much more assured.

"*. . . fifty-eight one thousand, fifty-nine one thousand, sixty one thousand . . .*"

One minute. I started over at one one thousand. Come on, Jesse, *I cried in my heart.* That's long enough. *I told* him *it wasn't going to work. Come back. Come back.*

"*. . . twenty-eight one thousand, twenty-nine one thousand . . .*"

A minute and a half. This was driving me crazy. I was hyperventilating. If I didn't stop breathing so fast, I was going to faint. Please, Jesse, please.

"*. . . sixty one thousand! . . .*"

That was it. Two minutes. Time was up. He had to come back now. Where was he? I got down on my hands and knees. I crawled to the edge of the water. I listened with all my might. The water was silent. Just that monotonous drip from the ceiling. Where was he?!

"*Jesse!*" *I screamed.* "*Jesse!*"

Was it possible that he made it through? What if he was waiting on the other side—waiting until he worked up enough breath to return? Then again, what if he was stuck? What if he was dying?! *Why hadn't we set a time limit? Some kind of signal?*

"*JESSSSSEEEE!*"

Tears shot out of my eyes. I'd stopped counting. It had been at least three minutes now. I had to do something. I couldn't wait any longer.

I plunged into the water. My adrenaline must have kicked into high gear because I barely felt a chill. The pool was about four feet deep near the wall. I located the tunnel. I dunked my head and listened. Sound carried for long distances under water, right? Yet I heard nothing at all.

I came up out of the water. This time I drew the deepest breath I'd ever drawn in my life. Again I plunged beneath the icy surface. I kicked off with my legs and squirmed into the watery blackness. I dragged myself along, digging my nails into the stones. The walls were slick. I couldn't travel very quickly. And yet the tunnel was so narrow that I couldn't use my arms to swim.

I remained completely blind. It occurred to me that if Jesse was on his way back, we'd crash heads. We'd create a bottleneck. We'd both drown. *This was nuts! Jesse was smaller than I was. Even if Jesse had made it through, I might still get trapped!*

I'd gone about thirty feet. I tried not to think about it. I'd have been paralyzed with claustrophobia. I couldn't stop now. There was no way of turning around. I'd have to crawl backwards. *My lungs were giving out. Even if I found Jesse, how could I ever help him?*

I reached the corner that Jesse mentioned. The tunnel curved sharply to the right. It was a tight squeeze. I turned on my side, pulling myself along more furiously than ever. Where had the rats gone? Rats couldn't swim this far underwater, could they? My head was starting to feel light. What had I done? I'd never get back now. It was too late! I'd just committed suicide!

I kept going. Forward was the only direction that offered any hope. God help me! My arms were going limp. I was dying!

Something kicked me in the head. Someone's knee. I felt a hand grab my hair and pull me upward. My head was pressed into the ceiling. What was going on? My face was being smashed into the stone! I heard someone's voice. Very muffled. Underwater.

"Breathe!" I heard.

It was Jesse. I could tell that much. He said something else—it was garbled. I didn't understand. I opened my mouth. My throat filled with water. What was he talking about? There was no air!

He cried out again, still underwater. This time I understood.

"Through your nose! Breathe through your nose!"

His fingers crawled over my face, trying to locate my nose. He was trying to line it up with a crack in the top of the tunnel. As soon as my head was lined up properly, he pressed my face harder into the crack.

I drew a breath! Air went into my lungs. Not a lot. But enough that Jesse no longer had to push. I pressed my own nose into the crack, digging my heels into the bottom. I snorted in as much water as air. I blew it back out my nose and pressed in even harder. The gap was only about three-fourths of an inch wide. There was no light. But there was air!

I breathed more steadily. If I opened my mouth, it only filled with water. It was so hard to keep it closed. But I learned fast. Only my nostrils stuck out far enough. It took all my concentration to keep from totally losing my mind. Something calmed my spirit. I was able to think straight. I was able to breathe.

It was incredible that Jesse had found this gap at all. I stuck my fingers into the gap and felt the open air. I couldn't reach in past my knuckles. I assumed it was just another section of the catacomb. This water tunnel might have once been a kind of sewer.

As Jesse realized that I'd gotten the hang of it, he let me go. He went back to trying to breathe for himself a little further down in the same crack. I reached out, found his hand, and held on.

After I'd satisfied my lungs for several minutes, stopping once or twice more to blow the water out of my nose, I yanked on Jesse's hand to indicate that we should try to go back. He resisted and yanked the other way. He still wanted to go forward! He still believed this tunnel might lead to freedom.

My nerves were fried. I didn't think I could go another yard. I was about to dunk back under and scream at Jesse, "Forget it! I'm going back!" when I heard Jesse's garbled, underwater voice calling into my ear.

"Air pocket! Come on!"

It occurred to me that Jesse had been on his way back *when I ran into his knee. He already knew what lay ahead. Air pocket. It didn't sound much more encouraging than where we were now. But if Jesse felt it was safe, I'd go along just a little farther.*

I brought Jesse's hand to my chin and let him feel it as I nodded my consent.

"Okay!" I shouted underwater. He squeezed my hand and began pulling away. I waited a few seconds. I was terrified of losing him in the tunnel, but I was more afraid of getting kicked in the head again if I swam too close. How far was the next air pocket? I knew I couldn't go as far as I had the first time.

Mustering the courage, I drew a deep breath through my nose and plunged in after him. I crawled hand over hand, kicking my feet like a demon. I had more confidence now. I forged ahead without fear. As I expected, my air ran out much sooner than before. I was on the verge of fainting when I ran into Jesse's hand.

I pushed upward. As my face broke the surface, I drew a deep gasping breath. It tasted so good. I began coughing and crying. The ceiling was only about six or eight inches above the surface of the water. I still couldn't see a thing, but oh! I could breathe!

"Where does it go from here?" I asked Jesse.

"I don't know," he said. "This is as far as I got. I'll scout ahead like I did before and then come back to get you."

"No way," I said sternly. "You're not leaving me again. I'm staying right behind you."

"I don't think we'll have to go much farther," said Jesse. "Do you feel it? The water is moving faster."

He was right. There was a distinct current pulling us along now. The tunnel was slanting slightly downward. I wasn't sure how this proved we wouldn't have to go much farther. But I'd give it a chance. I knew if the current became too *strong, we'd never get back to this pocket of air.*

My mind coursed back to that underground river that had started all this mess in the first place. Just don't be another time tunnel, *I told myself.* I couldn't take it. Unless of course it shot us out in the center of my front lawn in West Valley.

We remained there for several more minutes catching our breath and working up our nerves. I felt around. There were several crevasses and cracks. The air might have been coming through any one of them. I realized we were now surrounded by natural stone— not the cut stones that lined the walls and floors of the catacomb. Had we gone beyond the limits of the catacomb? The thought revitalized my faith. I was ready to go on.

"I'll count to three," said Jesse.

I drew several deep breaths. "Ready," I said.

Jesse counted. We dove back under. This time it was only about twenty seconds to the next air pocket. This one was large. And high. Jesse and I stood on our feet. The space was nearly five feet tall—with a full twelve inches for our heads. I could hear water dripping. Lots *of water. The sound echoed. The air pocket seemed to go quite some distance.*

"We can walk," said Jesse.

I held his arm. We continued down the tunnel with outstretched arms to keep from colliding into any hanging shelves. The current had grown swifter. Now and then we walked right under a shower of spring water. Something solid hit my face. It was a tree root. I pushed it aside. This was starting to get creepy.

Something slimy swam between my legs. I screeched and pressed against the tunnel wall.

"I felt something!" I rasped.

"I felt it, too," said Jesse. "A fish. There! I felt another one!"

"A fish! What kind of fish would live in here?"

"I don't know. But it's a good sign."

We continued to push through more tree roots. The current carried us along quite comfortably. My panic at being blind had almost subsided. I could make it. Who needed to see? Just as I thought this, the faintest of lights appeared up ahead. At first I thought it was an illusion. Then Jesse acknowledged it too.

"It's a way out!" said Jesse. "We're almost there!"

We scrambled that last hundred feet as fast as we could. It was definitely sunlight. The tunnel became narrow again. We had to get down on our hands and knees. The last ten-foot stretch was very *narrow. We pulled ourselves along on our stomachs. The ground was soft and muddy. When we came out we'd look like a couple of hogs fresh from the mire.*

At the very end the ceiling swung down very low. Only at the far right side was it wide enough to squirm through. In my impatience I'd gotten ahead of Jesse. I wanted desperately to feel that sunlight on my face.

The moment came. I stuck my head through the hole. The fresh air was almost too good to be true. The light was almost blinding. I paused to take it all in. I could feel Jesse at my feet.

"Hurry!" he said. "I want to see!"

I realized the water came out into some kind of stone pool. The pool overflowed into a stream at the far end. Flowers surrounded the pool. Hundreds of flowers. Suddenly the place seemed vaguely familiar.

As it hit me, I nearly choked. Just beyond the pool and garden stood a large building with terraces and columns. It couldn't be true. How could this happen? Of all the places in the world where this tunnel might have led us, why did it have to be here?

I began squirming backwards.

"What's the matter?" asked Jesse.

"We're back where we were last night," I said in anguish. "Right back where we least wanted to be."

"What do you mean?"

"It's Simon's palace! We're still locked inside the courtyard of the Sons of the Elect!"

CHAPTER EIGHT

We sat in the heat of the stockade under heavy guard. The only shade came from the spiked wooden fence that enclosed us. Not much protection considering it was about three o'clock and the sun was beating down like a hammer. Mary finally wore the hood of her cloak, but it had nothing to do with her disguise. It was the best way to keep from getting sunstroke.

The stockade was nearly a block long, situated just inside the demolished second wall of Jerusalem's outer quarter and just opposite the Roman siege wall. I imagined this spot had once been a thriving neighborhood with shops and clean city streets. All that was gone now. All around us were piles of rubble and stone and the remains of bonfires. The Romans had done their best to erase nearly every shred of evidence that this had ever been a peaceful and prosperous place.

Now and then I caught the guards whispering to each other and pointing a knobby finger in our direction. I should correct that. They were pointing at *Gidgiddonihah*. Once I heard a guy say, ". . . won the golden palm at Antioch." All the gawking was getting on my nerves. It was like they thought Gid was some kind of celebrity.

Then it hit me. The *sword*. Oh my gosh! They thought Gid was the *owner*. They thought he really was that trainer named Problius. Was Problius some kind of famous gladiator? As I thought back on the man that Gidgiddonihah had disarmed and knocked unconscious in the fighting pit at Salim, I wasn't all that impressed. Maybe in his younger days he was some sort of hot item. Now it appeared that Gid had unwittingly taken that reputation upon himself. Then again, maybe they were just trying to figure out what Gid was doing with a famous gladiator's sword.

Whatever the case, our treatment was a lot better than the prisoners in the main compound to the east. I had the impression that our little pen was reserved for prisoners of distinction, captured generals or kings or some such. They gave us plenty of water and even offered us some hardtack rolls.

The prisoners across the way were given no water or food or relief whatsoever. There were hundreds of them, mostly men, but also some women and children. These, I gathered, were war prisoners and deserters from the city. Their bodies were emaciated and their clothes were in rags. They may have been moving and breathing, but their eyes looked dead, as if their spirits had already departed to the next world. The sight tore at my heart. They couldn't all look like that inside the city, could they? The thought curdled my stomach. Several times I watched Roman soldiers enter their compound and drag away the youngest and strongest-looking of the men. As I watched, I gripped the wooden bars of our cage, my teeth clenching in anger. I realized it was likely from this place that the Romans found fresh victims for their crosses. What could I do? There was nothing. I was powerless.

The heat drained me of all my energy. I slumped against the bars and closed my eyes. I was sure that I only fell asleep for a few minutes, but when I opened them again, a strange awe seemed to have gripped the camp of the Romans. Nearly every soldier I could see had stopped to gaze in the direction of the temple. I turned and realized that the smoke had grown much thicker and blacker over there, making the buildings harder to see. Something new had been set on fire—something significant. It wasn't the temple itself. It appeared to be the tall porches surrounding the inner courtyard. Now I started to hear the flames.

Nearly all of the Jewish prisoners in the opposite compound were pressed against the timbers on the south, staring blankly at the temple compound. They stood like statues, their sights fixed. Was it disbelief on their faces? That didn't quite describe it. These people were stunned into silence. They looked like they were watching something totally incomprehensible, something they wouldn't have dreamed possible in a thousand years.

I sat there watching the whole thing in a kind of trance myself until I was jarred back to reality by the arrival of some Roman soldiers. They weren't ordinary troops. They had a special eagle insignia on their shoulders. The head honcho of the bunch went immediately to the officer in charge of the stockade and directed that the four of us be released at once. Behind him I recognized the soldier with the ruddy cheeks from the patrol who'd brought us here.

We emerged from the pen, a little dazed by our change in fortune. The ruddy-cheeked soldier approached us and said, "These men are with the royal guard. They will take you to Flavius Josephus."

"Then he is expecting us?" said Symeon, mildly surprised.

The man nodded. "Your story checks out. Lucky for you, you keep the right company." He glanced at Gidgiddonihah. Afterwards he saluted the lead guardsman and departed.

With elation I realized that several of the guardsmen were carrying our stuff! Even Symeon's mule was parked just outside the stockade. I went up to one of the men, who happily handed back my travel bag. To my delight the scroll of Matthew was still inside. The head guardsman approached Gidgiddonihah and held out Problius' sword.

"General Titus sends his apologies for any mistreatment you might have incurred," he said. "He's looking forward to seeing you again. As a boy he watched you fight in the Juvenalia."

I gulped like I'd swallowed a watermelon. So it was true. They thought Gid was Problius. Gid just gaped at the man. I felt a crawling dread. How would Gid respond? The man gestured again that it was okay for him to take the sword. Finally, Gid smiled and wrapped his fingers around the hilt.

"Thank you," he said simply. "I look forward to seeing him, too."

My eyebrows popped up. Gid shot me a look that said, *Be cool. Don't panic.*

What else could I do? Titus knew exactly what the real Problius looked like. He'd take one look at Gid and order him beheaded on the spot!

Calm down, I told myself. *The Lord is in control. The Lord is in control.*

"His Eminence is in counsel with his generals," the soldier told Gid. "But Josephus will see you now."

It was like a brief stay in our execution. Still, as the royal guard started to lead us east along the Roman siege wall, I seriously considered signaling to everyone that we should make a break for it. Symeon and Mary looked as jittery as I felt. Gidgiddonihah, however, had nerves of steel. The Nephite warrior looked unconcerned. I drew a deep breath, trying to feed off his courage.

As we approached one of the gate towers built into the siege wall, I noticed that one of the royal guardsmen—a gruff-looking old cuss with part of his right ear missing—was watching Mary quite closely. Her hood had fallen off and her feminine features were revealed quite plainly. Did the man see through the disguise? If he didn't, why was he glaring at her like that? I came to her defense.

"He doesn't talk," I said.

"Hm?" grunted the soldier.

"He's been traumatized."

The word didn't seem to make sense to him.

"He hasn't spoken since his mother was killed."

The Roman digested this. "How old is he?"

Symeon piped in. "Thirteen."

It was a smart answer. Making her younger than she was covered for any lack of masculinity. The soldier grunted again and faced forward, his curiosity deflected.

As we passed through the gate, the horrors of the war overwhelmed me all over again. Directly over our heads stretched a long row of crosses—maybe fifteen or twenty. I didn't stop to count. I tried not to look up, but I couldn't help it. Two of the victims were staring right at me, their lips cracked and bleeding, their faces black with sunburn. Their eyes cut into me like lasers. I turned away, shivering, again overwhelmed by a sinking feeling of helplessness.

"Will you give them water?" I heard myself ask.

The soldier at the gate laughed. His comrades tried to smile. They thought I was joking. But as they ushered us past, none of the soldiers could look me in the eye.

Beyond the tower I finally had my first clear view of the defenders atop Jerusalem's first and oldest wall. I heard their shouts of defiance. They were enraged. Enraged over the burning of those porches and columns around the temple courtyard. Some were yelling at *us*. I guessed they'd recognized the insignia of the royal guard. The sky was whistling with flaming spears and arrows. The Jews were trying to hit the Romans' catapult nests atop the timber embankments. We were only about fifty to a hundred yards out of range as we made our way through the rubble-filled streets toward a partly demolished building that stood directly northwest of the temple. It looked like it had once been a castle, but with only one standing tower. Inside was a large courtyard and a field of tents with red banners displaying the Roman numeral XII. This, I presumed, was the camp of the Twelfth Legion. Apparently it was also the headquarters of Titus and Josephus.

The smell of death was stronger than ever, so rank my eyes were watering. We passed a line of coffins filled with bodies. We even passed the rotting corpse of a horse. But all this didn't seem to explain the overpowering odor.

The head guardsman must have seen me wince, because he said, "The smell is from the ravines below the wall. The Jews toss their dead from the ramparts and leave them to rot. Over a hundred a day, just from starvation."

The comment made Symeon a bit defensive. "Jews would never treat a corpse so blasphemously."

The Roman huffed, "I've watched the Jews do a lot of things I heard they'd never do."

No more was spoken as we began to pass the first tents. We moved out of the way as a dozen horsemen thundered past us and galloped toward the temple grounds. A battle was raging in that vicinity at this very minute—right in the midst of the smoke and fire. It was happening just a stone's throw from the place where the battering ram inside the largest siege tower continued pounding. I could see part of the northern porch that encircled the inner courtyard. The gate was swallowed up in flames. Just east and west of the gate, a few of the Romans were raising ladders. I watched as several Jewish defenders dragged one of the ladders over and let it fall. A Roman soldier about two-thirds of the way from the top plunged to the earth. I didn't see him land, but I heard the shriek. It ended abruptly. The Jews atop the wall raised their shields and took cover behind the battlements. A volley of arrows rained on their heads. I saw it all right before my eyes!

The rows of tents became thick. My view of the action was hindered by the walls of the demolished castle. As I looked around I began to see a lot more men with royal insignia. The head guardsman received salute after salute. The Roman salute was just like in the movies when they pound their fist on their left breast and make a sign like a "Heil Hitler."

Finally we passed a long white tent that had eagle banners flying in six places. A host of guards were crowded around it, along with a lot of men bearing flags. The flags displayed the numbers X and XV, XII and V. Some also had the symbols of the foreign armies Rome had enlisted to help crush the Jewish revolt. This meeting must have been pretty high-level stuff. Every bigwig in the Roman army was in attendance. The Jewish defenders on the wall would have done well if they could have dropped a big firebomb right on top of us. Unfortunately, their catapults were barely out of range.

Through the various doorways and slits in the canvas I could see snatches of people. There was quite a hubbub, people arguing back and forth about some subject or another. I was sure I could see Titus himself sitting at the head of the gathering with about fifteen royal guardsmen behind him. He was listening intently to the discussion, his hands on his knees. Despite having what looked like a lean and muscular body, his face was rather chubby. He almost had a double chin. I might have expected the commander of the Roman armies to be a little older. This guy wasn't much over thirty. The fate of Jerusalem had been left in the hands of a fairly young pup. I guess when your dad is Emperor, no one asks your age. An odd thought struck me. It occurred to me that Titus was going to destroy Jerusalem at just about the same age as Jesus when He saved it.

Titus glanced in our direction. On impulse, I jerked out of his range of sight. Suddenly I felt foolish. It was *Gid* who needed to worry about being recognized, not me. At the moment Gid was behind the mule, unintentionally hidden from view.

The lead soldier in our escort whispered something into the ear of a sentry at the main entrance. This sentry whispered to another sentry who then slipped inside.

I listened to part of the discussion raging in the tent. Someone with a deep-throated voice—I assumed it was a general—was addressing the group. ". . . it will always be a focus for rebellion! I guarantee if we let it stand, they'll rally around it like wasps to a hive. Maybe not tomorrow, maybe not in ten years, but someday we'll be marching right back to this cursed land to fight this war all over again. By the gods, I guarantee it!"

A lot of men seemed to agree with whatever point the general was making. A loud clamor erupted inside. The sentry who'd been sent into the tent returned. Behind his shoulder walked a tall Jew with an alert, striking face. I had to look closely to confirm his nationality. After all, his clothes were Roman, his hair was cut like a Roman, and his presence among the Roman soldiers was so casual it was hard to believe he was Jewish. This might have explained the stunned look on Symeon's face. I think the transformation of his old associate took him by surprise. After all, this guy had once fought for the Jews.

I caught a strange scowl on the face of Gidgiddonihah. He was cordial enough as Josephus emerged and approached Symeon with open arms, but I perceived that he didn't like this person right from the start. I felt I understood why, too. Gid was a true-blue warrior. By all appearances, this man was a traitor to his people. I don't think Gid would have cared what army or nation Josephus had once fought for. To do what Josephus had done was an act undeserving of another soldier's respect.

I decided to reserve my own opinion for now. After all, this Jewish interpreter was our ticket inside Jerusalem. Josephus smiled broadly as he embraced Symeon, but I could tell that his mood was heavy. The discussion in that tent appeared to have taxed his energy. He seemed grateful for the break.

"Symeon bar Cleophas, what are you doing here?" Josephus said heartily. "I had heard you were in Pella with the others of your party. I had even heard that they gave you a position of some rank."

"Yes, Joseph," said Symeon. "We have traveled far. It's good to see you. Good to see you looking so well."

"Yes," said Josephus hesitantly. I think he'd interpreted Symeon's remark as a question. No doubt old friends would have been curious to learn how Josephus had come to look the way he looked, or to be in the position he was in. "What brings you to Jerusalem? It was a foolish journey to make. You shouldn't have made it."

"It is a matter of urgent—"

"Wait," said Josephus. "We'll talk in my tent. Come. Bring your companions."

Our escort let us go without a second glance, as if we were suddenly part of the regular scenery. Josephus' tent was only a short distance away. It was right in the midst of a network of other tents in the middle of the castle courtyard. More sentries stood around like statues. This, I assumed, was the headquarters of Titus and his closest advisors. Josephus had moved up the ranks from enemy to confidant as slick as you please. I had no idea what kind of man we were about to meet. But one thing seemed certain. Here was a guy who knew how to survive.

A woman appeared in the doorway of the main tent. Her dark hair was decked in pins and jewels. She had the most haunting dark eyes and bright red lips. I hadn't seen so much makeup and fine clothes since we'd arrived in the ancient world. And yet she looked very Jewish. I might even say she looked like a princess. I later learned she was.

"Joseph," she called over. "Is it decided?"

Josephus paused to speak with her. "Have no fear, my lady. The matter was decided before it was even discussed. This council was only convened in deference to the generals. Titus will keep his word. Be assured."

The woman tried to smile. Her eyes passed over us, then she retired into the tent. Josephus waved us into another tent a few steps to the west.

After we had entered, Symeon asked in mortification, "Was that . . . ?"

"Yes," said Josephus, interrupting. "Agrippa's sister, the Lady Bernice. Don't be so shocked. It may be the presence of Herod's granddaughter in Titus' tent that will save the temple."

"Save the temple?" Symeon asked.

"This is what the generals are debating in the council tent. Most of them are for burning it completely to the ground, even salting the soil so that nothing may ever grow there again. But Titus has promised Bernice—as he has promised me—the temple will remain."

Symeon shook his head. "It cannot be. The fate of the temple has been decided by prophecy."

"Ah," said Josephus. "Your messiah's old oracle. Well, I hope he did not mean for it to be fulfilled for a very long time."

"Sooner than you think," I said. I cleared my throat, realizing I'd spoken out of turn.

Josephus smiled at the remark, then changed the subject. "Forgive me. I have not been introduced to your companions."

"This is Harry," said Symeon. "Harry of Germania."

"Germania?"

"He is a follower of Jesus of Nazareth."

"The Nazarene has followers as far away as Germania? I'm impressed." He turned to Gid. "I understand this man needs no introduction. My master, Prince Titus, is looking forward to speaking with you. Are you also a . . . what is the word? . . . a Christian?"

"Yes," said Gid.

Josephus sighed, seemingly disappointed. He said to Symeon, "So your sect is converting gladiators now as well, eh? I wouldn't trumpet that bit of trivia among the troops if I were you. It might spoil the mystique. Romans like to think their heroes are above the passions of religion." Josephus turned from Gid and took Symeon by the shoulders. "Oh, Symeon, it's good to see you. It seems so long ago that we sipped wine together at your vineyard in Cana. The best wine in all of Galilee. Which, of course, means all the world."

Symeon looked at the ground. "The vineyard was burned when the Romans took Jotapata."

Josephus nodded sympathetically. "I heard. How is your family? How is your wife? Anna, wasn't it?"

"She . . . she has passed on."

"I see. I'm very sorry. And your daughters? You had three, if I remember. One had recently wed."

"Two are wed now," said Symeon.

"What about your youngest. She was quite beautiful, as I recall."

"Well, she . . . she is. . ." Symeon glanced at Mary.

Josephus followed his eyes. He gave the boy in the hooded cloak only a fleeting glance, perhaps wondering what he had to do with anything. Then Josephus did a double-take. His eyes opened wide. He approached Mary for a closer look.

"My word! Symeon!" Josephus said with alarm. "You have brought your daughter into the camp of the Romans?"

"We had no choice. There was nowhere else for her to go."

"You must get her out of here at once! These soldiers would show no mercy to a Jewess so young and fine." He raised a finger as if to touch her cheek.

I didn't like the look in Josephus' eye. I stepped closer to Mary defensively and said, "She has protectors."

Josephus saw that Gid was watching as well. He backed up a step. "Yes, well. It's still very dangerous."

"We have no desire to stay here long," said Symeon. "God willing, we will leave tonight. Tomorrow at the latest. But we need your help."

"My help? What is it that you need, my old friend?"

"We need to get inside the city."

He raised his eyebrows. "Inside Jerusalem?"

"Yes. Is it possible?"

"Whatever for?"

"We are seeking to retrieve some very important documents."

Josephus seemed amused. "Documents?! What documents could possibly be worth risking your lives to recover? Don't you know that the rebels have destroyed all the city's government records and archives?"

"Those are not the documents we seek," said Symeon. "We are looking for documents that pertain to our religion and faith."

"Christian documents? Don't be absurd. The Sanhedrin outlawed the dissemination of Christian writings years ago. I doubt very much that such writings could still exist inside those walls."

"We believe they do exist, Joseph." He placed a hand on Josephus' arm. "Years ago when we spoke at my estate, you professed a great deal of respect, even reverence, for the followers of Jesus of Nazareth."

"I admired your party's tenacity and zeal. That's all. Like Gamaliel of old, I never believed any of its teachings would survive into the next generation."

"But they *must* survive, Joseph," said Symeon. "It's the only hope for our nation and people."

Josephus grinned. "Oh, I think our nation and people will go on all right. They'll go on despite themselves. I've enlisted my services to Caesar and Rome to insure that very fact. The Romans must know that not all Jews are seditionists. I tell you,

Symeon, I was *never* a supporter of the rebel cause. Not even in the days when I commanded Galilee. Even then I did my best only to spare the people some semblance of pain and save them from the full fury of their inevitable fate. This has been a foolish and destructive war from the very beginning. We never stood a chance. Thousands have died in Jerusalem, Symeon. But not by Roman hands. They've been killing each other day and night for two years. They only stopped after we took the first and second wall. There was never any unity among them. Only tyranny and infighting. Idiots, all of them! Why, this siege might have gone on for years. The city certainly had enough food and grain. But you know what they did? They burned it! That's right. Burned nearly four-fifths of all their stores! The Idumeans and the Zealots and the tyrants of Eleazar did it while they were fighting *each other*. Criminals and idiots! All the common people could do was cower and watch. Now the rebels have nearly destroyed everything we hold most dear—our great city, our temple, our entire way of life!"

His voice was stirring. Almost enough to make even *me* hate those good-for-nothing rebels.

Mary, however, was more skeptical. "But . . . it's said that you defended Jotapata to the end. If you wished to spare the people, why didn't you surrender sooner before so many thousands were killed?"

Josephus smiled again, but there was pain in his smile. He stalled for several seconds, then he said, "My dear child, I am not a traitor, as so many of my countrymen have proclaimed. I was entrusted with a commission, and I fulfilled that commission. I am still a Jew, with the pride and spirit of a Jew. Though I might be scorned in the synagogues from Rome to Egypt, and though my fellow Jews will not come within seven paces of my presence, I know that time will vindicate me and prove me a patriot. Not to the Zealots—oh no! But to the *Jews*. Can anyone doubt that what has happened here is the will of God? The portents have all been clear. Just as God scourged us by Nebuchadnezzar and Babylon, he scourges us now by Titus and the Romans. This people will not learn from history! My role here has been to try to shake them from their stupor, convince them to abandon this futile war, and save what remains of our crippled culture."

"Why do the Romans call you a prophet?" I decided to ask.

He suddenly looked very smug. "Because I properly interpreted the ancient oracle."

"What oracle?"

"The oracle that states that the ruler of the world would come from Judea. Many still think this means someone of Jewish blood. It's one of the falsehoods that continues to fuel the rebel cause. When I was captured at Jotapata, I told Vespasian that *he* would fulfill this oracle. And I was proven right, because Vespasian was proclaimed Emperor on Jewish soil."

"You told him this right after you were captured?" asked Gidgiddonihah.

Gid's inference was clear. It sounded like a prophecy uttered in desperation—one designed to save one's own neck. But I had to hand it to Josephus. The plan had worked. Joseph, son of Matthias, may have been the luckiest man I'd ever met.

Josephus nodded to Gid's question, then said, "Now it becomes my task to witness all these sad events. I am commissioned by Caesar to write a history of all that my eyes have beheld and to publish it for all generations."

"It will be an invaluable book," said Symeon. "I support you in this venture. I support you for the same reason that I ask you to support me. The words of Jesus are the words of life. All we ask is that you help us to get inside the city walls."

"I might be able to help you get inside," said Josephus. "But I could never help you to get out again. Once you're in, you're a prisoner of the rebels. If the Zealots catch you trying to leave, they'll kill you on the spot. If the Romans catch you, they'll likely execute you just as swiftly. Titus hasn't much further use for deserters. The time of Caesar's mercy is past. I might never learn of it in time to intervene."

"We'll worry about that," I said. "We just need to get inside. Will you help us?"

Josephus started wringing his hands. "There might be a way, but you can't tell the Zealots that it was me who helped you. They'd flay you like an eel. But if I help you, I must have your word of honor that you will do something for me."

"What is it?" asked Symeon.

"My mother and my father are both in Jerusalem," said Josephus tenderly. "They have been there since the start of the war. I have heard that because of me the Zealots treat them quite miserably. My father, I've been told, is a prisoner in Phasael tower. My mother, I couldn't say. I heard that the rebels tormented her with the news of my death when I was struck on the head last month by a stone. I've heard nothing since. I don't even know if they're still alive. If somehow you could find them, explain to them why I have done what I've done. . ." Josephus looked sincerely stricken. I had my first real sense of the battle waging in his own conscience. "They may not accept it," he continued, "but perhaps they will understand. Please let them know that I never abandoned them. And tell them that when this is over, they can expect the full protection and hospitality of the Emperor."

"We will tell them, Joseph," Symeon promised. "If we find them, I'll deliver your words. You have my oath."

"You might find some of your own friends as well," said Josephus.

My ears perked up. "Who?"

"I've heard that a prominent Nazarene is also imprisoned in Phasael tower."

"Do you know his name?" asked Symeon, perplexed.

Josephus shook his head. "I heard the story about a week ago. They said he was first accosted by a Roman patrol on the Mount of Olives. This was just before one of the last raids by the Zealots. The Zealots captured this man and took him back with them. The last we heard he was accused of being a Roman agent and cast into prison. Apparently he made quite an impression on the Roman officer who found him. Something about a miracle—casting out demons or some other nonsense."

"But I thought all the Christians had fled from Jerusalem," I said.

"This one must have returned," said Josephus. "Perhaps for the same reason that you are returning."

It occurred to me that Barsabas had tried to rescue the scrolls long before we got here. Had another Christian leader set out to accomplish the same thing? Maybe an apostle?!

"I don't mean to give you false hopes," Josephus added. "Most likely such a man has already been executed. The Zealots consider all Christians traitors. For this reason you should keep your affiliations to yourselves."

"We could never deny the Christ," said Gidgiddonihah.

"Yes," smirked Josephus. "That might explain why there are so few of you left. Keep your sword, gladiator. You will most certainly need it."

Gid's conscience was pricked. "I am no gladiator. And this is not my sword."

We stiffened. At first Josephus thought he was joking. He laughed once, then he read the seriousness in Gid's eye. He looked around at the rest of us. Our faces confirmed the confession.

"This man is not Problius of Berytus?" asked Josephus in alarm.

"I am Gidgiddonihah of Zarahemla. And I am a soldier of honor to my people."

Josephus' blood pressure shot up. "But . . . if you are not Problius, then where . . . ?" He pointed at the sword.

"It's a long story," I said.

"Where is Problius of Berytus? Is he alive?"

"Oh, yes," I said. "He may have a headache, but—"

Josephus began to hyperventilate. "You're fugitives! You must get out of here. All of you!"

"But, Joseph—" said Symeon.

"No, wait! You can't leave. Titus is expecting you to be here. What am I to do? I could lose my post. My position of trust. The only reason Titus allowed me to liberate you from the stockade was because I vouched for your character, and because he wanted to meet Problius, the Syrian who won the golden palm. He is paranoid of spies. If this man is found to be a fraud, Titus will suspect that we have conspired together. Symeon, how could you do this to me?"

Symeon shook his head. "I-I didn't know his identity had been mistaken."

Josephus ranted, "A man is carrying the sword of a famous gladiator, and you didn't realize his identity might be mistaken?"

"I don't follow blood sports."

"Neither do I! But even I've heard of Problius of Berytus!"

"There's only one solution," I interrupted. I said to Josephus, "You come with us now and help us get inside the city. Tell Titus we had an emergency and had to leave."

He turned green. "An emergency? There *is* no emergency that supersedes the will of the Prince! *He* is your emergency! If you leave, I will be drawn and quartered for that fact alone. Oh, this is disastrous!"

"So what do we do?" I asked more humbly.

Josephus paced frantically. He stopped. "I have no choice. I must tell him everything. I must face the consequences."

Gidgiddonihah stood with Josephus nose to nose. "You would betray us?"

Josephus paled. Symeon came between them.

"Please, Joseph," he pleaded. "There must be another solution. One that will spare us both any dire consequences. We can still reach your mother and father. If they're alive, I promise we will do all we can to protect them."

Suddenly Mary, who had gone to the edge of the canopy, squeaked out, "I think he's coming!"

We could all hear the hubbub now. Who else could it be but Titus and his entourage? Maybe he wouldn't come here. I prayed he wouldn't come here first. No such luck. He and a half dozen of his men were headed right for Josephus' tent. They'd be here in seconds! Josephus wouldn't have *time* to betray us. Titus would know everything before his faithful interpreter could even open his mouth.

The prince of Rome burst inside, followed by several of his men. My life flashed before my eyes. It was too late to run. Too late for anything.

"Josephus!" Titus blustered. "Have no fear. Your precious temple will be spared. I have the commitment of all the generals. Tomorrow we attack with all of our forces and liberate the structure once and for all. What's the matter? I thought you'd be bouncing for joy."

"I'm . . . *thrilled*, your Eminence," faltered Josephus. "But . . . there's another matter I must—"

Titus wasn't listening. His eyes searched around until they found Gidgiddonihah. My heart stopped.

"Ah! There he is!" Titus stepped up to the Nephite, a boyish grin on his fleshy face. "My, my. It's been a long time." Titus glanced back at one of his generals. "You see, Cerealis? A man lives long enough, his life comes full circle. Just as all Rome is about to crown me a hero, I meet again one of the great heroes of my youth." He faced Gid. "You probably don't remember me, but I was the obnoxious little whelp who gave you a beaker of wine after you defeated Urbicus the Florentine at the *Juvenalia*. I was only thirteen, but it's still one of the most memorable days of my life."

Gid gawked back. I was gawking too, my heart in my throat. What was happening? Titus hadn't recognized him at all! One of the most memorable days of his life? I wondered if Titus would recognize his own mother.

"I'm afraid . . . I don't remember," said Gid.

Titus laughed and embraced his shoulders. "Just one of a thousand boys, I'm sure. But you might have at least tried to flatter me." He slapped Gid's shoulder good-naturedly. "It's marvelous to see you again. If only the circumstances were more propitious. Unfortunately, I have no time to reminisce. Perhaps another day."

"Yes," said Gid. "Perhaps another."

Titus turned back to Josephus. "Give your friends whatever they desire. Treat them as guests of Caesar."

Titus exited as brusquely as he'd arrived. The man named Cerealis followed last. He studied Gid's face. Then he smiled, almost absently, and exited behind his master. *He suspects something*, I thought. But what could he suspect? If Titus believed Gid was Problius, who would question it? Who would dare?

Josephus had beads of sweat on his forehead. He held his stomach as if the acids were churning like a washing machine. I still couldn't figure out what had happened. I realized I might never know. Another unexplained miracle. I even wondered if Heavenly Father had transfigured Gid's face in Titus' mind. Was it so far-fetched? After all, he'd made Brigham Young look like Joseph Smith that day in Nauvoo. In any case, Josephus' help was no longer a matter of choice. It was a royal command.

"Come on," said Josephus. "My heart can't take much more of this. The sooner you get inside that city and out of this encampment, the better."

CHAPTER NINE

My hands and my feet were wrinkled and withered worse than any prune. Jesse and I had been crouching in that cold spring water at the opening of the tunnel for hours, waiting desperately for the sky to darken. Now I was thinking it had been a mistake to wait so long. We should have taken our chances in the daylight. My legs had grown so numb, I wasn't sure I could stand, let alone run like a banshee.

I think it was just before sunset that the Sons of the Elect made the discovery that Jesse and I were missing from the catacombs. I heard ole' Menander caterwauling at the top of his lungs from inside the main house. I couldn't hear all that he was howling, but I did manage to make out the words, "Spread out!" and "Find them!"

As Simon's men began to pour out of the villa, I started to think this might be a godsend. Now there would be fewer cueball heads to stop us from escaping this darn courtyard. Jesse and I had been devising our plan of escape all afternoon. The courtyard was hemmed in by high stone walls on all four sides. They weren't walls, exactly. More like covered hallways with steep, tiled roofs slanting outwards. I could see at least three towers poking up in various places along the outer wall. I think the main tower was actually behind us, but we couldn't turtle our heads out far enough to see it. The outer walls had at least two stories. The upper story was open on the courtyard side with pillars to support the roof. There were window spaces in the upper-story walls. Each side had a stairway—

but only one. Our brilliant plan was to climb the south side stairway, hoping that one of those windows on the upper story would reveal a way down on the other side. I could see a pair of tall leafy trees, sorta like cottonwoods, sticking up over there. They looked fairly close to the wall on the other side, but I couldn't quite tell. I tried to visualize myself leaping from the window onto one of those branches like Zorro or Batgirl. It was a harrowing image.

The only other option was to try to barrel our way through to the front entrance. I'd been blinded by the hood when they'd first brought us in, but I had the impression there were several corridors and outer doorways that would have made escape in that direction far too complicated. I realized that once we climbed those stairs to the second story, there was no other way down if anyone spotted us. We'd have no other choice but to jump.

The sky was nearly dark now. Jesse and I continued to shiver as the water flowed around us into the courtyard pool. Poor Jesse's lips were as purple as grapes. Finally he stuttered, "It's t-t-time."

Not a single soul stirred in the lamplight. There were some areas of the estate that we couldn't see because of hedges and flowers at the head of the pool. Still, it was starting to look like Simon had marshaled every follower in the commune to try to recapture us. Or so we hoped. We could hide in the dark much easier outside the villa than inside.

As quietly as we could, Jesse and I crawled out of the narrow opening and into the open water of the pool. As I'd feared, my legs had hardly any feeling left in them. I practically had to drag them.

I whispered close to Jesse's ear, "We have find a place to hold up for a while. I have to get the blood pumping again in my legs."

"S-so do I," said Jesse.

We were completely exposed now. If anybody had been posted in the towers, they'd have seen us as plain as day. Fortunately, they all looked empty. I hoisted myself out of the pool. Oh, to be on dry ground! I swore I'd never go in the water again.

Jesse climbed out behind me. The two of us hobbled over to the thickest, tallest hedge and crawled inside the bed of flowers on the near side. We lay there in the warm soil waiting for our limbs to gather strength. Amazing what three or four hours of cold water can do to your muscles.

Jesse recovered before I did. He squirmed to the other side of the hedge to get a clear view of the main house. A moment later, he returned.

"Well?" I whispered. "See anyone?"

"No, but . . ."

"Yes?"

"I don't think we're alone."

"Huh?"

"It's almost as if . . . I can feel someone watching us."

"Don't get psycho, Jesse. No one has seen us. Give me another minute, then we'll go."

As the minute passed, I sympathized more and more with Jesse's paranoia. This place was far more creepy when it was quiet. There were ghosts here. I was sure of it. Evil spirits probably flocked to this place like Grand Central Station. A light breeze was blowing. I started to imagine that each rustle of the leaves or flowers represented a ghost passing by. I imagined them gathering around us, shouting to Simon and his cronies, "They're here! They're hiding right over here!"

I shook myself. I was freaking myself out for no reason. It was time to make our exit.

"Ready," I said to Jesse.

My voice made him jump. "Okay."

My legs itched from the new supply of warm blood, but at least I was strong enough to stand. Keeping low, we moved to the end of the hedge. In the lamplight I could see the stairs along the southern wall. It looked like clear sailing.

We looked both ways, then bolted across the courtyard. After reaching the stairway, I was prepared to rocket to the top three steps at a time. Instead, I gasped in horror and stiffened. Jesse collided into my back. When he saw what I saw, he froze beside me.

"So the hunted returns to the lion's den," said the shadowy figure at the top of the stairs. "Now there's an unexpected turn of fate."

The man took one step down the stairs, revealing his face in the lamplight. It was Cerinthus. We stood there, dumbstruck, too shocked to budge. He took another step.

"I've been watching you for several minutes," he revealed. "Next time, don't splash so much. Did you really believe you could elude a god?"

Jesse reached up and seized the metal-framed lantern above the base of the stairs. Cerinthus interpreted Jesse's actions immediately and postured himself for the attack. Jesse threw the lantern with all his might. Cerinthus dodged it. The lamp hit the top of the stairway and rolled across the platform, leaving a trail of oil flames behind it. Cerinthus glanced back at the fire, then riveted his attention back on us. The fire, he judged, could be dealt with later. First he wanted to dig his claws into us.

Jesse and I dashed back to the center of the courtyard. Some women emerged from a building at the side of the main house. We hesitated and looked about. Where could we run?

"There's no escape," said Cerinthus calmly. "Submit to the will of the divine!"

"There!" I shouted to Jesse, pointing toward the stairway at the northern wall.

Just then something bellowed—some kind of trumpet. I looked toward the tower at the northeast corner. Someone was sounding an alarm. The tower connected with the upper story of the northern wall. That way was blocked, too!

"This way!" cried Jesse.

He was bounding toward the back entrance of the main building. Was he insane?! He was running right into the snake pit! And yet, there was no place else to go. I pursued Jesse as fast as I could. He waited for me on the terrace. I'd almost reached him when a brutal hand grabbed my arm.

"Not so fast," said Cerinthus. "You and I still have a lot—"

My reaction was lightning swift. I utilized the best weapons in the female arsenal. My fingernails slashed right at his eyes. Cerinthus wailed and drew his hands to his face.

Jesse grabbed my hand and the two of us burst inside the main house. We were in a hallway off the central banquet room where Jesse and I had been interrogated the previous night. Several bald men had already appeared at the other end. It was Cleobius and Reuben, alias Ren and Stimpy, carrying clubs. More men arrived behind them. The alarm had brought the Sons of the Elect swarming back to the estate from all directions. I knew the main entrance was behind those men. It was impenetrable. Instead, we veered into the banquet room.

Ren and Stimpy pursued. Jesse leaped across the long wooden table, rolling off onto the floor on the other side. I followed in the same manner and gave my hip a nasty bruise. As the Sons of the Elect began rushing into the room, Jesse grabbed another lantern above the opposite doorway. The men started working their way around both sides of the table. Jesse smashed the lantern on top of it. The brass canister burst. Hot oil splattered everywhere, much of it landing on our pursuers. The oil on the table ignited into flames.

We flew through the doorway and into the next chamber. I remembered this hallway. It led to the sauna where Helga the Horrible and the other women had bathed me. One last lantern was hanging in an open window overlooking the courtyard. Beyond here the chambers were dark. I grabbed the lantern and led the way.

"It's a dead end!" Jesse declared. "We'll have no way out!"

"No!" I insisted. "There's a way!"

We carried the lantern through the hall until we found the sauna's heavy wooden door. Men were shouting. Our pursuers were only seconds behind us.

"In here!" I said.

We passed through a wide antechamber. The floor became slick and wet. This was the place. The fires that had created the steam were off, but the air was still humid and smelled of smoke. We stepped through the doorway and into the dressing area. I looked up. It was still there—the small ventilation hole in the roof. Beyond it glowed the stars. But how could we reach it? It was eight feet over our heads. We had only a few seconds to decide.

Jesse grabbed one of the stone benches. I took his cue and the two of us dragged it under the hole. I stood on top with my lantern. Shoot! It still wasn't high enough. Coming here was a very bad idea. I heard a commotion outside the antechamber. There just wasn't enough time! On impulse I threw the lantern up into the hole. It landed on the roof with a clatter. I jumped down, grabbed Jesse's arm, and dragged him into the darkest corner.

The dressing room filled with angry shadows. We pressed deeper into the corner. The first men to arrive had no lamps, but I could see the flicker of other lanterns coming up behind them. The room would be illuminated in seconds. I closed my eyes. These were our last precious seconds of freedom.

"Look!" someone yelled.

My eyes flew open. One of the men—I think it was Ren—pointed up toward the hole in the roof. A faint firelight was emanating through the hole—the glow of my lantern. They'd also noticed the bench pushed underneath it and drew their own hasty conclusions.

"They're on the roof!"

The room emptied as quickly as it had filled. The torches turned back as well. The ploy had worked! I couldn't believe it! But then I realized that the glow above us was growing considerably brighter. The roof was on fire! How could clay tiles burn? The oil had splashed on something flammable.

"Let's go!"

We fled from the sauna, slipping once on the slick floor. The hallway was filled with smoke. As we made our way back toward the banquet table, I checked several doorways. The rooms that were unlocked were all dead ends. The only way out was the way we'd come in.

The smoke was growing thicker. I coughed and held my sleeve over my nose. We reached the doorway to the banquet area. One look told us this would not be the route out. Flames were devouring the room. The table, the door posts, the crossbeams, the couches and fixtures—all of it was burning. Nobody was even trying to put it out! They were so consumed with catching us that everything else had been ignored. Now there were fires burning ahead of us and behind. We were hedged in!

"The window!" cried Jesse.

Jesse climbed into the window beyond the banquet hall where I'd grabbed the lantern. The ground was twelve feet down. We could jump that, couldn't we? But then we'd be back in the courtyard, right where we'd started.

Jesse reached toward the roof above.

"Help me!" he insisted.

I grabbed his legs to keep him from falling. He found a grip on the overhanging shutters and pulled himself up. I pushed his feet. He made it! I climbed into the window behind him. For me the stunt was a little trickier. The roof was slanted and there was no one to hold my legs. Add to that my staggering fear of heights.

"Take my hand!" said Jesse.

I clutched the roof tiles with one hand while Jesse pulled the other. I hoisted myself onto my chest. The smoke poured out of the window as Jesse dragged me to safety.

We stood on our feet and took in the scene. Simon's palace was burning in three different places. No one was fighting the flames at the top of the stairway on the south wall either. I saw why the roof of the sauna had caught fire. It wasn't tiled like the rest of the buildings. Just crossbeams of wood and plaster around a circle of chimneys.

"There they are!" a woman shouted.

We'd been spotted. Everyone started working themselves around to our position. Two men jumped onto the roof at the opposite end of the compound, closing in across the various arches and obstacles. Several more men appeared on the west ledge. One of them was Menander.

"Head them off that way!" he shouted to the others.

Jesse and I scrambled to the southern edge. Here the roof connected with the burning south wall. My attention continued to be drawn to the two trees poking up along the south boundary. They seemed to be our only way down.

We hesitated as we reached the section above the area that was on fire. The roof was only about six feet wide with a sharp slant. The flames were licking at the underside of the tiled roof. To reach the trees we had to grip the top edge and scoot our way across. We set out as swiftly as we could, Jesse leading the way. After just a few feet, the tiles became searing hot. They were burning my knees, scorching my hands!

"Faster!" I cried to Jesse.

I didn't have to coax him. He scrambled as fast as he could. All at once I heard a crack. The roof had collapsed! I screamed in terror as Jesse and I were split apart. Suddenly the roof jolted and became stationary again. I hung onto the hot tiles with all my strength. The roof had buckled about four feet. Jesse reached down to me. I could see flames through the open gap. I knew in seconds the roof would collapse completely.

"Come on!" shouted Jesse.

I ignored the pain in my burning palms and took his arm. Just as I'd planted my knees on firm tiles, the roof behind us caved in. It crashed into the courtyard, sending up an explosion of sparks and flames.

"Go!" I yelled to Jesse. "It's our last chance!"

My palms were throbbing as we scooted that last twenty feet. The nearest branch of the tree was about five feet out. The thought *of making that jump made the hair stand on my neck, but there was no other way. The trees sprang up from the stream bed that flowed out of the courtyard. There was a natural ridge to the east that cut off our pursuers on the ground. But to my dismay, I learned that the enemy had one more place of attack.*

The highest tower at the southern end brooded over us like a vulture. Inside that tower loomed the eyes of a sorcerer. I didn't have to see his cancerous face in the firelight to know it was Simon. And yet it was the other silhouette beside him that froze my heart. I hadn't seen him since Qumran, but I could still remember his close-set eyes and reddish beard. Right now I could only distinguish his bow. It was the archer whose arrow had pierced Harry's scriptures!

"Jump!" I cried to Jesse.

My hands released the topmost edge. There was no turning back. I threw out my arms and sprang from my toes. A second later I felt leaves and branches in my fingers. I flailed desperately to find a grip. Next thing I knew, I was hugging the trunk. My legs were dangling. But I'd made it! Jesse was still on the roof, working up his last ounce of nerve.

"Not the girl!" I heard Simon hiss. "Kill the boy!"

Jesse was just throwing his arms forward when I heard the bowstring snap. The arrow struck. Jesse yelped in agony, but his body was already in the air. The impact spun him around in mid-flight. He'd never catch himself! He'd crash to the earth! I reached out as he hit the branch and caught him under the armpit. His body was limp. I couldn't hold on! As he started slipping, my fingers seized the collar of his cloak.

"No, Jesse! Hang on! Hang on!"

Adrenaline took over. I supported his full weight with just one hand—one blistered hand.

"Jesse! Jesse!"

Finally, he roused himself enough to grab the limb. But with only one set of fingers. I realized the other hand was wounded.

The arrow had pierced right through his palm. It was still embedded there.

We were fifteen feet up, but we were behind the wall, hidden from Simon's archer.

"Can you climb?" I asked Jesse.

Stupid question. Of course he couldn't climb. And yet as I said it, he was already working his way down the tree. I released his collar. He continued to climb on his own strength, but about seven feet from the ground, he slipped and fell. I jumped down to him, landing on my feet.

"Jesse?! Are you all right?"

His groggy voice replied, "I think so."

He pulled himself up, using the tree for support. The arrow remained stuck in his hand. Blood dripped from his fingers. There was a gash in his cloak as well, right above the hip. I realized that the archer's arrow hadn't been off target. It had pierced Jesse's palm just as he was swinging his arms to jump. If his hand hadn't deflected it, the arrow would have gone straight through his abdomen.

"Down there!" Menander shouted.

He was on the ridge above us. The fire glowed behind him. His men scrambled to try to surround us. My mind reeled with panic.

"Jesse," I pleaded. "You have to run. Can you run?"

"Yes," he answered, his voice strong.

I was tempted to toss in the towel. How far could he go? Running would only make his injury worse. He'd lose too much blood. There wasn't even time to break the arrow's shaft and pull it out. But Jesse didn't wait around to analyze the obstacles. He propped the embedded arrow against his side and took off like a deer.

I followed after him. We tore off down the stream bed, dodging the trees and foliage and disappearing into the thickness of the brush. To our eternal relief, the voices of Menander and the Sons of the Elect fell farther and farther behind.

CHAPTER TEN

I've never heard such hatred and filth expelled in one unanimous breath as when I heard it from the mouths of the Jewish prisoners in the Roman stockade. They were yelling at Josephus as he led us past them to get to the place where we would try to infiltrate the city. I was surprised they'd even recognized him. After all, it was nearly dark. We were almost fifty yards away. But the prisoners knew him in an instant.

"God curse you, Flavius Josephus!" a man cried with all his venom, "Coward! Roman lover!"

This was actually one of the nicer things they yelled. I was also shocked when Josephus gave it right back to them.

"We'll see who's cursed, you wretches! You had your chance! Fools!"

We looked at Josephus like he was nuts. What kind of jerk would taunt condemned men? Gid could hardly stand the sight of him. Symeon still tried to be gracious, but I could tell he had a little different opinion of the tall, striking Jew who'd once bought his wine in Cana.

Josephus led us back through the gate and past the first tower of the siege wall. Symeon's mule had been left in Titus' camp with the assurance that it would be kept with the royal stock until we returned. Frankly, I never expected to see the beast again. All of our supplies, which included three days' worth of food, were flung over our shoulders.

Josephus took us around the east side of the siege wall, past the banners and cookfires of another army camp on a hill Symeon identified as the Mount of Olives. We walked directly beneath the temple again—this time from the front. Since it was dark, it was hard to appreciate the great Golden Gate. The temple porches around the courtyard still glowed with smoldering embers. We continued walking for several hundred more yards, climbing over rocks and crags until we reached a place Josephus called the Vale of Hinnon. Here the walls of Jerusalem were comprised of much of the cliff face itself. It was the easiest side of Jerusalem to defend and the hardest place for the Jews to launch a raid. Consequently, it was the area with the fewest Roman sentries.

The smell of death was the strongest yet. This had to be the area that the royal guardsmen had described—the site where the Jews tossed their dead over the walls. I thanked Heavenly Father for the darkness. I was spared the terrible sight. I wasn't sure how many more such scenes my mind could take.

Here and there we could see the flicker of cookfires, but for the most part the soldiers ignored us. At last we reached the only gate in the vicinity. Several dozen soldiers were manning it. A homely bunch, too. The man in charge had the face of a bulldog, and as far as I could tell, no teeth. This clearly wasn't Jerusalem's most envied post, assigned most likely to incompetents and troublemakers. We approached the fire as they were finishing a bawdy joke. When they heard us, they leaped to their feet.

"Who are you!" the toothless one gruffed. "Watchword!"

"Domitian, Prince of Rome," Josephus returned.

For a second I thought Josephus had taken on a false identity—one that was sure to get him hanged. Then I realized that the name of Titus' brother *was* the watchword. The soldiers relaxed.

"I'm Josephus, interpreter for General Titus."

"Josephus the prophet?"

"Yes," said Josephus shamelessly.

The four men looked awestruck. Even worshipful. What morons, I thought. The Romans were the most superstitious flakes I'd ever known. It didn't seem to matter what religion a person belonged to; if they thought you had magical powers, they'd kiss your feet.

"I have orders from Titus granting these men safe passage through this gate."

"This gate, your honor?" said the soldier. "Nothing over there but corpses and near-corpses, if you get my meaning."

"You're not to ask any questions," said Josephus. "Just do as you're told. Open the gate."

"Yes, your honor."

As the men did their duty, Josephus directed Symeon toward the dark ridge below the southeast wall.

"There's a tunnel at the base of that ridge," he revealed. "It'll take you into the city. The Romans ignore it since the opening is too small. Besides, it's an obvious place for an ambush. In the beginning Titus allowed the Jews to bring out their dead and bury them below the cliffs. Now the only ones who emerge are the ones who are nearly dead themselves. Their last hope is that someone will one day bury their corpse properly. The hope is vain. There are just too many of them now."

I peered through the gloom at the outline of the ridge. It was too dark. I saw no corpses. No dying bodies. Yet I knew they were there. We'd be walking right through them. I shuddered. *Please, God*, I prayed. There had to be another way in.

"What about one of the main gates," I asked. "Symeon says the Jews are required by ancient law—"

"Ridiculous," said Josephus, "The Romans would never let you past. You think they'd just let you stroll up to the gate with your food and reinforcements?"

"If it's such an obvious place for an ambush," asked Mary, "what's to keep them from ambushing *us*? Is there another watchword?"

Josephus became impatient. "I've brought you here. That's all I can do. The rest is up to you."

Symeon put his hand on Josephus' shoulder. "It's fine, Joseph. You've done more than we could have ever hoped. If we find your parents, I'll bring you news of their condition."

Josephus shrugged off Symeon's hand. "Don't come to me again, Symeon bar Cleophas. My reputation was nearly destroyed tonight. You must never make another appearance in Titus' camp. If you find my parents, show your gratitude by delivering my message. You don't really think you're ever coming out again, do you? I bid you farewell."

He turned and left us to ourselves. That was the last we saw of Flavius Josephus. I was never so unsure whether to call someone a friend or an enemy.

Gidgiddonihah urged us to move quickly through the gate. We climbed toward the cliff face. The shadows were thick. My stomach was tied up in knots. *Don't try to distinguish any shapes in the darkness*, I told myself. Still, I had to stay alert. The dangers were too great. If there were dying men under these cliffs, they'd have surely heard the gate open. How could they not think we were Romans? Gid had drawn his sword and dagger.

I began to hear breathing, sense movement. Dark forms began to appear on the ground around the narrow footpath. There were hundreds. Most of the shadows didn't move. A lump came to my throat. So much pain. So many broken hearts. No one attempted to stop us. No one begged for food. Most didn't seem to know we were there. It was a graveyard of the buried and unburied. My stomach curdled. I couldn't swallow. Vomit burned in my throat.

Mary started to faint. I caught her before she collapsed. With my support, she climbed over the last few stones. When we arrived at the face of the cliff, there was a dark, gaping hole where the pathway ended. The way appeared clear. No one was guarding the entrance. Gid went in first. He waved for the rest of us to follow. Mary trembled as I helped her to lean against the wall just inside the tunnel. She squeezed my arm as a sign that she was all right.

Before us stretched a humid, greasy passage, thick with the smell of filth and smoke. I saw the flicker of torchlight farther on, reflecting from an unseen corridor. We could hear shuffling and scurrying. Rats, maybe. Gid wanted to know for sure.

"Announce us," he said to Symeon.

Symeon cleared his throat. "Hello! We are Galileans! We come in peace!"

No response. Then someone laughed—interrupted by a fit of coughing. Gidgiddonihah edged forward, sword ready.

"They come in peace," someone muttered. "Peace. Galileans come in peace." The low laughter continued, like something bubbling in a pot.

A few steps farther, we found an old man lying in the pathway. He was little more than skin and bones. He didn't even look up at us.

"Peace," he continued mumbling. "Galileans come in peace."

Mary knelt down and touched his hand. The man didn't react. He was like the others outside. Apparently this was as far as he got. I tried to give him water. It just dribbled off his lips.

"Let's keep moving," said Gid.

We made our way deeper into the channels. More bodies lay strewn about. Some alive, most stricken with rigor mortis. Other tunnels branched off the main passage. The earth under Jerusalem was apparently honeycombed with tunnels.

At last we reached the corridor where the torchlight emanated. In it we discovered a Jewish soldier, fast asleep. His chain mail and armor looked too big for his chest. At his belt hung an empty scabbard. A rusty sword lay in his lap. His face was ashen. He didn't look like he'd had a whole lot more nutrition than the old man at the entrance. Our approach made him stir, but he didn't fully awaken until we were practically on top of him.

Suddenly he jolted to full attention.

"Who goes there?!" he demanded, his sword outstretched.

"Relax," said Gid, wielding his much larger weapon. "We're friends."

"Who are you? What are you doing here?"

Symeon moved forward. "I'm Symeon of Cana. This is—"

"Are you from the outside?"

"Yes, we—"

"How did you get in here? Why didn't the Romans stop you?"

"We're no threat to the Romans," said Symeon. "We just wanted to get inside the city."

"*Wanted* to?" The soldier grunted in disbelief. "Why would you *want* to get inside Jerusalem?"

Gidgiddonihah answered sternly, "We're looking for lost property. Stand aside and let us through."

"You can't just go through," said the man. "I'll have to report you."

He appeared to be the only soldier on guard. If we'd been the enemy, we might have simply killed him and moved on. Boy, if the Romans had known, they could have had a free-for-all. A couple hundred troops might have infiltrated these tunnels and reached the heart of the city before anyone noticed.

The man was shaking in his boots, yet he insisted, "You stay here."

"No," said Gid. "We'll follow you."

"All right," he said reluctantly. "But I'll follow *you*. Leave your weapons."

"We'll do nothing of the sort," said Gid.

The man stewed over this, then said, "Just give me your bags."

He snatched the travel sacks from both Symeon and Mary. When he came to me, I held on with a grip of steel. "No way," I said.

One look at Gid told him he'd get the same response. He brushed it off as if it wasn't important in the first place and flung the other sacks over his shoulder.

"Through here," he directed.

He followed us at a distance of several steps, presumably to keep an eye on us.

"Turn here," he said at an intersection. "Keep going. It's right up there."

The tunnel opened up, revealing several caverns and chambers on both sides. At the head of the central chamber, a stone stairway was carved into the rock. As we reached it, I glanced back. Our military escort was nowhere to be seen.

"Hey!" I cried. "He's gone!"

We heard the echo of his feet as he scurried through one of the side passages. I couldn't tell exactly which one.

"Our food!" said Symeon.

Gid scolded himself. "Little vermin. I saw it coming and didn't prevent it."

"I'd have given him food if he'd asked," said Mary.

"He couldn't take that chance," said Gid. "He was starving. Let's go. Before we meet more just like him."

We climbed the stairs and entered another labyrinth of tunnels. There were very few lamps or candles. For the most part our eyes had to pierce the darkness. I heard whispering and saw moving shadows from time to time, but no one else confronted us. I doubted any were soldiers. Just people who were sick or in hiding. These tunnels were likely a way station for deserters.

At last we reached a hall with fresh air coming in. Fresh for Jerusalem anyway. But the passage seemed to go nowhere. Then Mary grabbed Gid's arm.

"Up there."

She pointed toward a square plate in the ceiling, almost like a sewer grate. Gid reached up and lifted the metal plate out of its grooves. I doubted it was the main exit, but it suited us fine. The ceiling was low. After Gid had pushed it aside, he easily jumped up inside. Then he reached his arm back down to assist us. Mary went first, followed by Symeon. I handed up my travel bag and followed last.

The room was some sort of storage house. Large clay vats, waist high, lined the walls. Some were broken. All were empty. The room was long. It had no windows, but there were slits in the left wall and a door at the other end. Through the slits we could see the reflection of torches and lamps from the outside street. Shadows hurried past. From somewhere down the street, a voice barked, "You there! Inside!"

More shadows passed, marching in unison. Soldiers. A door slammed somewhere up the avenue. Then the street fell silent. Other commotion rattled in the distance, shouting and running. And, of course, the eternal drum of the battering rams.

"What's happening?" I asked Symeon.

He shook his head. "I don't know."

"Curfews, I'd wager," said Gid.

That made sense. If the Zealots wanted to discourage deserters, they'd have to force the citizens to stay inside after dark. We maneuvered toward the doorway. Mary stepped on a broken shard from one of the vats, and it made a loud crack. We hesitated. No response came from outside. Gid reached the door. Locked.

He raised his knee and kicked it open. I peered around Gid out into the narrow street. It was filled with garbage and filth, but there were no soldiers. No sign of anyone.

Gid turned to Symeon. "Where are we?"

"The Lower City," said Symeon. "Yes, I'm sure. That way is the pool of Siloam. Over there is the temple."

"What about the house of James?" I asked.

"It's ten minutes from here," said Symeon. "Not far at all. At least in daylight."

Ten minutes. I felt a rush of energy. We were here. We were inside Jerusalem. In ten short minutes we'd have the object of our quest.

"Perhaps we should stay here until daylight," Mary suggested.

"The street is clear," I protested. "We should find the house and get the Scroll of Knowledge as soon as we can."

Gid seemed to agree. "It might be easier to retrieve in the dark."

Symeon nodded. "All right. But it may take longer. We shouldn't pass by the Essene Gate. Too many soldiers. We'll take the gate above the valley of the Cheesemakers."

"Fine," said Gid. "Lead the way."

We entered the cluttered street and started north. The smell of smoke continued to hang heavy over the city. The buildings were all claustrophobically close together. Many of the houses nearest to the city walls had been burned, or showed big chunks missing in the plaster. The result, I assumed, of stones and flaming arrows from the Roman catapults.

Ahead of us arose the outline of the temple, its white walls and golden plates flickering slightly from the reflection of fires still burning around the outer court. The battering rams continued to shake the earth. It occurred to me that this sound had been going on nonstop for months. It was a wonder the population hadn't been driven insane.

The streets were dark. Unlit lamps and lanterns hung in doorways and above street corners, evidence of a time when lamp oil had been more plentiful. I could hear much whispering and babbling. These apartments were all occupied by frightened people. The whispering and babbling were the sounds of prayer. It was going on everywhere, mournful and anguished.

In one window I saw a man kneeling over a small candle, bobbing back and forth as he mumbled the words:

"Our skin was black like an oven because of the terrible famine.

"They ravished the women in Zion, and the maids in the cities of Judah.

"Princes are hanged up by their hand: the faces of the elders were not honored.

"They took the young men to grind, and the children fell under the wood.

"The crown is fallen from our head: woe unto us, that we have sinned . . . ."

His words faded in with all the other voices as we passed by. We turned a corner and entered the next narrow street. It was pitch dark. No voices; no praying. The stench of death was overpowering. The houses themselves smelled as if they were crammed with bodies. A stabbing nausea returned to my guts. I shut my eyes, trying to block out the horror.

We turned another corner. The new street had two lighted lamps. The way looked clear, but as we stepped out into the open, several soldiers emerged from the darkness at the far end.

"You there!"

We stopped cold.

"Go!" said Gid, directing us into an alley.

We scampered like jackrabbits.

"Come back here! Halt!"

We crossed under a hanging roof and entered the next street. We could hear footsteps pursuing. Someone blew a whistle. Other footsteps approached from somewhere else. My heart faltered. We'd run smack into angry soldiers around the next corner! Suddenly a shadow appeared in the passage ahead.

Gid raised his sword. But the man held up his hand in peace and urged us toward a doorway.

"In here! Hurry!"

We looked at one another. We didn't know this guy from Adam. But it was our best hope. Again he waved us inside. After we'd entered, Gid and the stranger closed the door. The room was small, only about ten feet square. A tiny lamp illuminated the frightened faces of a mother and two children. Make that *three* children. There was a small baby wrapped in linen on the mother's lap. All of them, including the father, looked gaunt and sickly. The children were like rails. The infant hardly moved. *Dear God*, I thought. It was barely alive. The two children—a boy and girl about ten and eleven—stared up at us with worried faces. Their clothing was tattered, their hair tangled. The only thing that didn't look filthy were the whites of their eyes—clear as pearls.

They looked terrified. If they were so frightened by us, why did they invite us in? Harboring curfew breakers must have carried severe penalties. Perhaps the flame of humanity hadn't entirely gone out in this desperate city.

"Don't worry," the father told us. "The soldiers won't look in here."

After a minute, I started wondering if the soldiers were looking at all. As the father peered out through a crack in the door, no one came rushing past. The man glanced at us frequently. He was very nervous. Finally, he stuck his head outside. Then he stepped all the way into the street.

"Come inside," said Gid. "If they see you, they'll come here for sure."

The father nodded. "Sorry. You're right." He entered again and shut the door. "Are you deserters? Trying to get out of the city?"

"No," said Symeon. "We were trying to get in. We thank you for—"

"Trying to get in?" The man was perplexed. "You're not deserters?"

"Not exactly," said Symeon.

He seemed disappointed. "Then why are they chasing you?"

"We came up through the tunnels," I said. "We didn't know about the curfew."

"You're from the outside?" he asked in astonishment.

"Yes," said Symeon. "My name is—"

"Don't tell me your names!" he insisted. "If you're fugitives, I don't want to know."

"We're not fugitives, really," I said.

"If you're out after dark, you're fugitives. You must stay until morning. Or at least until just before daybreak. The patrols are wearier before daybreak."

The mother continued to clutch her children closely. She didn't appear to approve of our presence one little bit. Gid peered through the crack in the doorway one more time.

"We'll stay for a while," he said. "But only a moment. Then we'll be out of your way."

"Perhaps you should sleep," said the man. "You should be well rested before you try to escape into the hills."

"I told you," I said, "we're not trying to—"

Gid looked at me as if to say it was better not to explain. "Thank you," he told the man. "You may have saved our lives."

He tried to take the man's hand in friendship. The man rejected it and moved over by his family.

"We will sleep here," he said. "You may sleep over there."

They continued to glare at us. It all felt very strange, as if they considered themselves our hostages. But Gid was right. They'd saved our lives. They could treat us however they wanted.

The four of us huddled on the floor in the opposite corner. Gid lay his travel bag aside. Inside were the barley loaves and sunflower seeds purchased in the same village as Mary's tunic. I felt famished. I hadn't eaten a full meal since we'd laid eyes on Jerusalem. As I pulled a fig cake out of my bag, the family stirred anxiously. The children's mouths watered. The little girl licked her lips. I couldn't eat it now. I couldn't have taken a single bite.

I handed it to the little girl. She took it greedily. But before she could get it into her mouth, the boy snatched it out of her hands. The cake was reduced to crumbs. The girl lashed out savagely at her brother.

"Wait! Don't!" I pleaded. "There's plenty! *Plenty!*"

The boy lapped up the crumbs. I handed the little girl a fresh cake. She popped the whole thing into her mouth and swallowed.

"Not so fast," I said.

Mary came up behind me. She had one of the barley loaves from Gid's sack. Symeon and Gid made no protest as each of the parents received a loaf of their own. They devoured them as ravenously as the children. My heart swelled painfully. They fed like animals, not even looking up to acknowledge who had given it to them.

Gid also urged them to eat more slowly. "A little at a time. So long without food, your stomachs might burst."

His advice did little to hinder them. Within minutes every scrap of food we'd brought into Jerusalem was gone. The Jewish soldier stole the first half. This family ate the other. None of us got a single crumb. Our next meal seemed an eternity away.

I didn't see any evidence of indigestion. Maybe their stomachs weren't as unused to food as we thought. If they'd survived this long—little children and all—they might have been a little more fortunate at finding food than others.

I could tell Mary wanted to hold their baby. The mother clutched it closer. It was obvious she'd never allow it. The father looked at Mary strangely. I think he knew she wasn't a boy. Not that it mattered now.

I had a dark feeling that our supplies would do little to help the frail infant. It appeared destined to become a casualty of the war. It was only a few months old. I tried to imagine the mother's horrible experience of having to give birth in the middle of the siege.

I sat back against the wall, my stomach rumbling. I was so tired. Mary laid her head on my shoulder. Symeon's chin had dropped onto his chest. He was already asleep. It no longer looked as if we were leaving any time soon.

"How do you feel?" I asked Mary.

"My stomach is empty," she said. "But my soul is full."

I couldn't have said it better. It was the last thought to touch my mind before I faded off into dreamland.

* * *

I awoke suddenly to the threatening voice of Gidgiddonihah.

"Where's the boy?" he demanded. He was holding the father by the collar of his cloak. "Where is he? Where did he go?"

"To cover his feet," the father replied. I guessed this was a Jewish expression for going to the bathroom.

"*Where?!*" Gid demanded again. "He's been gone too long!"

The father didn't answer. He was as white as a ghost. Why was Gid being so harsh? The mother became hysterical. The little girl started crying. Gid released the man and turned toward us.

"Get up!" he shouted. "We're leaving! *Now!*"

"Wait!" said the father.

Gid drew his sword. The man cowered back into the corner. He threw his arms over his head, as if death was inevitable.

Gid was seething. "We feed your family and this is how you repay us?"

We were all up and alert. Gid ushered us swiftly out the door. I was still rubbing my eyes, trying desperately to figure out what was wrong. I'd been sleeping an hour at the most. Just seconds ago I'd been dreaming about my motorcycle. Now I was running pell-mell down a dark Jerusalem street.

The father came to the doorway. "You're deserters!" he shouted after us. "Your sins bring God's wrath down upon us all!"

We turned a corner. Gid spotted a tight alleyway.

"In here!" he whispered harshly.

We slipped into the alley and pressed our backs to the wall. Seconds later we heard footsteps. A squad of heavily armed Jewish soldiers tromped past us on their way to the house of the man who'd taken us in. The boy was leading the way.

It was clear to me in a flash. Now I understood why the father had stepped out so far into the street to see if the soldiers were pursuing us. He'd *wanted* to draw their attention. He'd wanted them to find us. He was planning to betray us all along!

The soldiers continued marching past.

"There's likely a reward for deserters," Gid grumbled in a low voice. "Probably food. It may be the only thing that's kept that man's family alive. He's made a *profession* out of betraying deserters and curfew breakers."

"But we gave him all we had," said Symeon.

"Didn't you hear?" said Gid. "The man thinks he's doing the work of God."

"That way!" someone shouted from down the street.

Gid led us to the other end of the alley. I feared it was a dead end, but then it circled around and came out into another narrow street. Gid looked unsure. Symeon took over.

"The gate into the Upper City is over there," he said.

The temple walls loomed much closer than before. I heard shouts and the clash of metal. The sky suddenly lit up with *fireworks*—a volley of flaming spears. Soldiers were fighting inside the outer courtyard. A battle on temple property! I'd have sworn that the flaming missiles had been launched from the temple roof itself. It was past midnight, but the armies were clashing even now. This might have been why the boy had taken so long to bring the soldiers.

Suddenly Gid halted. "We can't go this way. Soldiers are massing in the street ahead."

"But it's the only way into the Upper City," said Symeon.

"What about over the wall?" asked Mary.

We looked up at the thick stone barrier about a hundred feet to our left. The Upper and Lower cities had been divided in half by this wall, likely as old as David and Solomon. The Romans had built an aqueduct for bringing water into Jerusalem along the top ridge. Much of the aqueduct had been torn down. The buildings of the Upper City arose behind it. Buildings on this side of the wall sat right up against the stone.

We took a sloping street, then crossed a small courtyard filled with rubble. The courtyard extended to a row of apartments that sat against the dividing wall. The apartments were three stories high with stairways and balconies nearly reaching the battlements. We started to climb. At the second story, I heard a door slam. Whoever it was didn't want to be seen with curfew breakers.

From the third floor we climbed onto the roof. The wall was only about eight feet over our heads. Gidgiddonihah jumped and caught the edge. Mary, however, was a little more astute. She found a wooden ladder at the other end of the roof.

"Help me," she said.

Symeon and I helped her drag it over and lean it into place. As we joined Gid on the battlements, I had my widest view of the city yet. Despite the late hour, it looked like every Jewish soldier in Jerusalem was awake and manning his post along the exterior walls. I heard crashes and shouts and the snap of catapults. Missiles were being launched from every station—Romans firing in and Jews firing out.

"It's a decoy," Gid observed. "The Romans are trying to occupy the Jews at every battlement to draw attention from the main assault over there."

He indicated the temple. Most of the Zealots hadn't been fooled. The biggest block of Jewish soldiers that I could see were crammed in the streets just outside the temple's western wall, ready to defend the sacred house.

I looked out across the buildings and tried to imagine the thousands of citizens shivering in corners, waiting for the end to come. They must have realized it was hopeless. They *must* have. Why wouldn't the Zealots surrender? So many lives could yet be spared. Were some of them still deluded enough to believe they could actually win?

Looking northward I made out the silhouettes of three tall towers. I thought again of Josephus' remark that a prominent Christian was imprisoned in one of them.

"Which tower is Phasael?" I asked Symeon.

"The tallest," he replied.

I studied the formidable structure. No wonder they'd made it a prison. It looked impregnable. Even situated where it was, fully exposed to the Roman guns, I felt sure after everything else was demolished, that structure would be the last thing standing. It seemed insane to think anyone could ever be rescued from such a place.

"James' house is over there," said Symeon, pointing west.

He indicated an area fairly close to the west wall. Several houses were burning nearby. *Great*, I thought. To find the Scroll of Knowledge, we might be dodging boulders and flaming arrows.

This particular battlement appeared mostly unoccupied at the moment. Several smaller towers rose up along its length, but there was no point in manning them now. As soon as the Upper or Lower City fell, these battlements would become the last line of defense. Until then, this appeared to be the most private spot in all of Jerusalem.

"There," said Gid, directing us toward the closest tower, twenty yards north. "We'll rest in there until dawn."

Relief swept through my tired muscles. I might get a few more hours of sleep after all. It was a good thing. Tomorrow might prove the most important day of our mission. If I couldn't have food, I at least needed rest. But what we needed more than anything was another day full of miracles.

CHAPTER ELEVEN

Jesse was still asleep as I made a pouch with my cloak and filled it with as many wild grapes as it would carry. Neither of us had eaten since that night in Simon's banquet hall. The sight of those grapes, about thirty feet from the shed where we'd bedded down for the night, was like a pot of gold at the end of a rainbow.

We'd chosen the most secluded spot we could find in the dark, nestled in the brambles and trees. As the dawn grew lighter, I realized that this had once been a farmer's vineyard. The wooden trestles had all been cut down and burned, but the marauders hadn't been all too efficient. Many of the vines had survived. Bushels of purple gems sprouted in all directions. I was already engorged before I started gathering for Jesse.

I wanted Jesse to sleep as long as he could. He'd had a torturous night. We'd broken the shaft and removed the arrow from his hand, but this only seemed to make it worse. The wound was more serious than I'd first suspected. The tip had gone in at the base of his wrist and come out through the knuckles between his middle and index fingers. Much flesh had been torn. I'd washed his hand in the stream and wrapped it in the black sash from around his waist. He'd lost a lot of blood. We'd been running for over an hour. By the time we felt satisfied that we'd lost the Sons of the Elect, Jesse was staggering with delirium.

As I approached with the grapes, I could see that Jesse's wrappings were soaked with blood. The wound must have been dread-

fully sore and inflamed. I couldn't believe he was sleeping at all. Tough kid. If it were me, I'd still be squalling.

I knew the wound should be redressed. But if I took off the bandage, would it reopen the wound? First-aid classes in school had never covered this. They just told you to stabilize the victim until help arrived. There was no help around here. I was it.

As I knelt down, Jesse awoke with a start.

"Oh, Meagan," he said, closing his eyes again. "It's just you."

"Just me?" I teased. "Who would you rather it be?"

He grinned. "We burned it down, didn't we, Meagan? We burned it to the ground."

"That's what it looked like," I confirmed.

"That old scorpion and his followers will have to find someplace else to live, won't they?"

"I guess so."

"We make a good team, don't we, Meagan? We messed him up good."

"We make a very good team. Are you hungry, Jesse? I've got a whole pile of grapes. They're really sweet. It must be just the right season."

"Grapes? Yes. Yes, I'm very hungry."

I laid out the berries on a bed of grape leaves. Jesse ate with his uninjured hand.

"Are you feeling better?" I asked.

"Yes," he said through a mouthful of grapes. He swallowed the seeds right down with the rest of it.

"We can't stay here, Jesse. Simon's men must still be searching."

"I'll make it all right," said Jesse.

"Are you sure?"

"I've been hurt before. This is nothing."

Even as he said it, he had a hard time focusing his eyes. Blood loss was making him dizzy. This was terrible.

"Jesse, we have to find a village. Someplace with people. Do you think we might find a doctor?"

"You mean a priest?"

"Is that who treats people who have been injured?"

"Depends. The Greeks have doctors. I've heard they do nothing all day but help the sick."

"Fine. Priest. Doctor. Where can we find one?"

He tried to rise. "I don't need one. I'll be fine."

I steadied him. His balance improved after a few steps, but I stayed close just the same. I knew finding a village was only a temporary solution. What I needed was to find Harry. I could only imagine where he was about now. I wasn't even sure he was still alive. Would he have really gone to Jerusalem to find Simon's scroll? Maybe if I found a place to care for Jesse, I could go after him. Or maybe, I thought, I should just find this Mount Gerizim and try to meet him on the specified day. I knew Harry would be there, even if he didn't have the scroll. I knew he'd try to rescue us. I figured we had four days left. How far away could this mountain be?

I saw two large hills to the south. Not exactly mountains. But I was from Utah. I just needed to find a village to verify their names. There were some houses on a hillside to the west. That would be our destination.

We worked our way through the brush until we reached the stream, although it really wasn't much more than a trickle. I helped Jesse kneel down for a drink. The edges were crawling with tiny black bugs, and I just knew I was gonna suck in a whole mouthful as I drank. I spread the water with both hands and set my lips into the stream.

I heard the snort of a horse.

My heart dropped. Water sucked up my nose. Coughing, I tried to turn. I tripped and sat down in the mud. Jesse rolled onto his side, trying to focus up at the intruder.

Someone was laughing. I could make out the horse—white with brown patches—but the morning sun was directly behind the rider's head. I could make out leather sandals, armored leggings, and the *sheath of a sword, but the face was washed out. I could also tell the color of his tunic—red.*

He was Roman.

"What have we here?" the voice resounded. "A couple of mud ducks?"

The man dismounted. At last I perceived the features of his face. A very young face. Eighteen or nineteen. He wore no helmet. Locks of curly brown hair framed his forehead. I must admit, it was one of the most handsome faces I'd ever seen. Once when I was little girl I had a fantasy about meeting a knight in shining armor in the woods. My knight had a very rugged, beautiful face with a mischievous, but warm-hearted grin. The face of this Roman—I'm not kidding—looked just like the face in my fantasy.

"You two look like you've had a rough night. Can I ask who you are and where you're from?"

We stood there gaping. In any other circumstance I'm sure Jesse would have lashed out or tried to run. He just stood there. He didn't have the energy.

"I see," he said finally. "You don't speak Greek. I'm afraid my Aramaic is a little rusty. How about Latin?"

"I understand you fine," I said.

He raised his eyebrows. "Well, well. Your Latin is perfect. Are you a Roman? I can't quite tell under all that dirt."

He reached out as if to brush the hair out of my face. I deflected the hand—a little tae kwon do move I still remembered. I felt horribly self-conscious. I was still covered in dried mud from head to foot. Not to mention smoke and soot from last night's fire. Every inch of my white cloak was a slimy brown. I looked like something from the Black Lagoon. In my fantasy I'd been wearing all gold and silks. This wasn't how it was supposed to be at all.

On impulse, I replied, "Yes. Yes, I am a Roman. What's it to you?"

I glanced at Jesse, hoping he'd go along with me. Jesse grimaced with pain. While standing up, he'd accidentally put some weight on his injured hand. Still, he looked ready to take on this Roman ruffian if he had to.

"What's your name?" asked the soldier. "Where are you from?"

"Meagan," I said. I wished I'd said something a little more Roman. Julia or Augusta.

"Meagan," he repeated. "Unusual name. Sounds more like the name of a slave."

"Then you obviously don't know much about names," I replied. "Meagan is a very popular name where I'm from."

"And where is that?"

I didn't miss a beat. "Sicily, if you must know."

"Sicilia, eh? What town?"

Uh-oh. "A very small town. You've probably never heard of it."

"Try me."

I paused another second, then said, "Provo. Ever heard of it?"

"No."

"I told you it was small."

"In Sicilia, you say?"

"Have you ever been there?"

"Well, no—"

"Then stop asking stupid questions. Can't you see we need help? Can't you see this boy is hurt?"

"What happened?"

"He was shot through the hand by an arrow. He's lost a lot of blood."

"He's Jewish, isn't he?"

"Does that matter?"

He shrugged. "Well . . ."

I decided to use Harry's old tactic. "He's my slave. And he needs a doctor. Don't you belong to some sort of fort or something? Don't you have doctors on staff?"

"Yes, but . . . we don't normally—"

I stepped up to him. "Listen. My family is very rich. They own ships. Many ships. Our ships sail all over the world. All the way *from Sicily. They'll reward you beyond your wildest dreams. Don't you understand? You've* rescued *us!"*

"*I have?*"

"*Yes! We were kidnapped! Kidnapped by Simon Magus and the Sons of the Elect.*"

"*Who?*"

"*They're a band of religious freaks who live back in those hills. Last night we burned down their villa and escaped. They're trying to* kill *us!*"

The soldier looked off into the hills, then turned back. "Back in those *hills, you say?*"

"*Yes!*"

"*What a coincidence. That's just where I was headed. The ridge near the old Assyrian catacombs. We saw the flames from our barracks last night. My father—the garrison commander—sent us to check it out.*"

"*Us?*" *I glanced around and became aware of a half dozen horsemen watching us from the woods.*

"*Me and my men,*" *the Roman clarified.*

"*You're not going there anymore,*" *I declared. "First you're going to take us to your fort and have your doctor treat my slave.*"

He smiled with one corner of his mouth. "Oh, I am, eh? Not likely. My father would have me horsewhipped. He shows no favoritism to his son."

I became frantic. "Are you crazy? Simon has over fifty men! You have seven. You want to take on Simon and his archers and swordsmen with only seven men?"

His face grew serious. "What makes you think they'd attack us? There's been no uprising in Samaria for over a year."

"*These are not ordinary Samaritans,*" *I said. "They're pursuing us even now. Chances are, you'd be ambushed before you ever reached that ridge.*"

He surveyed the woods and hills. After digesting the information one more moment, he said, "All right. We'll take you to our camp. You can tell my father everything you know. I'm not saying I believe you. *This country is full of religious fanatics. I don't see how one stray band of men could pose any real threat.*"

"*They kidnapped me, didn't they? A Roman citizen!*"

"*I'm not sure I believe that either.*"

He called over to his men, and their horses emerged from the woods. The soldiers looked a lot older than their youthful leader. Honestly, some of them looked too old to be soldiers. Maybe that explained why they'd been assigned to a two-bit outpost in Samaria rather than with the legions at Jerusalem.

Jesse looked like a cornered fox. It occurred to me that he hadn't understood a word that the Roman had said. And yet he would have understood me just fine. This gift-of-tongues thing was getting rather sticky. No doubt Jesse considered me more incomprehensible than ever. To him it would have looked like I was carrying on a conversation with a man who wasn't even speaking my own language. I tried to quell his fears.

"*It's all right,*" I said in a low voice. "*They're going to take us to their army camp. There's a doctor there who'll look at your hand.*"

"*But they're* Romans," he said, as if that should have expressed the stupidity of such an idea without further explanation.

"*I know what I'm doing,*" I said. "*Have I ever led you wrong before?*"

"*You've come awfully close.*"

"*Trust me. And remember—*" I whispered in his ear "*—you're my slave.*"

The young officer explained the situation to his men. Finally he turned and walked back to us. He had a lovely walk. Cocky and confident. I could have watched it all day. Another man dismounted to help Jesse onto his horse. Jesse looked at me one last time for assurance, then let himself be lifted onto a horse.

"*You'll ride with me,*" the young Roman told me.

No problem, I thought. He jumped gracefully into his saddle and reached down a hand to me.

"*Do I sit in front or behind?*" *I asked.*

"*Behind,*" *he said.* "*I'd rather your filthy cloak soiled my back than my front.*"

I frowned. Still, I let him pull me up. I wrapped my arms around his armored chest and latched onto some leather straps.

"*I don't know your name,*" *I said.*

"*Apollus Brutus Severillus,*" *he replied.*

"*Do you go by Apollus or Brutus?*"

"*Apollus.*"

"*That's good.*"

"*Oh? Why?*"

"*I don't know. Never much cared for the name Brutus. Blame it on Popeye.*"

"*What?*"

"*Never mind. Private joke.*"

"*Brutus is my father.*"

"*On second thought, it's a lovely name.*"

"*I'm sure he'd be happy you think so.*"

"*Apollus, eh? Can I call you Apollo? Maybe Paul?*"

"*If you want to walk behind the horse.*"

I pulled in my chin. We definitely needed to work on this guy's sense of humor.

* * *

The Roman military camp was located on a hillside near a village called Neopolis. The fence around it was made of wood, as were most of the buildings. It looked fairly permanent, and yet I had a feeling that the whole thing could have been torn down and set up somewhere else in a matter of days. Maybe even hours.

We earned some curious glances from the sentries as we rode through the front gate. I don't think a female was a real common sight in these camps. A Jew might have been even less common.

The buildings were all laid out in nice, neat rectangles. All very grim and "male"—no concern for appearance or color. Still, despite the starkness, I hadn't felt so safe since arriving in the ancient world. Simon and his cronies couldn't reach us here. Neither could bandits and hyenas. I wondered if I'd ever been so secure in my life. These men belonged to the most powerful army on earth. If they couldn't protect us, who could?

The camp didn't look fully equipped by any means. Maybe a couple hundred men. This included everyone—soldiers, cooks, horse handlers, and men like the doctor who would be treating Jesse. Every eye was on us as we entered the main complex of buildings in the center of the camp. Men were practicing with lances in the middle courtyard. Most were as old as the men who rode with Apollus—late thirties and forties, some even into their fifties.

Jesse was taken toward some offices at the south end of the complex. Apollus and I rode up to the central door in the north wing. There was a covered boardwalk, just like in a western movie. As we approached the door, a gray-haired gentlemen with bright blue eyes came out and leaned on the rail. There were crumbs on his chin. I assumed he was just finishing up his breakfast.

"What's this, Centurion?" the gentleman inquired.

Apparently the commander preferred to call his son by his military title.

"Sir, may I introduce Meagan the Sicilian," said Apollus. "She's a refugee from the fire that we saw in the hills last night. Claims to be a Roman citizen. She also claims to be the victim of a savage abduction by a band of crazed religious fanatics."

He was making fun of me. I didn't appreciate it at all, but I held my tongue.

"She claims all that, does she?" said the gray-haired man. "Well, bring her in. I was about to supervise the construction of the new

latrine. This sounds far more entertaining."

Apollus helped me down from the horse. We mounted the board-walk and entered the gentleman's office. It looked as austere as the rest of the camp, except for a curious little bronze statue on his desk. It looked like a woman in a large headdress, holding a spear. A tray with a half-eaten bread loaf and a pitcher of honey was also on the desk. Two other men were in the room with us—orderlies, I assumed. As soon as we got inside, the formality of military titles was dropped.

"I thought I sent you to reconnoiter a fire, Apollus," said the commander. "Not carry off and seduce the local gentry."

"Well, her story does seem credible to a point, Father," said Apollus. "And she does speak fluent Latin. Even has an Italian accent."

"What are you doing in Palestine, girl?" asked the father. "How did you get here?"

I was ready for this. I'd been working it out in my head all during the ride to the fort.

"My father is a merchant," I said. "He owns a fleet of merchant ships and sells goods from Sicily all over the Mediterranean. My brother and I were traveling with my father when we landed at Ceasarea."

"Your father, eh? What's his name?"

More Italian names. Okay, I had one. "Romeo," I said. "Romeo . . . Travolta."

"Travolta?" Apollus repeated dubiously.

"That's right," I said.

So much for lies. Now I was determined to tell the truth. To a point, anyway. Heck, maybe I could recruit these old soldiers to help me find Harry.

"Simon Magus and his followers took my brother and me prisoner, along with our slave, Jesse."

"Simon Magus?" asked the commander.

"Oh, I forgot to tell you," Apollus informed his father. "This is the leader of these crazed religious fanatics."

I wanted to wipe that patronizing smirk off his face with a wet mop. "I'm sure you must have seen these guys. Each one of them is as bald as a hen's egg."

That rang a bell. "As a matter of fact, I think I have seen these men," said Apollus. "They come into town from time to time. I had the impression that the locals were afraid of them."

"That's them," I said. "These are the people who kidnapped us."

"Why would anyone kidnap the son and daughter of a Sicilian merchant?" asked the commander.

"Somehow Simon got it into his head that we knew the location of a secret scroll in the city of Jerusalem—"

"Back up," he said. "A secret scroll?"

"Yes. It's a religious scroll. Simon believes that it contains all sorts of spells and magic that will make him the world's most powerful sorcerer."

My listeners were thoroughly entertained. "Go on," said the commander.

"Simon threatened my brother that if he didn't go to Jerusalem, find this scroll, and bring it back, he'd kill me and Jesse on the spot."

"Go to Jerusalem?" said Apollus incredulously. "You mean inside the city walls?"

"Yes."

"And how does your brother expect to get past all the legions and come out again in one piece?"

"Honestly, I don't expect him to go to Jerusalem," I said.

"That sounds sensible," said the commander. "So what happens now?"

"The plan was to meet at the summit of a mountain called Gerizim in four days. Do you know where it is?"

"Of course," said Apollus. "Just look to the southeast."

"Really?" I said excitedly.

"Exasperating little mountain," said the commander, wiping some crumbs off his desk. "If there's ever an uprising in this district,

that's where it starts. The Samaritans consider it some sort of Mount Olympus."

I continued, "In four days my brother was supposed to exchange the scroll for our lives. Even if he doesn't have it, I think he'll still try to come and rescue us."

"So your problems are solved," said the commander. "You seem to have escaped easily enough. You can meet your brother on the appointed day, sail back to Sicilia, and live happily ever after."

"But I believe Simon is going to be there on the appointed day, too. He'll try to ambush my brother just in case he does have the scroll. If Simon finds any of us, he'll slit our throats without a second thought. I'm sure he's looking for us even now. Don't you see? We need protection!"

Father and son looked at one another.

"Palestine," the commander grunted. I think he was expressing his opinion of all the religious wackos and fanatics in this country.

"Your story is remarkable," said Apollus. "Some Greek should put it to verse. But what makes you think the Roman army would be interested in wasting their time on such a trivial matter?"

"Oh, forgive me," I said sarcastically. "I forgot how busy you were here in Samaria. Building latrines and all."

The commander laughed. He liked me. I was sure of it. His son, however, was another matter. He wore a heavy frown. I think he resented being stuck here in Samaria. He wanted to be in Jerusalem where the action was. I wondered why he wasn't.

"Get this girl some breakfast," the commander told an orderly. "Get her cleaned up as well. She can use my private bath if she likes. Do we have any women's clothing in the camp?"

The orderly raised an eyebrow. "Uh . . . no, sir."

"Then run into town and buy her some. Buy whatever other frills you think a young girl might like as well."

The orderlies looked at one another blankly. I don't think they had the foggiest idea what a young girl might like. I looked into the commander's warm blue eyes. I couldn't believe he was being so nice. The old soldier named Brutus seemed to be getting soft in his old age.

"Then you'll help me?" I asked.

"Why not?" said the commander. "I'll make it my son's personal mission. If the army can't protect its own citizens, what are we here for?"

"But, Father," said Apollus, "we don't even know if she is a citizen."

"What do you mean?" said the commander. "She speaks the language better than I do."

"Which tells me she's probably a tutor. A slave just like her companion."

"Nonsense. Look at that pierce in her nose. That's the custom of a seafaring Sicilian if I ever saw one."

I touched my nose. Who'd have thought that that obnoxious pierce would someday work to my advantage? I was flabbergasted. What luck! We had the whole Roman army on our side now. Was it possible that all our troubles were at an end? With these men patrolling the area, Simon and his followers wouldn't dare hang around Mount Gerizim waiting for Harry. In a matter of days we could all be reunited. Then Harry and I could finally devote our energies to finding a way home.

Home. It was almost too much to comprehend!

The question was, where was Harry Hawkins now? The very thought caused apprehension to well up inside me all over again. No, I had to confess. This adventure wasn't over yet. Not by a long shot.

CHAPTER TWELVE

The first rays of sunlight streamed through the windows of the tower. I wasn't sure if it was a welcome sign or not. But at least it meant I no longer had to lay on the hard floor listening to the growls in my stomach. I drank about half the water left in my pouch and gave the rest to Mary. Then I joined Gidgiddonihah at the window overlooking the Upper City.

All was relatively calm at the moment. The only fighting was in the vicinity of the three tall towers in the northwestern corner. Just a few stones being hurled back and forth, steady as clockwork. Of course, this didn't include the area around the temple where smoke continued billowing from the outer court-yard and the battering rams had never stopped booming.

The city was starting to come to life. The curfew had certainly been lifted. I could see people gathering at a few of the fountains and wells, filling their pots and buckets for the day. To the west I could see part of an open market. Some shops actually looked as if they were opening for business. For some reason the scene made me feel a depressing emptiness. Even in the face of certain destruction, the citizens still went about their normal activities. Tomorrow it might all be gone, but today life still had to go on.

"You can almost see it," said Symeon. He joined us at the window and directed our eyes toward the precise location of the house of James. "It's there, across from that water trough, right beside those tenements. Most of the rubble has been long since cleared away. But there's still one wall and part of another. And the foundation is still there. Or at least it was three years ago."

"It had to have been there just a few *weeks* ago," I said, "before the Romans built that siege wall surrounding the city. That's when Barsabas took the first eleven scrolls—the ones he carried to the Dead Sea."

"All right," said Gid, standing up straight. "I suggest we climb down from this wall and walk there as casually as possible—as if we're just headed to the market or refilling our water pouches at one of the troughs. If we make our way calmly, but swiftly, we shouldn't draw too much attention."

We climbed down a staircase inside the tower. At the bottom we found a strong wooden door. The lock was already broken. We stepped into the street. I tried to act casual, as Gid had suggested, but my nerves were as taut as piano wires. People were milling about, shuffling through the garbage and debris in the streets, foraging for food. They looked almost like ghosts, their faces gray and sunken. They wouldn't lift their gazes to look at us or each other.

After a minute I began to notice faces in shadowed windows. They were watching us quite closely. We weren't quite as inconspicuous as Gid had hoped. Maybe it was because we still looked fairly healthy, a good amount of meat still left on our bones. That alone made us stick out like sore thumbs.

Or maybe it was more simple. This city was accustomed to seeing the same faces every day. Ours would have immediately seemed unfamiliar. Besides, at least two of us didn't look Jewish at all. I was starting to think Gid and I were the only males in the whole place without beards.

The attention seemed to increase with every passing street. Everyone was whispering about us now, pointing. As we passed one doorway, I heard someone say, "Spies!" under his breath. This was very bad. My heart started pounding. Genuine fear settled in. What had ever given us the idea that we could blend in?

The deadest giveaway might have been Gidgiddonihah's sword. No citizens were armed with anything fiercer than an eating knife. Gid was obviously no Jewish soldier. Again that sword was complicating things in ways we could have never anticipated.

Gid quickened his pace. We quickened ours to match. Looking behind, I noticed that several people were following us. They tried to conceal themselves around corners. This was getting downright eerie. I thought back on that old movie *Invasion of the Body Snatchers*. It was almost like we were the only human beings left in a world being taken over by aliens.

Someone threw something. It splattered on the street ahead. Gid halted and assessed the situation warily. Every step was becoming more dangerous.

"How much farther?" Gid asked Symeon.

"Just up this next street," he replied.

"We should have come at night," said Gid. "We should have taken our chances in the dark."

I was becoming convinced there *was* no safe time to retrieve this scroll. Clearly we'd never get away with it now. They'd be watching our every move. We might be mobbed in minutes. I felt sure someone had gone to fetch the soldiers.

"I have an idea," said Mary. "We need to find a place to hide."

"That's your idea?" I asked.

She shook her head. "I'll tell you when we're in hiding."

"Through here," said Gid. "Hurry!"

He led us up a flight of stairs and across a causeway that dropped down into another part of the town. It was a wealthier area with fancy architecture and lots of gates and gardens. It was also a little cleaner, despite the fact that the vines were brown and the gardens were bare. To our relief, there seemed to be a lot fewer peering eyes. We made a couple of sharp turns to be sure that no one was following, then Gid approached the archway of a private yard. The gate had a chain and padlock, just like any gate in the twenty-first century. Gid's patience had worn thin. He threw his shoulder into it. The rail snapped and the gate opened cleanly. We closed it behind us.

The yard was small and covered with flagstones. Nothing stirred in the house above us. The gate area had a covered walkway with trellises overgrown with leaves. We huddled beneath it and gathered our wits.

"The problem is me," Gid admitted in frustration. "I'm a foreigner and they know it."

"I should have anticipated this," said Symeon. "I didn't realize the populace had become so wary and suspicious."

"Father," said Mary. "You and I should go alone. Harry and Gidgiddonihah can stay in hiding. We'll recover the scrolls and bring them back here."

"This isn't the best hiding place," said Gid, staring back at the house. "I'm not sure how long we can remain."

"We'll work swiftly," said Symeon.

"You have to find the Scroll of Knowledge," I said.

"We'll find it," Mary promised.

"You have one hour," said Gid. "If you're not back, we'll come looking for you."

"Agreed," said Symeon. They turned to leave.

"Wait," I said again. "Do you know how to find the secret library?"

Symeon hesitated. "The foundation isn't very large. It shouldn't be too difficult."

Anxiety trickled up my spine. I had a feeling it was anything *but* obvious. If it had survived all these years, it must have been pretty well concealed.

"Keep on your toes," I said.

Mary smiled. Then she and her father slipped through the gate. Gid and I looked at each other, both of us wondering if this had been such a smart idea. I realized it was possible that I'd never see Mary and Symeon again. I drew a deep breath. This could easily turn out to be the longest hour of my life.

Gid and I got comfortable and waited. The minutes passed. The shutter of a window above us creaked in the breeze. The battering ram pounded in the distance. A half hour passed. Gid made frequent trips to the gate to peer through the cracks. I started biting my nails. Every minute became more and more anxious. Finally, the hour was up.

"Where could they be?" I whispered.

"Perhaps an hour wasn't enough time," said Gid.

"But we promised we'd come looking for them."

I realized now it was a ridiculous promise. We'd only face the same wrath and suspicion. If they'd been captured, our best bet was to wait until dark. But what then? What options would be left? We couldn't just leave them. The rebels would cast them into prison. They'd be executed for sure. I fought down a wave of dread. *Please*, I prayed. *Please let them return.*

"A few more minutes," said Gid. "Then we'll—"

He stopped abruptly. Someone was outside the gate. I sighed with relief. But as I started to rise, Gid caught my arm. He put his finger to his lips. I became deathly still. My relief changed to apprehension.

The person behind the gate made no effort to come in. We could see him through the slats in the wood, but the slats were too close together. I couldn't tell if it was a soldier, a citizen, or even Symeon, acting with extra caution. The prowler lingered a good twenty seconds. We knew now it wasn't Symeon or Mary. Gid pulled out his dagger. A hand reached up to rattle the chain still hanging from the top rail, as if to verify that the lock was broken. Then the stranger backed away. His footsteps took off down the street.

"They know we're here," said Gid. "Come on!"

My veins rushed with adrenaline. We bolted from the shadows and threw open the gate. One glance up and down the street revealed the prowler's identity. It was a soldier. Both ends of the street were *bristling* with soldiers!

"There they are!" someone shouted.

The troops converged. Terror knotted in my chest. We fled back into the yard. I crossed the flagstones and smashed through the wicker door at the back of the house. Gid was right behind me. The soldiers began pouring into the yard, their swords drawn. The house was a shambles. Ransacked—probably months ago. We dodged the broken furniture and reached a back entrance. But looking into the alley, the sun reflected off the helmets of more Jewish troops. We were surrounded! Gid veered to the left. We exited another doorway leading out onto a terrace. There was a stairway leading up to the second story.

The soldiers had entered the house. We climbed to the upper story, then followed another narrow stairway onto the roof. It was a flat roof enclosed by a three-foot containment wall. We ran to the edge on the east side. The neighboring roof was only about nine feet away.

"We'll have to jump," said Gid. "Are you ready?"

"Yes," I said, my heart thumping. Such a jump would mean we'd have to run the length of the roof, place a foot atop the three-foot wall, and then sail nine feet to the other side. It would be awkward, but I felt sure I could do it.

The soldiers were climbing the stairs. Gid started his run. He stepped up to the containment wall and sailed out into space. His arms were swinging as he came down on top of the neighboring roof. He collapsed and rolled. Two seconds later he was back on his feet, urging me to follow.

"Come on, Harry! Throw me the shoulder bag!"

I threw him the bag with the Book of Matthew. The soldiers reached the roof. I leaped up to the edge. But my footing wasn't solid. As I propelled myself outward, I slipped. I wasn't going to make it!

I came up short, smashing into the neighboring wall. Gid scrambled to catch me. His fingers caught part of my left hand, but I was just too far below him. I slipped through his fingers and plunged to the earth.

As I hit, stars exploded behind my eyes. I blacked out for several seconds. When I opened my eyes again, Gid's face was staring down at me from the roof. His image blurred. When my focus returned, Gid was gone. Above me now were the faces of a dozen Jewish soldiers. I was their prisoner. I assumed they'd caught Gid, too. I was also certain they'd captured Symeon and Mary.

Our miracles seemed to have run out. We were at the mercy of the Jerusalem rebels.

* * *

There were six other prisoners lying beside me in the dank holding cell below one of the three tall towers. None of them were Gidgiddonihah, Symeon, or Mary. For three hours, maybe four, I lay in the dark, the fate of my companions completely unknown. The side of my face was bruised and bleeding. My eye was swollen half shut. I felt bruises in several other places, and my wrist was sprained. As far as I could tell, only the injury to my wrist had been caused by the fall. The others had been inflicted by the soldiers.

I tried to remember what had happened. It was all so blurry. They were dragging me back across the causeway and into the neighborhood where we'd been earlier that morning. I guess I stumbled or something. This had perturbed the soldiers to no end. They were annoyed anyway at having to chase us; it didn't take much to provoke them. The first blow to my eye was the last thing I remembered. After that I must have gone unconscious. I hadn't felt the other blows at all. But I sure felt them now.

A heavy chain had been fastened on both of my wrists. My sprain ached horribly from the chains. I tried to balance the chain's weight on my chest. Then I lay back in the dark, trying desperately to figure out what had gone wrong.

What did I do, God? I asked. *Did I make a mistake?* I was totally baffled. And yet I refused to let my faith waver. God was still in control. The only mystery was how He was going to reveal it. Hopefully, I wouldn't have to wait long.

Moments later the cell door opened and sunlight filtered in. Three Jewish soldiers in bronze armor entered the room. The other six prisoners started begging for water. The first two soldiers pushed them back.

"Get down!" they warned. "You don't need water. You'll be dead by sundown. Traitors!"

"My wife," pleaded one of the prisoners. "Where is she?"

The soldier slapped him. "I said get down!"

The third soldier, a large man with a triangle-shaped beard and narrow eyes, glared down at me. He was sweaty. Soot covered his face, as if he'd come here fresh from the battle at the temple courtyard.

"Is that him?" he asked the others.

"That's him," they confirmed.

"What about the other one?"

"He'll be in custody soon, general."

So they haven't caught him, I thought. Gid was still free. My heart soared. And yet I still had no idea what had become of Symeon and Mary.

"Bring him," the general commanded. He turned and left the cell.

I was seized by both arms and dragged out into the daylight. The general with the triangle-shaped beard tromped on without glancing back. My escorts would have gladly dragged me all the way. Luckily, I found my feet and was able to walk.

They took me past a tall row of columns, through an archway that tunneled through a thick stone wall, and out into a wide courtyard with many buildings that were scarred with fire. At one time this place might have looked magnificent. Now the lawns and gardens were trampled. Tall marble statues were lying cracked in half, their faces chipped until there were no features. It struck me that it might have once been the palace of a king, but the rebels had turned it into a junkyard. One large structure still stood at the north end—a meeting hall with a big, open roof. It was into this hall that the soldiers delivered me.

The place was packed with Jewish soldiers, all of them tired and battle worn. The odor of fresh meat nearly knocked me off my feet, causing my mouth to water. Nine or ten roasted carcasses—I guessed they were sheep—had been spread out on large silver platters in the middle of the floor. Soldiers were slicing off large chunks and returning to their places to gobble them down. It was a regular feast. Not exactly a sight I'd expected to see in a town that was starving.

The general, walking a good ten yards ahead of us, was hailed by his men as he entered. He took his place on some steps near the front. A generous pile of meat awaited him on a bright golden plate. In fact, I saw a lot of golden plates, as well as jeweled goblets and silver knives. They seemed to have pulled out all the stops. To me it had all the signs of a last grand meal.

As the general started eating, he motioned to my escorts to bring me forward.

"Set him down," he commanded.

I was forced to kneel on the marble floor in front of the Jewish general and another man with gray in his beard and dark, sunburned skin. I glanced to my right. One of the roasted carcasses sat only about four feet away. I stared at it, almost transfixed, the juicy flesh glistening in the sunlight. The only thing hindering my movements was the chain on my wrists. It would have been so easy to make a quick lunge, tear off a piece, and stuff it into my mouth before anyone could stop me. The general and his companion watched as I struggled with the temptation. They were enjoying it.

"Sacred meat," the sunburned man said to me. "I guarantee, boy, you've never tasted anything so sweet."

"Sacred?" I asked.

He smiled. "You can thank your precious Prince Titus for that. Since the days of Antiochus, king of Syria, the daily sacrifice on the temple altar has never ceased. Two hundred and thirty-seven uninterrupted years. Until now, that is. A few days ago that sacrifice ended again. Why? You see it spread before you. This meat was meant for God and His priests. It must now be consumed by His warriors." His raised his voice for all to hear. "Eat up, men! The power of God is inside you now. Today you will fight the most important battle of your lives. As you feel His power in your bellies, think about God's sacrifice for *you!*"

A cheer went up, but it died rather quickly as the men recommenced feeding their faces. The general with the triangle-shaped beard grinned at the sunburned man. "You always were the speechmaker, John," he said in a low voice.

John grinned back. "Why thank you, Simon Giora."

So the meat had come from the temple. Apparently they'd plundered the last lambs meant for the sacred altar. God's sacrifice for *them?* Not long ago, I felt sure, nothing would have been considered more sacrilegious.

Simon Giora turned back to me. This was the second man named Simon I had met in this land. I was beginning to think the name itself had negative connotations. "I'll make you a deal, boy. Tell us what we want to know and maybe we'll let you have a few bites."

"Who are you, boy?" asked John. "What are you doing in our city?"

I didn't see any point in not telling them. "Looking for a scroll."

The answer made them raise their eyebrows.

"A what?" asked John.

"A scroll. Once I found it, I was planning to leave."

"A scroll?" said Simon dubiously. "What kind of an objective is that? How did you get inside?"

"Through a tunnel. The one used by the dying in hopes that they'll get buried outside the walls."

"Impossible," said John. "You think we're buffoons? How would you have gotten past the Roman defenses?"

"I had help," I replied.

"Help from who?"

I hesitated. Josephus had warned us that the mere mention of his name would bring instant death. "A friend," I said.

"You mean a *Roman*, don't you? Now stop your lying. What are you really here for? What information were you and your companion—the man with the sword—supposed to gather and bring back to that old fox, Titus?"

"No information," I said calmly. "Titus didn't send us. I just wanted to find the scroll."

"*Liar!*" John snapped. "You're a spy. The Romans sent you here to discover our strength and report our plans. Isn't that right?"

I scrunched my forehead. "Why would the Romans need a spy for that?"

The men glowered at me. To suggest that the Romans no longer even cared about their strength or their plans made them burn with resentment.

"Maybe I'll send him back to the Romans," Simon told John.

"What?" said John in dismay.

"Yes. I'll cut off his hands and send him right back." He leaned toward me, his eyes searing. "You want to know our plans? I'll tell you *exactly* what our plans are, boy. Our plans are to watch the Emperor's legions obliterated by the wrath of God the instant they try to mar His holy house. From that moment you'll see the armies of Israel sweep them off the earth like the dews of dawn. God has not abandoned His people. The Roman scourge will be crushed. So say the prophets. So says God Himself." He leaned back again and said smugly, "Do you know who I am, boy?"

"I don't have the foggiest idea," I replied.

Simon raised up and put the question to the soldiers. "Who am I, men?"

"The deliverer!" came back the reply. "The prince of peace! The messiah!"

Almost on cue, the men on the opposite side of the hall started to protest. "*John* is the deliverer! *John* is the messiah!"

A shouting match ensued. I realized the hall was pretty much divided right down the middle by men devoted to Simon and men devoted to John. On the whole, the contest seemed fairly good-natured. John and Simon lapped it up like Dobermans, even slapping each other on the back. Something told me this contest wasn't always so friendly. There was a very real tension in the room. These two men were rivals. I figured they'd come together only because of the Romans. If by some miracle the Jews ever won this war, I felt sure Simon and John would have been right back at each other's throats.

As the shouting died, Simon said to me, "What do you say, boy? Your freedom for your hands? I'll chop them off right here and now if you like. You can leave by way of the gate of the Essenes and be back in the arms of your Roman nursemaids to deliver your message in less than half an hour. Are the terms agreeable?"

I tried to keep my voice from quivering. "I wouldn't know who to deliver any message to. No one is expecting me to return."

"Is that so?" said John. "Well, then your other choice is to die. Is that your preference?" He filled his right hand with a dagger.

I swallowed hard. Then I gritted my teeth. I wasn't going to die today.

"What I'd really like to do, if it's not too much trouble, is get my scroll and leave the city in peace."

I sounded like some character in *Leave It to Beaver*. John and Simon were dumbfounded. Then they perked up again, greatly amused.

"The scroll again, eh?" said Simon. "So what is this scroll? Some nobleman's will leaving you all his property?"

"The words of Jesus," I replied.

"Jesus? Jesus who?"

"Jesus of Nazareth," I said. "Jesus the Messiah."

Their expressions changed. Not exactly to contempt, but I think my answer had genuinely surprised them. I could hear muttering in the hall behind me.

"Jesus of Nazareth?" said John in bewilderment. "You're a Nazarene?"

I nodded. "Yes."

Simon grunted, shaking his head. "Another gentile Nazarene. What is the world coming to?" He took a bite of meat.

"Do you really want to know?" I asked.

Simon stopped chewing. He narrowed his eyes, then swallowed. "Yes. Yes, why don't you tell me, young Roman. What *is* this world coming to?"

The hall was quiet. I realized I had a captive audience.

"The Romans are going to take this city," I declared. "I think everyone here already knows that. They're going to burn it to the ground. Everything—including the temple. There's not much time left. If only you'd recognize it. Do something about it. Just put down your weapons. So many people could still be saved."

The muttering behind me grew louder. Some men laughed. But not very many. I could feel the anger rising. Insults started flying. "Nazarene scum! Roman pig!" A wad of spit hit the back of my head. Another one splattered on my cheek.

John stood up, his dagger in hand. "So you *are* a spy. A spy sent to deliver Roman lies and propaganda. I've heard enough." He started toward me.

Simon grabbed his arm. "Wait, wait. Don't be so impetuous, my friend. Learn how to savor the moment. We'll put him with the other Nazarenes in the tower. I'm told we caught two more just like him this morning. Isn't that right, Nathan?"

One of Simon's guards nodded. "A man and a boy. Caught them worshipping at the old burned-out house of that beggar James."

Symeon and Mary, I thought breathlessly.

"Traitors, all of them," said Simon. "Corrupters of the faith. Worshippers of a savior who couldn't even save himself. We'll catch the last one, then we'll get rid of them all. I'll behead them myself in the center of the amphitheater in view of all the Roman towers. Then I'll prop their heads on a pike atop the Hippicus. The red-haired one, too. I've amused myself with his nonsense long enough. His arm clock doesn't work anymore anyway."

I watched Simon reach beneath a golden band on his right wrist and slide something nearly to the middle of his forearm. My jaw dropped like an anchor. My eyes blinked in disbelief. It had to be an illusion.

He was wearing a *watch.*

It wasn't possible. And yet I could see the word engraved on the face—Seiko. A genuine modern-day Seiko watch with a flexible silver wristband! The digital face was blank. Somehow he'd broken it. But how did he get it? Where had it come from?

The answer hit me like a baseball bat. A modern-day watch. A man with red-hair. There was only one possibility in the entire universe.

CHAPTER THIRTEEN

I'd barely taken three bites of my breakfast of deep-fried honey bread and stuffed figs when I heard a blood-curdling scream from the opposite side of the compound. I went pale with guilt. I'd been so concerned with my own needs that I'd completely forgotten about poor Jesse.

I sprang from the table and ran across the yard, interrupting several dozen men still practicing with their lances. I entered the infirmary where the camp doctor was supposedly taking care of Jesse's wound. Another terrible scream shook the room as I entered.

My heart stopped. Tears sprang from my eyes. Jesse had been tied to a table. He was convulsing violently, his eyes rolled back in his head. Standing over him was the camp doctor—a short man with flaring nostrils—and two attendants. In the doctor's hand was a glowing firebrand. I smelled the sickening odor of burning flesh. He'd just seared Jesse's wound!

"What's the matter with you?" I shrieked.

They looked at me in confusion.

I stepped up to the doctor and yanked the burning stick out of his hand. He was so stunned he hardly reacted. But now I had a potentially nasty weapon. He backed off so rapidly that he knocked over a tray of primitive surgical instruments.

"What are you? The village torturer!" I yelled in his face.

I plunged the firebrand into a water basin and let it sizzle out.

Then I started to untie Jesse. Apollus had followed me inside. The doctor looked at him, totally incensed.

"What is this, Centurion?" he demanded. "The girl is insane!"

"It's all right, Demeterus," said Apollus. "She's just looking after her property."

"My property?" I raged. "Jesse is a human being! You people are cavemen! You think you can just stab him with a burning stick?"

"The wound had to be cauterized," said the doctor.

I finished untying his hands and held him tightly against my chest. He continued shaking, but his eyes were closed. His uninjured hand gripped the sleeve of my tunic.

"Don't you use anesthetic?" I asked.

"Anesthetic?"

"Yes! Anesthetic! The word is Greek, you moron! Pain killers! Don't you use pain killers?"

"The boy is a slave," said the doctor. "And a Jew. We reserve our opium and mandragora for Roman casualties."

"Give it to him!" I howled. "You give him a pain killer right now!"

The doctor looked at Apollus.

Apollus nodded. "It's all right. Give him whatever he needs."

The doctor went to a wooden counter. He took the lid off a black vial and measured out a portion of yellow powder. He then opened Jesse's mouth and placed the substance right under his tongue. Within a minute, Jesse's muscles relaxed. He fell asleep. The other attendant began wrapping Jesse's hand in bandages.

Apollus touched my shoulder. "Come on, Meagan. He's in good hands, I promise you. Demeterus is an excellent doctor. He'll take good care of the boy." He gave Demeterus a stern look to make sure this would be true.

I squeezed Jesse's arm and allowed Apollus to lead me from the infirmary. Maybe I shouldn't have flipped out. After all, this wasn't the Mayo Clinic. It was a Roman army camp in 70 A.D. Maybe Jesse was getting the best care around. After we left the doorway, I swear I heard the doctor and his attendants laughing.

"You seem to care about your slaves a great deal," said Apollus as we walked back across the compound.

He had a queer emphasis on the word "slave." He was testing me again. My story about being the daughter of a rich Sicilian merchant still didn't fly with him. My fit in the infirmary hadn't helped my case. It probably seemed more like the reaction of a fellow slave than an owner.

"Of course I care about them," I said. "Especially this one. He's almost part of the family."

"I see. Just how many slaves does your father own?"

"About twenty. Why? How many does your family own?"

"We don't own any."

"That's good."

"Why?"

"You can tie your own boot latchet for a change. Get off your rear end and do some real work."

"I have all the men I need to tie my boot latchet," said Apollus. "That's what it means to be an officer. You have all the slaves you could ever desire and it doesn't cost you anything."

"Is that why you became a soldier, Apollus? So you could boss everybody else around?"

He stiffened his jaw. "I became a soldier because every boy in my family becomes a soldier. My father fought in Britannia with Vespasian, my grandfather rode with Germanicus across the Rhine, my great-grandfather was an advisor to Augustus in Asia Minor, and my great-great-grandfather fought with Julius Caesar in Gaul."

"Quite a heritage," I said. "So how does someone like you end up here in Podunkville?"

Apollus bristled. "I'm here because it's my father's will. Finish your breakfast."

He turned and departed. I'd offended him more than I'd intended. I don't know why I felt the need to offend every guy I met.

No, I take that back. I did know why. Most of them deserved it.

After breakfast I took up Commander Severillus on his offer to let me bathe in his private facilities. The baths were located just behind his barracks. They consisted of two different pools—a cold bath about five feet wide, made of wood and shellacked with some kind of resin, and a smaller cement pool heated from underneath by vents in the floor, much like the ones at Simon's palace. All of it was housed in a nice wood building with neatly cut decks and an open roof. There were even rough white towels for drying. Pretty fancy for an army camp, I thought. Romans seemed obsessed with bathing. A habit of which I highly approved.

"Do you have any shampoo?" I asked an orderly outside the door.

"Shampoo?" he repeated.

"Or just soap?"

"Soap?" he said with equal perplexity.

Goodness! Didn't these guys know what soap was?

"The commander says you may use may his oil and strigil," said the orderly. "They're on the bench."

"Oil and what?"

His expression said I definitely should have known what he was talking about.

"Never mind," I said, scooting inside. "I'll find it myself."

Twenty seconds later I was out of that disgusting tunic and sinking rapturously in the heated water. Oh man, oh man, oh man, it felt good. I closed my eyes and let the steam swirl around me. The only thing missing was a Jacuzzi jet. I even glanced at the wall for an "on" switch. With as many other luxuries as these Romans enjoyed, seeing some mechanism for producing air bubbles wouldn't have surprised me one bit. No such luck, however, so I sat back and soaked, determined not to come out until I was well-done.

Suddenly some lout pushed open the outer door. I panicked and grabbed a towel from the edge and wrapped it around me, even though I was hidden by the pool wall.

It was Apollus. His arms were full of clothes and other items.

"Get out!" I barked.

"Sorry," he said. "My father's secretary just returned with a cloak and some other things. I'll just set them here and—"

"GET OUT!!!"

He bumbled out the doorway and disappeared. What an arrogant clod! He didn't even think to knock! I no longer regretted anything I'd said to him. Or anything I was about to say. He'd be darn lucky if he got through the day without having his eyes gouged out.

My towel was drenched. I dunked my head several times, climbed out, and found another towel by the bench. I saw the oil and some sort of curved stick. I wouldn't have had the first clue how to use them.

To my surprise, the outfit they'd bought me was quite beautiful—a long blue tunic of soft material. Gold embroidery lined all the hems and sleeves and crossed at the neck. There was also a belt, some bronze brooches, and even a hairband with pink stones. There were earrings, too, shaped like little clusters of grapes, and a sleek pair of leather sandals. My tennis shoes were coming apart anyway. I set them aside and tied on the sandals.

There were also bracelets and hairbrushes. Who said these oafs didn't know how to shop for a girl? What I found most curious was a little corked vial. I pulled out the cork and took a whiff.

"Whew!" I wiped the tears from my eyes.

Strong, but not unpleasant. Rather nice, actually. Flowers and spices and cinnamon. I dabbed a little on my neck, donned the blue cloak, and combed my hair with painful determination to get out the knots. Afterwards, I found Apollus pacing outside.

He faced me quickly. But before he could speak, he took a good long look at me from head to foot.

"You look . . . better," he stammered.

I scowled. "I have to check on Jesse."

"Wait!" said Apollus.

I turned back, still scowling.

"I want to apologize. For walking in on you, I mean. I just wanted to see you—"

"You what?"

"I mean, I just wanted to see what you would do."

"Excuse me?"

"I mean—" He sighed in frustration and began again. "What I'm trying to say is, I believe you. I no longer think you're a slave or a tutor or anything other than what you say you are. We both know that a slave wouldn't have ordered me out like that. It wouldn't be in their nature."

"So if I was a slave it would be okay?*"*

He looked stymied. I honestly don't think he saw any moral conflict whatsoever.

I rolled my eyes and turned away. "Never mind."

"No, wait!"

He grabbed my shoulder. I turned back, ready to deck him.

"I wanted to declare peace between us. My father wishes me to assist you in any way I can. I'm determined to obey."

He straightened up, his jawline taut. It was a pretty jawline, by the way.

"Fine," I said. "Just keep three steps behind me and I'll whistle if I need you."

The jaw quivered, but he controlled his anger well.

I continued inside the infirmary and found Jesse still fast asleep. I figured it was best to leave him like that. I sat beside him and brushed the hair from his eyes. I hated seeing him so helpless. His face looked flushed and fevered. The doctor said that was normal.

"I've treated a thousand war wounds like this," he proclaimed. "Your slave will be fine in a few days. He mostly needs rest and nutrition to rebalance his humors."

"His what?" I asked.

"Humors—yellow bile, black bile, blood, and phlegm. Later I'll

give him an elixir of viper's flesh and doves' blood to hasten the balancing process."

I cringed. *"Let's save that for your next patient, doc. He'll do just fine with the pain killers."*

The doctor was about to protest, then gave up. After all, Jesse was just a slave. I walked away thinking this guy should be practicing medicine with a bone in his nose.

I ate supper that night with the soldiers in the garrison—all two hundred and sixty-eight of them. There was no cafeteria or mess hall. We just lined up at the cook's cabin, filled our trays with bread, cabbage, leeks, and a boiled hen's egg, and ate out in the open courtyard. Everyone was very polite. I was told there was a lot less belching and bawdy jokes than usual. The story of my ordeal had spread. I felt sure every man in the camp knew all the details by heart. I was told there was a man in the camp from the town of Syracuse in Sicily who wanted to hear news from the homeland. That was my cue to announce that I didn't feel very well and to retire to my quarters.

I'd been given the official guest chambers, originally meant to accommodate generals and other Roman officials. But no one important stopped in Neopolis these days. The room, however, was wonderful. Not because it was fancy or decorated. Actually it was just as spartan as the rest of the camp. But there was a bed! A real bed! I hadn't slept in a bed since I'd left Utah. In other words, it felt like I hadn't slept in a bed for two thousand years.

I leaped into the feather mattress and let it suck me right in. After a few minutes, I opened my eyes. Despite my exhaustion, I just couldn't fall asleep. My mind was spinning.

I climbed out of bed again and walked across the compound. The men were drinking large goblets of foul-smelling ale. I passed by several dice games and other forms of gambling. Some women with white-painted faces and bright red lips had come in from the village. I didn't guess they were here to sell Avon. In reality, these old soldiers were a *fairly disgusting lot. I started to question the wisdom of thinking they could really protect me from a force as evil as Simon Magus.*

I wandered to the lookout tower in the southwest corner and climbed the ladder. The two sentries recognized me from dinner.

"Would you mind if I looked over the rail?" I asked.

They had no objections. I moved to the far end and gazed out at the rounded summit of Mount Gerizim in the last light of the setting sun. It wasn't nearly as ominous as I might have imagined. No jagged cliffs. No dark clouds and lightning. Nevertheless, that hill was the key to putting this nightmare behind us once and for all.

Harry's out there, I thought. Our rendezvous was barely four days away. Then it occurred to me: What if Harry was up there already? What if all this time he'd been waiting, hiding? The more I thought about it, the more logical the idea became.

"Would you like to go up there?" said a voice from behind.

Apollus had climbed the ladder. He saluted the sentries, then joined me at the rail.

"The summit is only a few hours' ride," he continued. "Maybe we could find your brother and ship you back to Sicilia a few days sooner than you'd planned."

"That's amazing," I said. "I was just thinking that very same thing. Do you really think he might be up there?"

He shrugged. "How would I know? He's your brother. But if you want to go, I could have ten of my best horsemen ready at sunup. We could be back again in time for the noon meal. Unless you'd like to ride around a while. Then I could bring our lunch with us."

"Ten horsemen?" I felt a shiver. My eyes scanned the walls and fences of the army camp. In here I felt safe, protected. But out there . . .

Where had Simon and his men gone after the fire, I wondered? Did they sink back deeper into the hills? Had they already climbed Gerizim? Were they spread out looking for us across the countryside?

"Make it twenty horsemen," I said.

"All right. Twenty it is. What's the matter? You look afraid."

"Sorry. Force of habit, I guess. I've been afraid a lot these past few weeks."

"You have nothing to fear anymore," said Apollus. "I've sworn to protect you with my life. So will any other man I ask to make the same pledge. Your days of fear are over, Meagan. If we find these men, I promise I'll personally line them up and drive a single lance through all of their hearts."

I crinkled my nose. It wouldn't have been so bad, except he was totally serious. Then I smiled. Male bravado. It did have some appeal, didn't it?

"I'm glad you're here in Samaria, Apollus," I said. "But why aren't you fighting for Rome on some front line somewhere?"

Apollus gazed out at the sunset. "My father is getting old, I guess. Old and sentimental. He'd be in Jerusalem right now if his health were better. He has a bad back and gouty joints. Whatever the case, he made a deal with the Legate to keep me as far from any action as possible."

"Why's that?"

"I'm his youngest son," said Apollus. "He lost two sons in Cestius' flight from Jerusalem four years ago. Two years before that my mother was killed in a carriage accident on the Felsina Road. My little sister, Albia, was killed as well."

"I'm very sorry," I said.

"It was all a long time ago. But it may be why my father has taken to you."

"Oh? Do I look like your sister?"

"No," said Apollus. "Not at all. But she would have been just about your age."

"So your father doesn't wish to lose his last child, eh?"

"Something like that," said Apollus. "So here I am, in the middle of—how did you put it?—Podunkville?"

"I'm sorry. I didn't understand."

"Maybe someday my father will realize if I can't serve Rome with honor, dying if necessary, it's hardly worth living at all."

I'd heard of patriotism, but this was ridiculous.

"Isn't anything more important than the honor of Rome?"

"What could be more important? As the poet says: 'Remember, Roman, your task is to rule nations, And your genius shall be to lead men into peace, To be generous to the conquered and to stand firm against the proud.'"

I smirked. "You really believe that?"

Apollus frowned. "Of course. It expresses the sacred duty of all *Romans. Even Sicilians."*

"Rome won't be around forever, you know. Maybe you should think about devoting yourself to something more permanent."

"What could be more permanent than Rome?"

"A lot of things. Family. Friends. Ideals—"

"Ideals?"

"—and God, for example."

"The gods? The gods change with every crisis and season. And their numbers increase with every nation we conquer."

"Not gods," I said. "Just one God."

"And what god is that?"

Uh-oh. *What was I getting into? I couldn't talk about the gospel. This was Harry's department, not mine. And with a Roman? I felt totally unqualified. It's not as if I didn't have a testimony. I did. I just hadn't borne it since I was in Primary.*

But it wasn't just that. If my religion offended Apollus, I might get booted out on my rear. Could I afford to take that chance? Then again, considering all that my Heavenly Father had done, could I afford not to?

"He's the God of the whole universe," I replied to Apollus.

"Like Jupiter?"

"No, not Jupiter."

"What's this God's name?"

"He has a lot of names, actually. But only one that's important now. He's our Father in Heaven."

"You call this god 'Father'? That seems rather presumptuous."

"That's what He is. He's the father of our spirits."

"Spirit of who? Who has a spirit?"

I could see I had to start at the very beginning. "We all have a spirit. It comes into our bodies when we're born and leaves our bodies after we die."

"Ah, like our ghosts. The part of us that goes to the Underworld."

"Sort of. But we call it heaven. That's where our Father lives, and when we die we go back to Him."

"Where did you hear of this 'Father'? He sounds very much like the God of the Jews. These bald-headed Samaritans didn't warp your mind while you were with them, did they?"

"No, no," I said. "I knew about my Father in Heaven long before that. I think I've always known Him. I'll bet if you concentrated and opened your heart, you'd realize that you've always known Him, too."

He shook his head. "The only gods I know are Roman. My father pays particular obeisance to Minerva, the goddess of wisdom. He keeps her statue on his desk. Sometimes I hear him talking to her."

"What about you?" I asked. "Do you talk to any gods?"

"I make sacrifices on festival days, like any Roman. But I've never felt the need to ally myself to any particular one. I've never had the time for it."

"Haven't you ever felt the need to just kneel down, close your eyes, clench your fists, and say out loud, 'Hey, is there anyone really up there?'"

Apollus looked at me strangely, then he laughed. But it was a warm laugh. "You're a funny girl, Meagan Travolta. Curious and enchanting. Perhaps tomorrow you can tell me more about this Father-God."

"Yes," I said. "I'll tell you whatever you want to know."

I realized that we were staring at each other.

I looked away. "Well. It's getting dark."

"Yes," said Apollus. "You're probably exhausted. You'll need a good night's rest if we're to ride to Gerizim. I'll have my men waiting at the stables at sunup."

"I'll be there," I said.

He nodded and climbed down from the tower, directing one of the sentries to escort me back to my quarters. I watched him depart, my heart pounding for the first time in weeks with something other than fear. I wasn't sure what to think of Apollus. Handsome, yes. Brave, yes. But sensible? I highly doubted it. Besides, he was way too coarse for my tastes. At least that's what I told myself as I watched him walk back into the central compound. There was that walk again. Mercy!

Settle down, girl, *a voice said in my mind.* You're not even sixteen. *I think it must have been the voice of my mother.*

I gazed at the shadowed mountain one last time and drew a heavy sigh. Time to concentrate on more important things.

"Hang on, Harry," I whispered. "If you're there, we'll find you."

I happened to glance down at the covey of shops and houses outside the gate and noticed that they, too, were closing up for the night. As I started to turn away, something horrifying caught my eye. I turned back quickly, but as I searched to find what I'd seen, nothing was there. My heart was hammering hard.

"Something wrong?" asked the sentry who'd been told to escort me back.

I stared at the place where I thought I'd seen it. Nothing moved. I rubbed my eyes. Had it been a mirage?

"I'm fine," I told the sentry. "Let's go."

As the night progressed, the image I'd seen seemed to grow and enlarge in my mind. I became convinced that somehow it had to have been real. At one of the corners of one of the shops, I could have sworn that I'd seen a man in a white robe, his face half-eaten with cancer.

Real or not, I felt sure that Simon Magus knew that I was here.

CHAPTER FOURTEEN

Phasael Tower wasn't quite the dungeon I might have envisioned. In fact, it was decorated from floor to ceiling with incredible tile designs and mosaics, some of which had fallen apart and never been repaired. At one time it might have been a luxury apartment complex, but the apartments had all been gutted. The Zealots had turned the place into a prison, likely because it was the most accessible location to house traitors and criminals without any hope of escape.

Still in chains, I was taken to one of the upper stories. We stopped in front of an intricately carved door scarred by the points of daggers and swords. It looked like the vandalism had been done by the guards to relieve boredom, especially since one guard's dagger was still embedded in the wood.

"Open it," my escorts commanded the guard.

The guard plucked his dagger from the door and turned a large rusty key in the lock. As the door fell open, I saw two or three people inside, but before I had a chance to recognize them, I was knocked to the floor. The door slammed behind me.

A pair of gentle hands wrapped around my shoulders and helped me to my knees. I looked up into the sweet, angelic face of Mary. Symeon took a hold of my other shoulder and helped me to my feet. But it wasn't the sight of Symeon and Mary that took my breath away. It was the sight of the man standing behind them.

"Uncle Garth!" I cried.

My emotions welled up and overflowed. I threw my arms around his chest. He hugged me back with all his strength.

"I can't believe it's you!" I wept.

"Believe it, Harry. It's me. In the flesh. All that's left anyway."

Every muscle and vein in my body surged with joy. It was my Uncle Garth! Tears glistened in Garth's eyes, too, as he held me back a few inches for a better look. I flinched as he touched his thumb just below my right eye. I concluded it must have shown a pretty ugly shiner.

"What have they done to you?" he asked.

"Nothing much," I said. "Nothing I couldn't handle."

"It's good to see you, Harry," said Garth. "I thought it was hopeless. I was beginning to think I'd never find you."

"What are you doing here, Uncle Garth?" I asked. "My note said that I was going to the land of the Nephites. How did you know to look for me here?"

"A pair of socks, a package of beef stew, several candles, and the right shoe from a pair of Nikes," he replied. "You left a trail, Harry. It was as easy to follow as any trail of bread crumbs."

Of course. I remembered now. Meagan had been attacked in the cave. The Arab had ripped a hole in my backpack. Several things had fallen out in the struggle.

"Then you saw it?" I asked. "You saw the Galaxy Room?"

"Yes, I saw it," said Garth. He took me by the shoulders. "Harry, now tell me from the beginning. Symeon and Mary have filled me in on some of the details. I want to hear it from you. *What happened to Meagan?*"

He listened grimly as I revealed everything that had transpired up to Meagan's abduction. I told him about the Sons of the Elect and Simon Magus. I told him how they'd attacked us at the river. Then I told him about the Scroll of Knowledge and our mission to Jerusalem.

"Where is this scroll now?" Garth asked. "Have you recovered it?"

Symeon answered. "We tried. We couldn't find it. The soldiers arrived and demanded to know why we were snooping around. They didn't like our answers, so we were arrested."

"They knew we were Nazarenes," said Mary. "We couldn't deny it."

I stared at Symeon and Mary. I wondered how much they now knew about our true origins. Garth had obviously discussed a lot with them before I arrived. Garth had known that I was in Jerusalem even before I arrived at the tower. Mary looked at me with more curiosity than ever before. I doubted if my story about being from Germania was going to fly any longer.

"What have you told them?" I tried to ask discreetly.

"They understand that we come from a land very far away," said Garth. "Symeon is convinced—"

Symeon interrupted. "I'm convinced that God has sent you here to fulfill a very sacred work. I've even wondered if you are not part of the lost ten tribes of Israel, come here to pave the way for the great gathering before the end of the world."

I raised an eyebrow. Symeon could sure draw some bold conclusions. Whatever the case, it seemed to get us off the hook from having to explain that we were time travelers.

I turned back to Garth. "But why did you come to Jerusalem? When did you realize you were in Israel?"

"The exit on the opposite side of the Galaxy Room emerges near the fortress of Masada," said Garth. "I recognized it almost at once. I've been there several times doing studies for the University. From there it seemed only natural to come to Jerusalem."

"We met Josephus," I said. "Josephus the historian. He told us that a prominent Nazarene had been accosted by the Romans, then captured by the Jews and imprisoned in Phasael Tower."

"Josephus told you this?" Garth was impressed. "My fame

seems to have spread to some distinguished circles. I told the Romans that I was a Christian. They asked if I was a leader. I said I'd been a bishop. I guess that was prominent enough for them."

"But they said you performed a miracle. Cast demons out of a Roman officer or something."

Garth smiled. "I suppose to them that's how it would have appeared. All I said was to take two of these and call me in the morning." From his pocket he revealed an empty plastic container of Motrin. "The officer had migraines, not demons. The Romans took half of the pills. Simon, the son of Giora, took the rest. He wanted the container too, but when he couldn't get off the childproof cap, he threw it back at me."

"Did he also take your watch?" I asked.

"Yes. And my wallet. Thankfully there aren't too many places around here where he could use my credit cards."

"What about your other supplies?" I asked. "Did you bring anything else?"

"Backpack, sleeping bag—all the necessities," said Garth. "Everything is hidden on the Mount of Olives. Or at least it was a week ago. I sure do miss some of those modern conveniences."

For the first time I realized how weak and gaunt Garth appeared. I wondered how much he'd eaten in the past week. His eyes were moist. It wasn't just his backpack that he missed. It was his wife and two children. My heart tightened with regret. He'd come here because of me. This was all my fault.

"I'm sorry, Uncle Garth," I said. "I don't know what to say."

Garth sighed. "Oh, Harry. I know you were doing what you thought was right. But you never considered the danger. Did you really think that no one would come looking?"

"But I found him, Uncle Garth. I found Marcos."

Garth was struck with amazement. "You found him? Where?"

"Here in Judea. He was with us just a few days ago. I sent him back to be with Melody. I'm hoping he's already reached her."

"What was he doing in Judea? How in blazes did he get here?"

"It's a long story," I replied. "I found Gidgiddonihah, too. Do you remember Gid?"

"Of *course* I remember Gid."

"He's here in Jerusalem."

"He came *with you?*"

"The Jewish soldiers haven't caught him yet. Knowing Gid, maybe they never will."

Garth shook his head, still reeling with astonishment. "Gidgiddonihah and Marcos in the land of Judea. Nephites in Jerusalem! I can't believe it."

"He's helping me to rescue Meagan and a Jewish boy named Jesse. Without Gid, I didn't think I could ever succeed."

Garth stepped over to a small square window facing east. It was situated about thirty feet above the nearest ledge and eighty feet from the ground. The view overlooked the entire city, including the smoke and rubble surrounding the temple.

"I'm surprised you've made it this far," said Garth. "You couldn't have picked a more inauspicious time to fulfill such a mission. Tomorrow is the tenth of Lous—August 30. Tomorrow the temple will be destroyed."

"But," said Mary, "we heard Prince Titus make a firm promise that it would be spared."

Garth shook his head. "It won't be any act of Titus that destroys it. It will be the fury of his soldiers. They'll destroy it against his direct orders. And when he commands them to stop, they'll ignore him until it's too late. I half suspect that Titus' heart isn't really set on saving it at all."

We gazed solemnly at the great white and gold edifice. Even with all the fighting that had taken place—all the ruined walls and buildings around its perimeter—it was still hard to believe that something so beautiful could ever be demolished. And yet we all felt the finality of the moment. The sun was setting. It was the last time any sunset would ever reflect off the building's gleaming walls.

"We've known this day would come for a long time," said Symeon. "No earthly prince can retract the words of the Messiah."

As we settled in to await the darkness of night, Symeon remained by the window. He was determined to catch every last glimpse of the edifice that had represented the glory and triumph of his people for so long.

Garth told me everything he knew of my sister's condition since I'd left. It only included about five days. But he still seemed to feel that Melody was steadily improving. The news thrilled me beyond words.

Next I told Garth about the scroll of Matthew and everything that had taken place at Qumran.

He listened in awe. "You think that this is the original manuscript?"

"I'm not certain. But I'm afraid it is."

"Where is this scroll now?"

"Gidgiddonihah has it. Meagan and I wanted to give it to an apostle. But the nearest living apostle may be John the Beloved. We were told he lives in the region of the Seven Churches."

"Seven churches?" said Garth. "You mean in Asia Minor?"

"Yes," I said. "Somehow we have to find a way to get it there."

I sighed. Such an objective seemed so far down on our list of priorities. Garth sensed my frustration.

"Don't go gray at fifteen, Harry," he urged. "If the Lord wants that scroll to reach the Seven Churches, He'll provide a way."

It was exactly what I needed to hear. I was so tired. So exhausted. My stomach was burning with hunger. Still, I felt so glad to be here with my uncle. The man had an incredible spirit. He had a way of giving me newfound courage and strength.

And yet I had to tease him. "It seems like you get cast into prison every time you visit an ancient world."

He smiled glumly. "It does appear that way, doesn't it. At least when I was imprisoned in Jacobugath, they tossed food to us once in a while. Feeding prisoners isn't much of a priority in Jerusalem. I've received a few scraps from Simon in exchange for showing him certain things—the watch, the medicine—but I haven't even seen him for three days."

"He's determined to kill us, Garth," I said. "He plans to execute us as soon as he captures Gid."

"Then we'll have to hope Gid remains free," said Garth. "Don't worry. I have a feeling that the Zealots will be too preoccupied fighting the Romans for the next few days to be concerned about Gidgiddonihah. Be patient, Harry, and trust God. I've never felt that my life was meant to end in Jerusalem in 70 A.D."

I stepped back to the window. Symeon's head was bowed in prayer. I looked over his shoulder and out into the darkened city.

Where are you, Gid? I wondered. It was clear that our key to escape rested with him. And yet what could he do? How could he ever storm the tower by himself? I wasn't even sure he knew we were in here. But if he *did* know, he was surely planning something. No doubt about it. Whatever it was, he'd have to pull it off soon. My hunger was sapping all my energy. More importantly, after tonight there were only three days left to reach Mount Gerizim. I prayed it could be reached in so short a time.

I sat down by Mary and asked her, "When you searched around James' house, what did you find?"

She shook her head. "We didn't find anything, Harry. We looked for a long time before the soldiers arrived. We just couldn't find any secret niche. Are you sure Barsabas told you it was located inside the area where the house once stood?"

"Yes," I said urgently. "I'm sure of it."

"Then we must have missed something. I'm not sure how. Maybe if we'd searched a little longer."

I sat back and drew a dreary sigh. After all our troubles and trials to get here, the Scroll of Knowledge wasn't even where it was supposed to be. Maybe, I thought, I hadn't been *meant* to acquire it. Maybe God had sent me to Jerusalem to find Garth and that was it. Did this mean if we escaped I was just supposed to go to Mount Gerizim without it? It seemed unthinkable. What would I have to bargain with? Then again, as Gid had once stated, even if I had the scroll, what guarantee did I have that Simon would keep his end of the bargain?

I started to wonder if Mary was right. Maybe Barsabas had been mistaken about the secret library's location. He'd been delirious and near death when he'd told us. As I closed my eyes, a part of me even wondered if this scroll had ever existed at all.

Seconds later my eyes popped open. My whole body must have jolted because Mary asked, "What's wrong?"

"I know where it is," I declared.

"Where what is?" asked Garth.

"The Scroll of Knowledge. The secret niche. I know exactly where to look."

"How could you know such a thing?" asked Symeon. "We searched every crack and crevasse in the foundation."

"Because I *saw it*," I said. "I saw it as plain as day!"

The image still burned in my mind—the image from that first night as we'd slept in the cave near Qumran. Until this moment I'd never thought of it as a vision. But now it was hard to think of it as anything else. Just before falling asleep I'd seen the half-standing walls of blackened brick. I'd seen a certain stone in the corner. And underneath it, I saw a hidden niche outlined by shimmering shafts of light. Yes, I knew the place. I knew it as precisely as if I'd played on those ruins a thousand times.

So, I concluded, God *did* want the scroll to be found. Or He wanted us to find some other scroll in that niche. A way would be provided. We were going to escape.

CHAPTER FIFTEEN

My heart was beating fast as we passed through the fort's front gates and headed toward the slopes of Mount Gerizim. I scanned the crannies and corners of the various houses and fields, keeping my eyes peeled for the shiny heads of any followers of Simon Magus. There was no sign of them. Just humble villagers going about their morning chores.

Maybe I shouldn't have felt so jittery. After all, there were twenty tough-as-nails Roman soldiers riding on all sides of me. Of course, this wouldn't have made any difference to Simon's archer if he chose to pick me off out of the crowd. This didn't seem likely. What good was I to them dead?

I felt if Simon did anything, it would be to try to separate me from my bodyguards and take me alive. I wasn't about to let this happen. The soldiers were under direct orders to stay close to me at all times. I told Apollus specifically to never stray farther from me than twenty feet. I think he was flattered by the challenge.

I stared up at the mountain. If Harry was up there, he was hiding near the top. Somehow I had to make myself visible in spite of all the men around me. He certainly wasn't going to pop out in front of a Roman patrol. But if he could see me riding in the midst of them, safe and unthreatened, he'd have to make himself known.

"Don't look so nervous," said Apollus as we entered the forest at the base of the mountain. "The people around here know that to

attack a Roman means swift and ruthless retaliation. They've seen us destroy entire villages in response to a single Roman casualty."

"How nice," I said wryly. "But the Sons of the Elect don't live in villages. Since we set fire to their villa, they probably live in the woods."

"Then we'll burn down the woods." Apollus grinned.

The guy was incorrigible. It might have been charming if it didn't involve so much blood and mayhem.

"Is there any problem you think a Roman might solve without *burning and pillaging and plundering?"*

"Like what?"

"Like anything."

"What method do you have in mind?"

"How about generosity and love?"

He wrinkled up his nose. "Generosity and love? Are you serious? You want me to treat the men who kidnapped you with generosity and love?"

"I'm talking in general."

Apollus straightened up proudly on his saddle blanket. "We introduce civilization in regions where before we arrived there was only chaos. We build aqueducts and roads. We bring commerce and opportunity. We've introduced the superior ways of Rome all over the world. If that's not generosity, I don't know what is."

"What if other people don't like *Roman ways? What if they like their own ways just fine?"*

"Then it's only because they don't know any better. It's our responsibility to teach them. There's a high price to pay for peace in this world. Romans are the only ones willing to pay it. We pay it with our own sweat and blood. Imagine a world where there are no tribes or borders. No wars or invasions. A world where everyone is an equal citizen of the Empire. That's what we're fighting for, Meagan. You and I are a part of it."

I shook my head. His devotion to Rome was his religion. How could anyone reach someone whose heart was anchored to such a cause?

"Maybe there's a better way to conquer the world, Apollus," I said. "One where a single drop of blood is never spilled. It transcends borders and languages. It binds people together with more loyalty and devotion than they could ever feel for any emperor or country."

"And what way is this?" asked Apollus dubiously.

"The way of our Lord Jesus."

"Who?"

I swallowed. I was in the thick of it now. There was no turning back. "Jesus the Messiah."

"Never heard of him. Is this man a king?"

"Yes. But his kingdom isn't of this world."

Apollus huffed. "Where is it then? In the stars?"

"His kingdom is in heaven."

"Ah, I get it. We're speaking of your God again. You believe your religion could somehow conquer the world?"

"I do. It's going to happen. It just might take a while."

Apollus chuckled. "Well, until then, I'll put my faith in Rome. You sound very naive, Meagan. Even religion is best spread by fire and sword. Though I've never heard of a religion worth fighting for."

"This religion can't be spread by fire and sword," I said. "It can only be spread—"

"Let me guess. By generosity and love?"

Several of the closest horsemen snickered. Apollus was patronizing me. Oooh, there was nothing I hated worse than being patronized. Maybe this whole thing was useless. What was I trying to do? Convert a Roman centurion? Maybe it was all part of some silly fantasy I had. I could hardly fall for someone who didn't know about the gospel, even if he was the most gorgeous male I'd ever known.

"Exactly," I said. "Generosity and love."

"So is this Jesus the One God that you mentioned yesterday?"

"Actually, the One God is His Father."

"But I thought you told me this God was the Father of us all?"

"He's the Father of our spirits. To Jesus, He's also the Father of

His mortal body. Jesus was born into this world just like any of us. His mother was a mortal mother. But His Father was a God."

"So this Jesus is half-god, half-man? Like Hercules?"

"Not exactly. Besides, He's perfect, just like His Father."

"So He's a God?"

"Yes."

"I thought you said there was only One God. Now there are two?"

Man. This was hard. How did missionaries do this all day long? "As far as we're concerned, there's still only one God. We worship our Father in Heaven with all our heart, might, mind, and strength. Jesus worships Him, too."

"So why is this Jesus important? How is His religion supposed to conquer the world?"

"Because," I said, "Jesus is our Savior."

"Our Savior? What did He save?"

"He saved all of us."

"From what?"

"From our sins. He saved us from death."

Apollus pulled in his chin. "From death? Rather ambitious undertaking. How did he go about saving us from that?"

"By being resurrected from the dead. He paved the way for all of us to one day live again."

I realized that a few of the horsemen had started listening a little more intently. Either the subject was becoming more interesting or—

Or I was finally getting the help that I desperately needed. The Spirit was playing its part. At least I hoped that's what it was. I realized now that I couldn't do this by myself.

"Well," said Apollus, "everyone I've ever known who died is still very much dead. My mother, my brothers and sister. When is this Jesus supposed to bring them all back to life?"

"At the end of the world."

"And when is that?"

I sighed. "Not for at least two thousand more years."

"Gracious!" said Apollus. "This Jesus is in no hurry, is He?"

"I'm not explaining this very well," I said, exasperated. "But believe me, it all makes perfect sense. You will see your mother and your sister again. And you'll be resurrected. That was Jesus' promise to everyone."

"How did He die in the first place?" asked Apollus.

"He was crucified," I answered.

"Crucified?! He was a God and He let someone inflict such a horrible death?"

"He did it willingly," I said. "For the sake of all mankind. He was the perfect sacrifice for the sins of the world."

I felt calmer now. My words flowed more smoothly. I almost wondered if they were mine. Apollus looked uncomfortable, as if there was a bug in his armor. I think the words had touched him. He didn't like it though. Leave it to a man to shrug off the Spirit like a mosquito.

"I don't buy it," said Apollus. "If He was really a God, He'd have crushed His enemies to dust and made all His followers richer than kings. Resurrected from the dead, bah! Where did this crucifixion take place anyway?"

"In Jerusalem."

"Jerusalem? Hundreds of rebels are crucified there every day. Which one was He?"

"It happened thirty-six years ago," I said.

A nearby horseman spoke up, a crusty old soldier, probably in his mid-fifties. "Was this Jesus also called Jesus of Nazareth?"

"Yes," I said. "That's Him."

"I remember this man," he said to Apollus. "I was stationed at Antonia that spring. Strange business. Strangest I've ever seen."

Wow, I thought. This was incredible. An eyewitness!

"Why was it so strange, Scribonus?" asked Apollus. "What did you see?"

"I saw the man she's describing. I saw Him nailed to the cross. I was just a kid, still cuttin' my teeth on my armor. Me and the boys from the Antonia shook some dice for His coat. Ole' Tigellinus thought His clothes might be worth somethin' someday. I lost the roll. I was glad, too, especially after this Jesus died."

Apollus was listening closely now. "Why's that?"

"It was real strange," said Scribonus. "The sky was real dark. Never seen it so dark in the daytime. After he died, there was a quake."

"An earthquake?"

"Shook the whole hill. Made some rocks tumble. I had to catch myself. I remember ole' Tigellinus, he looked up at that man and called Him the Son of God. I remember it like it was yesterday."

I realized I was hardly breathing. This man was there. He'd actually seen it happen!

"So was He?" asked Apollus.

"Was He what, sir?"

"Was He the Son of God?"

"He was something," said Scribonus. "Don't know what. But He was something."

I stared at Scribonus dumbly. This man had cast lots for the Savior's raiment. Hearing it from the lips of an old hardened soldier made it feel more real than I'd ever felt it before. Scribonus was no prophet. Yet his description of the event matched every detail in Matthew, Mark, Luke and John.

Our horses continued up the rocky trail. Apollus remained skeptical. "So did you see Him rise from the dead?"

"Nope," said Scribonus. "The man was dead. I know it because I helped take Him down. Some of His men—disciples—took Him away. That's the last I saw."

Apollus turned to me. "It seems your Jesus wasn't resurrected after all."

I faced Scribonus. "What else did you hear? Did you hear anything about the matter three days later?"

"Sure did," said Scribonus. "I heard His body got stolen. Grave robbers. That's what I heard."

"Did you believe it?" I asked.

"No reason not to," said Scribonus. "Never gave it much thought."

I became rankled. "You watched an innocent man die—you felt an earthquake—and you never gave it much thought?"

"Well now, I guess that's not entirely true," said Scribonus. "I thought about it some. But what was I supposed to do? It was festival time. Lots of rowdy Jews to keep in line."

"What makes you think He was innocent?" Apollus asked me. He turned to Scribonus, "What crime was He accused of committing?"

"I never was clear on that. I think He called Himself a king. That might have made ole' Pilate a bit antsy. We just passed it off as one of them Jewish things. Crazy people, these Jews."

Apollus turned back. "Well, Meagan, your rumors of a resurrection appear to have been started by grave robbers."

"There were other witnesses," I said, somewhat testily. "In fact, there were lots of people who saw Him after He arose from the dead. My brother is one of them."

Apollus raised His eyebrows. "Your brother was in Jerusalem thirty-six years ago?"

"He didn't see Him in Jerusalem."

"Oh?"

I paused. I had to be careful. I couldn't talk about Nephites and Lamanites. Man, I wished Harry was here. He'd have put all these Romans in their places.

"All I can tell you is, it's true," I said. "Jesus was really resurrected. And one day every knee will bow and every tongue confess that Jesus is the Savior of the world."

Apollus softened. "I didn't mean to offend you, Meagan. As a Roman you can honor whatever God you like. As long as you also honor the image of the Emperor."

I shook my head. "In just a few years the Romans will be feeding

*our people to the lions right and left. Nero has already killed
hundreds. He even accused us of setting fire to Rome when in fact he
set the whole thing himself to make way for his royal gardens."*

*I saw something click in Apollus' memory. "I know your religion
now. The people of Christus. Of course! They say you practice canni-
balism and sacrifice your children by drowning. Is this the religion
we've been discussing all this time?"*

"Oh, please," I said dryly. "Do they have National Inquirers *at
the checkout stands in Rome, too?"*

*Apollus drew his eyebrows together, not understanding the refer-
ence. He opened his mouth to speak, but I never heard the words
that he uttered. His voice was suddenly drowned out by the shrieks
and shouts of his men.*

*I looked around in confusion. What was going on? The horses at
the front and back of the company were rearing. I saw the blur of
arrows flying from the trees as well as the long shafts of spears. My
heart flew into my throat. We were under* attack!

*A spear struck Scribonus in the back, penetrating right through
his armor. He cried out and fell from his horse. My own horse reared.
I screamed. Apollus tried to grab the reins, but it was too late. I hit
the ground with a dizzying thud. Pandemonium had broken out in
the Roman ranks. I rolled onto my stomach to avoid the hooves of a
bolting horse. I covered my head as my own horse came down again
on its front legs. The attackers were flying from the trees in all directions—men with lances and swords and studded iron balls on
chains. Some I recognized as the bald followers of Simon Magus, but
others had full heads of hair. What was happening?*

*A wounded Roman fell on top of my legs. I cried out. Soldiers
were dropping everywhere. Others were scattering—fleeing for their
lives. I'd lost track of Apollus. Was he already dead?* Dear God,
please! Why did I come here? *I knew* we might be attacked. *My
worst fears were coming true.*

A hand grasped my shoulder. It was Apollus!

"Come on!" he yelled.

He pulled my legs out from under the wounded soldier. A bald attacker suddenly appeared from the woods aiming a lance at Apollus' head.

"Look out!" I cried.

Apollus ducked and rolled. He stabbed upward with his short Roman sword. The man grunted and buckled to his knees. With his last ebb of strength, he lashed out at me! His fingers clasped my throat. I recognized him. It was Reuben—the man I called Stimpy. As he squeezed my neck, I watched his eyes roll back. He was dead. Apollus pried away his hands and threw him aside.

Apollus stood me on my feet. I was disoriented. I couldn't have said which direction was up. As he led me through the melee, his sword struck another attacker. My legs started to run. The sun hit my face in bursts as we passed through the trees.

"Get her!" someone seethed. I knew that voice. It was Menander.

My orientation steadily returned. We were crashing through the brush, dodging the trees. Apollus still gripped my hand. We began scrambling up the side of a hill. I glanced back. Dozens of men were pursuing us. I couldn't even count them. Over a hundred men must have been involved in this attack.

We reached the top of the hill. On the opposite side was a winding ravine, twisting down the mountainside through a bed of sharp boulders. I felt sure Apollus would go in that direction. Instead we descended into the ravine at an angle that took us up the slope. The ground leveled out. We climbed another short rise. But on the other side Apollus put on the brakes. We'd reached an edge.

Below us stretched a sea of briars—not like the typical brambles I knew from Utah. This was a tangled nightmare of leaves and branches with thorns as long a toothpicks—utterly impenetrable. We ran along the edge. It seemed like our only way to run. But it was suicide! We were still out of view, but any second the attackers would pour over the hill. We'd be cornered!

Apollus looked at me. "We have to jump."

"Into that?!" I stared at the briars and shuddered.

I heard their shouts. They were almost in view!

Apollus grabbed my arm. "Now!"

My feet left the ground. I braced myself for the pain shock of my life. The briars sucked us in and closed over the top of us like a Venus flytrap. It was like leaping into a pit of porcupines or a net barbed with a million fish hooks. I could feel my skin as it was torn and pierced and shredded. The thorns penetrated my clothes. Apollus was wearing armor to protect him. I had nothing!

When I landed I was still half-suspended in the branches, my head and neck pinched at an angle against the ground, my body too stunned to feel the pain. Apollus was at my right. The weight of his armor had taken him all the way to the bottom. The leaves overhead had all but extinguished the sunlight. Only small triangles of sky shone through.

I knew I was bleeding in a hundred places, but I couldn't cry out. A minute later I heard voices: "Do you see them? Check down that way!"

Some men were running along the edge above us. I felt sure someone would catch on. There had to be clear evidence of where we'd disappeared—footprints, broken foliage—something to betray our hiding place. I imagined a spearhead thrusting through one of those triangles of light and mercifully ending my life. But the voices drifted away. The mountain went quiet.

The pain started to sink in—excruciating! Like a thousand bee stings. I wanted to move—just a little to try to relieve some of the torment. But I couldn't risk it. I'd never be able to contain my cries of agony.

I felt Apollus' fingers touch my right hand. "Be still," he whispered. "They're coming back."

Several men returned to try to retrace our steps. I tried to hold my breath, to smother my emotions. Several lances poked down into *the briars to try to see down inside, but this was quickly judged to be a waste of time. Who would be stupid enough to leap into something like this? Even if such a person crawled back out, there'd be nothing left but a bare skeleton.*

As I glanced up through the briars, I saw a pale patch of white. But it wasn't sky or cloud. Someone in a pale cloak was standing there. Did he know we were here? Why was he standing there?

But then the cloak moved on. There were no more footsteps. The attackers were searching farther down the mountain.

My face was streaming with tears. I could feel blood trickling down my legs, down my stomach. I could taste it on my lips. Even if I managed to climb out of here, what would I look like? I'd be a complete mess. Would I have the strength to walk?

We waited twenty more agonizing minutes. Finally Apollus said, "All right. Let's get out."

Apollus used his sword to chop away at some of the branches that pinned me. Nevertheless, as I started to move, it was like rolling on a bed of nails. Pain shot through every nerve. I gritted my teeth. I could do this. Please, Father, *I prayed.* Help me do this! *I built up my momentum. I untangled my legs, ignoring the pain, pretending it didn't exist.*

Apollus was on his feet. He was crashing though to the other side of the briar patch, cutting a trail with his blade. I stumbled behind him, tucking one bleeding arm close to my body and using the other to protect my eyes. We were making enough noise to wake the dead. If any of the Sons of the Elect were within a hundred yards, Apollus would plunge out of these briars right into the head of a spear.

At last Apollus emerged. I fell out of the briars after him. My fall only drove the thorns deeper into my flesh. I lay there moaning and crying. Apollus leaned over me. He was hardly injured. A few thorns in his arms, scratches on his face. His helmet, armor, and leather leggings had protected him. As for me, I must have looked like I'd just been through a paper shredder.

"Hang on, Meagan," he pleaded. "You'll be all right. I'm going to pull out the thorns. Are you ready?"

I was so delirious with pain that I didn't bother to answer. For ten or fifteen minutes he plucked the needles from my legs, from my garments, and from my face and back. He didn't even pull out his own thorns until all mine had been removed.

"I'm sorry, Meagan," he said. "It might have been better if we'd fled down the mountain."

"How do I look?" I asked dazedly.

It was a ridiculous time to feel vain. But I had to know.

Apollus smiled tenderly. "You look beautiful, Meagan. Like the face of a dove."

"Liar," I said.

"We need to find water," said Apollus. "We need to wash all these scratches and punctures. I have some in my water pouch, but not enough."

"I don't think I can make it," I responded. "I don't think I can walk."

"That's all right. I'll carry you."

His eyes scanned the area. As soon as he felt it was clear, he hoisted me over his shoulders and carried me fireman-style. I could still feel a few thorns, but overall the relief was incredible. Now all I wanted to do was sleep. My emotions and my nerves had all frayed. I didn't want to fight anymore. If Apollus couldn't rescue me, I'd just lay here and let fate take its course.

I shouldn't have thought such a thing. When faith wavers, the vultures swoop in. As Apollus passed the trunk of a tree, I saw movement. He hardly had a chance to react as an iron ball smashed down on his helmet. The blow split the metal in half. His body went instantly limp. He was unconscious or dead before he even hit the ground. I landed on his shoulders and rolled off onto the dirt. It happened so fast. I didn't even register the horror.

But that terror set in as I saw the pale robe. The man with the iron ball and chain was standing over my face.

"Oh, Meagan," he said. "Thank the Aeons you're alive. You're safe now. The others are far away. It's just you and me. We're together at last. Together for eternity."

I recognized the long grizzled beard, the tiny, darting eyes.

It was the face of Saturninus.

CHAPTER SIXTEEN

All through the night I lay awake and listened to the war cries of the legions of Rome and the howls of the rebels and citizens of Jerusalem. Just before dawn I watched Mary creep over to Symeon, who had not moved from his place by the window.

"Come, Father," she urged. "You should rest. Get some sleep."

Symeon refused. "The temple has stood for six hundred years. I can certainly pay it the proper respect by giving it my attention during its last twenty-four hours."

At dawn Garth and I joined Symeon in his vigil. The sunrise was the deepest purple I had ever seen. It never really became orange or red. The purple just faded until it became the full light of day. I'd always thought of purple as a peaceful color. Not after today.

All the violence was now contained inside the courtyards of the temple. Even the battering rams in other parts of the city had gone silent. From the height of our prison cell in Phasael Tower, we could see just over the temple's western wall. The fighting was more furious than ever. Smoke continued rising from the outer structures. The bodies of the dead littered the ground everywhere the ground was visible, mostly the bodies of men without red tunics—the bodies of the Jews. The horror and waste made me shake my head with incomprehension.

We watched hundreds of Jewish troops storm across the bridge that led to the western gate. It looked like one last grand effort to try to drive the Roman soldiers permanently from the temple grounds. The Romans met the attack with a cavalry charge. With their shields held over their heads like the shell of a great tortoise, they drove the Jews back across the bridge. The Romans had now reached the inner courtyard. The sanctuary of the temple was entirely at their mercy.

About twenty minutes later we heard a horrible wail. I couldn't pinpoint its source, whether it came from the battle zone, some other part of the city, or from the cloudless sky. It seemed to resonate from several different places at once. As I squinted, I could see smoke seeping up from the sanctuary. The temple was on fire.

All four of us stood transfixed at the window. Symeon appeared passive, his chin rigid, his face streaked with tears. Garth's eyes were also moist. It was the culmination of so many days of desperation and waiting. Garth had been watching the horrifying scene from this window for a week. He looked drained, as if he'd been enduring a long vigil by the hospital bed of a loved one, and now the dreaded moment had arrived.

"It will be seventeen hundred and fifty years," he said quietly, "before an edifice like that will ever be built again upon the earth."

Mary slunk into the corner and buried her face underneath her arms. She'd seen enough. Before long we didn't have to squint to see the smoke. It was churning from the temple doors like a smokestack. The howls and wailing were growing louder with each passing minute. I witnessed the frenzied agony and frustration as hundreds of Jews—soldier, priest, and civilian— fought desperately to put out the flames. The Roman cavalrymen showed no pity. They unleashed their fury and venom on every living soul, cutting down anything that moved. The entrances to the sanctuary were crammed with people. They were *crushing* each other. Some were trying to beat out the flames. Others were tossing candlesticks and other sacred treasures out of the temple windows. Everywhere we looked the Romans were storming the temple grounds with flaming torches, setting fire to anything that would burn.

So much for Titus' promise, I said to myself. I wondered if any general in the world could have controlled such a fever of savagery. Later the flames themselves could be seen shooting out of the windows and doors. The smoke became so thick that it started to darken the sky. Anyone looking on from a few miles outside the city would have thought that all of Jerusalem was ablaze.

The noise and tumult became almost deafening. Even from inside the tower we could hear cries. The prisoners were no less panicked and grieved than anyone else. It was amazing that through all the screaming I was able to distinguish a single voice.

"Harry!"

The voice was faint. It had come from the lower part of the tower. I went to the doorway. "Gidgiddonihah! Gidgiddonihah!"

Soon Garth and Mary shouted with me. We screamed Gid's name at the top of our lungs, hammering on the thick wooden door.

"Harry!" we heard again. "Symeon!"

"We're in here, Gid! In here!"

The voice now rang from just outside the door. "Harry? Are you in there?"

"We're here! We're *all* here!"

"Stand back!"

We moved away from the door. The room vibrated with a heavy blow. The blow repeated. After several more hits the wood around the lock splintered and split. One more strike and the door burst open. Standing outside was Gidgiddonihah, his arms wielding a heavy iron mallet. Mary couldn't contain herself. She rushed forward and embraced him.

"Well now," said Gid with surprise. "That's worth a rescue any day of the week."

I watched as his eyes fell on Garth. He blinked in astonishment. "Garplimpton?!"

Garth had a grin as big as the Mississippi. "It's me, Gid. Boy, are you a sight for sore eyes."

They embraced in a flurry of laughter and tears.

"When did you come?" Gid asked. "How did you get here?"

"Let's find a safe place, and I'll tell you the whole story."

"No place like that for at least ten miles," said Gid.

"Then I suggest we get started."

"Where are all the guards?" I asked anxiously.

"The guards are gone," Gid said. "Every soldier is at the other end of the city, defending the temple hill."

I looked at my shackles. "What about these?"

I was the only one in chains. But escape would be far more difficult with twenty pounds of iron on my wrists. Gid reached behind his shoulder and pulled out his long gladiator sword. He pointed at the stone panel beside the doorway.

"Hold it right at the first link," he directed. "And duck your head."

There was no one in this world I'd have trusted to do this except Gidgiddonihah. I raised up my arms and set the first iron link against the stone. Gid raised his weapon. I closed my eyes to keep them from catching any sparks.

He swung. A direct hit! The link chopped right in two. Iron was no match for Damascus steel. Better yet, there were still five fingers on my right hand. I opened the hinge on the wristband and flung it aside. Gid did the same to the link on my left wrist. I was free!

"Let's move," said Gid.

"Wait!" said Symeon. "The parents of Josephus. I made a promise. I have to find them."

I started to panic. There was no time. We'd have to check every cell! "What if they aren't here?" I said.

"I gave my word," said Symeon.

He ran into the hall and began calling out, "Matthias! Matthias, the father of Josephus!"

The rest of us joined in the shout. What else could we do? I took Gid's iron mallet. We ran through the hallways and chambers crying out, "Matthias, father of Josephus!" We could hardly hear ourselves above the clamor of the prisoners. Not a guard was in sight. The tower had been abandoned of all personnel.

Finally, from one doorways we heard, "Matthias is here! He's in here!"

I brought up the hammer and swung it with all my might against the lock. My sprained wrist might have lessened my strength. Nevertheless, after three strikes the door burst open. The prisoners—those who could still walk—began to emerge. They were listless and pale. The odor was horrid.

"Where is Matthias?" Symeon asked them. "Where is the father of Josephus?"

No one replied. They walked in a daze toward the stairwell where the sunlight streamed through the hole in the open roof. I wasn't even sure who'd called to us from inside.

"Matthias isn't here," said Gid. "They just wanted out."

Symeon entered the cell. Over fifty people had been packed inside. A third of them were still strewn about the room, too weak to appreciate freedom. Many were already dead.

Symeon called out, "Matthias, the father of Josephus!"

No one responded. But then a man's eyes directed us toward two people in the corner—an older man and woman. The man was sitting up. The woman lay in his lap. As I drew nearer, I froze. The woman was dead. I think she'd been dead a long time.

I stepped back in revulsion. These people had been left to starve. I couldn't believe such inhumanity.

Symeon approached the man. "Matthias? Are you Matthias?"

He raised his eyes. The face had absolutely no color. It wouldn't be long before he would join his wife.

"Your son sent me," said Symeon. "He sent me to tell you—" Symeon tried to steady his voice. Josephus' message was meaningless now. But he was determined to keep his oath. Symeon stumbled out the words, ". . . He says to tell you he has never . . . never forgotten you or abandoned you. He says . . . when this is over, you can expect the full protection and hospitality of the Emperor."

Matthias looked at Symeon blankly.

"We'll take him with us," Gid told Symeon.

"No," said the man in a dreadful whisper. "Leave here. Leave me with her."

"But your son," said Symeon. "He's outside the wall."

Matthias' bony, quivering hand seized the collar of his tattered cloak. Using all his remaining strength, he tore it. His wrathful eyes were glowing as he hissed, "I have no son. Now go."

* * *

We wasted no more time and fled from the tower, fearing the return of any guards. Smoke from the temple continued to fill the air, giving the streets a gray and misty haze. The citizens—thousands of them—were perched on rooftops and walls, watching the spectacle of the burning temple in the afternoon heat. It must have seemed like the end of the world. The wailing continued. Tears streaked every face. People could be heard cursing the Romans. Some were even cursing God.

It took us only a few minutes to reach the ruins of the house of James. This time the nearby square was vacant. The ruins were just how I'd envisioned them—two crumbling walls and a foundation littered with stones. Garth stepped inside the ruins and looked around solemnly. He'd been told that this was also the site of the Last Supper and Jesus' first appearance to the apostles after his resurrection. There was so little left to hint that Jesus or James or any other righteous soul had ever walked here.

I quickly located the precise spot in the northeast corner that I had seen in my mind. I found a large flat block of stone on it. A tingle ran up my spine.

"Give me a hand," I said.

Gid and Symeon and even Mary found a grip around the stone's edge. We started to lift. I thought of Joseph Smith prying up that stone atop the Hill Cumorah. The treasures I might find inside seemed no less fantastic.

The stone lifted without much effort. We stood it on its edge and let it fall the other way. Sure enough, there was a small niche covered over by thin wooden planks. I threw off the planks. A dark, dusty hole curved back underneath the floor, barely wide enough for a single person.

I squeezed into the nook, poking my head deep inside. The chamber was dark. I crawled in out of the sunlight. Suddenly the details became clear. The walls were lined with neat round holes carved into the rock, like little torpedo chambers. There were three rows on each side, ten deep, enough to hide dozens of scrolls. Each space appeared to have been designed for a specific manuscript. Most of the holes were vacant—a lot more than eleven. Either someone besides Barsabas had been here before us or the spaces had never been filled in the first place. Several holes—ten to be exact—were stuffed with a rolled-up piece of papyrus, just like the Book of Matthew. *Ten!* This was incredible! I could potentially add ten new books to the Bible in a single pop!

"Eureka!" I cried.

I thought back on that first day when Meagan had found those clay jars. I laughed at myself as I recalled my lack of

interest. I'd come a long way in my reverence for ancient manuscripts. There was no question what had to be done. I couldn't
leave a single one. All of them had to be saved. I began pulling
them from their compartments one by one and packing them in
my arms. I had six in the first load as I emerged.

"Take these," I said to Garth. "There's more!"

I dove back inside and began removing the others. The very
last scroll sat in a lone compartment at the back—as if set apart
from the rest. My heart fluttered. I could hardly breathe as I
pulled it out. It wasn't much different than the other nine—
certainly not longer or heavier. But there were three thick clay
seals along the edge. This was it. I knew it. The Scroll of
Knowledge.

I was bouncing off the walls with jubilation as I dropped the
last four scrolls on the ground and handed the scroll with the
three seals to Garth.

"What does it say?" I asked frantically. "There's writing right
here. Read it."

Two small blocks of ancient letters sat between the three
seals. I knew Garth read ancient languages. I decided he had to
know every ancient language known to man. Not that I was
worried. No doubt Symeon or Mary could have read it more
easily than Garth.

"This one's Aramaic," said Garth, pointing to the one on the
right. "This one's Greek—'*Hoi logio hierophantikes gnoseos tou
Iesou Christou tou zonto tois hierois apostolois gegrammenoi tou
Petrou, Iakobou, kai Ioannou.*'"

"What's it mean?"

Mary read the square on the right:

"'*The words of most sacred knowledge of Jesus the Resurrected
Messiah to His holy apostles and written by Peter, James, and John.*'"
We looked into one another's eyes. My heart was pounding. I
had it! The Scroll of Knowledge—the object and passion of

Simon's existence and the key to Meagan and Jesse's freedom. It was right in my hands!

Then the gloom dropped over me like a shroud. The scroll suddenly felt as heavy as the Titanic. I set it on the ground and looked at it. Then I looked at Garth.

"We need to read it," I said. "If it's really the sacred knowledge of Jesus Christ, taught after His resurrection, how could I ever give it to Simon Magus?"

Garth sighed deeply. He shook his head. "That title says it was meant for the eyes of the apostles. The apostles *only*. They gave it three seals. I'm not sure I feel . . . *qualified.*"

"But," I said desperately, "we need to make a decision."

"We might not have to make it today," said Gid. "Maybe we won't have to make it at all. I say we go to this mountain and decide then."

Garth pondered this, then nodded. I could tell he was tempted. After all, he was a scholar. This was his life. And yet the very nature of the scroll might have made anyone hesitant.

"Okay," I said. "We'll wait. But sooner or later we're gonna have to read at least some of it."

"When that moment comes," said Garth, "I think we'll know."

I continued to revel in the find. Ten scrolls—enough to weigh down a pack mule. Actually, they weren't that heavy. Just bulky and awkward. I fit two more in my travel sack, including the Scroll of Knowledge. Gid fit three in his. Mary's and Symeon's travel sacks had been confiscated. Mary made a sack, or satchel as she called it, out of some cloth and twine among the garbage in the streets. We used it to tie up the rest, and Symeon carried it. Garth would have done it, but his scarcity of food for so long had taken its toll on him. Honestly, I was going to be happy enough if Garth just carried himself. We all needed to find food. And *soon*. Symeon had confirmed that we could reach Mount Gerizim in two days. But would we have enough strength to travel? I knew God understood all these things better than we did. Again, it was in His able hands.

Gid's idea was to get out of Jerusalem exactly the way we'd come in—by way of the subterranean tunnels. There was a good chance that the Roman soldiers at the gate in the Valley of Hinnon would recognize us and let us through without much hassle. The trouble was, all the soldiers were massed in the Lower City. We'd probably run into some of them while trying to locate that storehouse where we'd come up from the tunnels.

The smoke was thicker than ever. It almost looked like a fog bank had settled over Jerusalem. We held our sleeves over our noses and mouths as we moved cautiously from street to street, choosing alleyways and roundabout paths. As we neared the wall between the Upper and Lower cities, it was clear that this route was no longer an option. The battlements were packed with hundreds of mourning citizens. There were few places that offered a better view of the burning temple. The echo of their cries sounded ghostly in the smoky fog.

"We'll cross over at the gate of the Essenes," said Symeon. "There will be soldiers, but I don't know any better way."

"I do," said Gidgiddonihah. "We'll take the sewers. That's where I hid last night."

The idea of crawling through a sewer didn't even faze me anymore. I'd totally lost my sense of revulsion.

"But what about the scrolls?" I asked.

"We'll carry them over our heads," said Gid. "There's space."

We backtracked several streets. At last we came to an old fountain whose water flowed into a gutter that ran several hundred feet. The gutter ended at a narrow drain that flowed under a wall. Iron bars had once blocked the drain, but several had been broken off.

Gid slipped in first. He took our bundles and set them inside. Then we all crawled in after him. The gutter was flowing, but only a trickle. The passageway was arched and descended deep into the darkness. I'd have given anything for a flashlight or a torch. As before, we had to brave it in the dark.

After twenty yards we heard more water flowing in from various gutters. The floor became slick. The squeak of rats was all around us. They swam through our feet. I tried not to think about them. I thought only of pushing forward, getting out of this city, and leaving all these black memories behind. At certain junctures sunlight seeped in from other drains. Toward the end, the passage became very steep. Steps had been built into the floor, but the water flowed swiftly. Garth slipped. Symeon caught one arm. I caught the other.

"I need to rest," Garth said. "Just for a moment."

"There's another tunnel up here," said Mary, pointing toward the ceiling on the right.

The tunnel emitted a faint yellow glow. There were grooves in the wall that allowed us to climb up inside it. I decided it was an access tunnel. Jerusalem was teeming with tunnels. Maybe we wouldn't have to locate that storehouse in the Lower City after all. Maybe this tunnel could take us exactly where we wanted to go.

Safely inside, we stopped to rest. I heard voices. They were coming from the direction of the light.

Gid started to rise. "I'll check it out."

"I'll go with you," I insisted.

We crept through the passageway. The light increased, but we heard no more voices. The tunnel intersected with another chamber. The light was coming from a corridor off to the left. Gid peeked around the other side. There was no one there. Just an abandoned oil lantern. I followed as he stepped out into the open.

"Where do you think they went?" I asked Gid.

He started to shake his head, then he stiffened. He turned abruptly to the left. I heard another noise coming from behind. As I spun around, a man charged out of the shadows. He held a raised dagger! Fury exploded inside me. I grabbed the arm before it could stab down. I fell backwards. Using my free arm I threw the man over the top of me. He smashed into the wall, but I didn't let go. My strength surprised even me. I rolled onto his chest, ramming his dagger hand against the stone. It dropped to the ground just as I heard another voice shouting, "Wait! I know these men! They're Romans!"

My attacker relaxed. He'd have likely gone limp anyway since I'd totally whomped on him. Gid was facing off with two more men—both Jewish soldiers like the one sitting under me. As of yet Gid hadn't delivered any blows. In fact, the soldiers were turning their weapons hilt out, as if to surrender.

I recognized one of the men. I'd seen him yesterday in the hall where the soldiers were having their feast. He was one of Simon Giora's henchmen—Nathan, if I recalled correctly. He'd reported to Simon about the capture of two Nazarenes at the house of James. The other two had been part of the Zealot leader's entourage as well.

I released the man I'd subdued. He stumbled to his feet, holding his injured hand. Gid disarmed the others.

"You're the ones who were spying, aren't you?" asked Nathan. "The Nazarenes?"

"We're Nazarenes," I confirmed, "but we're not spies."

"But you're with the Romans—"

"No," said Gid. "We're not with anyone."

The men looked stricken. They'd just surrendered to two strangers with no connections to Rome or anyone else.

"We're deserting the city," said Nathan. "We're seeking the clemency of Titus."

"We can't help you," said Gid. "You'll have to surrender to someone else."

Symeon and Mary appeared, followed by Garth.

Nathan persisted. "But you have friends among the Romans.

You *must*, or how could you get past the siege wall?"

Gid and I looked at each other. We were both thinking the same thing. To deliver a few deserters might make it easier for us to get through the gate. The Roman sentries might think this had been our mission all along.

"Are you sure you want to surrender?" I asked. "I don't know if Titus has any clemency left."

"The temple is burning," said one of the others. "The war is lost. It's either this or we die anyway."

I realized there was another advantage. These men knew the way through these tunnels. We followed them closely, moving as fast as our feet would carry us. Garth didn't take any more rest stops. Like the rest of us, he was operating on pure adrenaline. Twenty minutes later we reached the final passage. The tunnel was clogged with dying men and women. I didn't even look at them anymore. I'd seen so much death. My mind had learned to block it out. We fought our way through the stench and filth until at last we emerged into the light.

The scene below the cliffs was indescribable. Hundreds of the dead and dying—*thousands!* Two nights ago we'd been spared this grisly scene by the darkness. It was the final culmination of all the horrors and abominations I'd seen in Jerusalem. It was a city gasping its final breath. Soon it would be over. It was time for the jackals and hyenas, vultures and ravens to move in.

As we'd hoped, the Roman sentries remembered us from two nights ago and allowed us to pass without any complications. They received Nathan and the other deserters, but they acted like it was all so routine. They'd seen hundreds of deserters. The stream never seemed to end.

"So what's it like in there?" asked one of the sentries before we left. "Are the Jews ready to surrender? Sure would like to go home."

I stared at the man blankly. My emotions were numb. I was almost sure they were dead.

"You'll be home soon enough," Garth answered.

The man seemed pleased by that. We left without saying another word.

It was already evening as we started climbing the Mount of Olives to retrieve Garth's backpack. We found it exactly where he'd left it—in a small cave beneath a stone embankment in the midst of several olive trees that had somehow survived Titus' war machines.

The night was falling fast. We remained there in that olive grove and devoured nearly all of the food supplies in Garth's pack. He'd brought several packaged dinners, just like the ones I'd brought from our food storage back home. He'd also packed several Mars and Snickers bars. Mary had her first taste of chocolate. I ate one as well. I might have thought the flavors would sent my tastebuds into ecstasy. To be honest, I don't even remember what it tasted like. It could have been sawdust. With all that I had seen, I wondered how anything could ever taste or smell or look beautiful again.

Directly below us the temple was fully engulfed in flames. The gold plating had all melted and seeped into the earth. As darkness stretched over the landscape, the embers glowed brighter and brighter, as if the temple mount had been detonated by a massive firebomb.

"It'll take another month before the city is finally defeated," said Garth. "By then the ramparts will be vacant. Most of the city will already be dead. As to the survivors, Titus will spare no one. A few will become slaves for Rome's triumphal parade. Others will become fodder for wild beasts and gladiators in the arena. Everything you see, except for the tower where we were imprisoned, will be burned and leveled."

I hardly heard him. The words certainly didn't affect me the way they should have. My heart was cold. As we sat there, the entire north wall of the temple collapsed. The noise shattered my nerves one final time.

As the echo faded, Garth sat beside me. "Are you all right?"

I shook my head. "Why, Uncle Garth? Why did I have to see this? Why did I have know how blind and cruel people can become?"

Garth sighed. "I don't know. Maybe you were destined to see it. Just as you were meant to see the destruction at Jacobugath and the glory of the Savior. Sometimes we have to see the abyss before we can appreciate the light."

"I miss the light, Uncle Garth," I said. "I need something. Something to balance it out."

"Perhaps if you knew where you were sitting," said Garth.

I drew my eyebrows together. "Where I'm sitting?"

"Look around," he invited. "Can you see it? Over there. The fence. The gate."

I looked around at the gnarled olive trees, the crumbled stone fence, and the broken wooden gate. It was clear that this had once been a garden, though it was now overgrown with thorns and weeds. Garth didn't need to say anymore. I knew exactly where we were.

It was the Garden of Gethsemene.

My heart started to melt. Tears pricked at my eyes and streamed down my face. I no longer felt like I had to ask God why. I just yearned to know when all the pain would end. Not just the suffering of this blighted city, but all the suffering every-where, from the beginning to the end. I'd been told that what had taken place right here in this garden had exceeded all of the suffering that anyone had ever experienced. I'd been taught that it had spared us from an eternity of torment. The whole thing was beyond my understanding. And yet I believed it. I knew it with all of my heart. Once again the familiar burning inside my chest confirmed that it was true. As I pondered all the crimes and sins paid for in that moment—including the ones I'd witnessed over the last several days—I was staggered into silence.

For several minutes I couldn't utter a word, though my tears continued to flow.

For a moment I forgot about our trials and the difficult journey that still lay ahead. Instead, I felt an incredible sense of release. Nothing else mattered. All of the things I had seen, the turmoil that we were going through. It was all just a split second of eternity. One more blink of the eye—just one more blink—and I'd be swept up into a state of incomprehensible happiness and peace. It was a gift. It had been paid for on this small patch of ground thirty-six years before.

We didn't stay the night in the garden. The dangers of remaining anywhere near Jerusalem were still too great. We wanted to get as far away as we could under the cover of darkness.

So with our shoulders weighted down with scrolls and supplies, we started north, carefully avoiding the campfires of the legions. Ahead of us awaited our final confrontation with Simon Magus on the slopes of a mountain called Gerizim.

CHAPTER SEVENTEEN

Saturninus poured water onto a rag and began washing the blood from my face. I was still lying in the dirt on the hillside where he'd smashed Apollus' helmet with an iron ball. I stared into his face with utter terror and loathing. And yet Saturninus tried to sound consoling.

"There now," he said. "I'll bet that feels better. You'll be just fine."

I was still in shock. I bent my neck and looked over at Apollus. He was lying motionless on his stomach about five yards away, the pieces of his broken helmet covering his face. I couldn't tell if he was breathing. Oh God, please! He can't be dead!

"We have to leave here, Meagan," Saturninus continued. "The others are still searching. I'll take you to my father's house in Sebaste. He's dead now so we'll have all the solitude that we require. From there we will found the new order of things. You and I, Meagan. I believe in your gifts. You see the future and the past the way others see only the present. I have seen an angel of light. He has confirmed to me everything you revealed three nights ago. He has also confirmed that you are to be the new Earth Mother of the Unknown God."

I still couldn't speak. This guy was certifiably nuts. Did he think I was going to help him found some new religion? I squeezed my fists. I wanted to run away as fast as I could. I was still too weak. But I could feel my strength returning fast.

I looked again at Apollus.

"You don't need to worry about him anymore," said Saturninus. "His soul has returned to the primeval darkness. Along with all the others who were with him."

"Oh, please, no!" My voice was quavering. I tried to roll over and push myself up on my hands.

Saturninus was confused. "You're concerned about the Roman? Why? The Romans are the Sons of Darkness. You must know it. They are the empire of evil."

He laid his hand on my shoulder.

"Don't touch me, creep!" I wailed. "Get away!"

I crawled over to Apollus' body.

Saturninus was deeply offended. "I don't understand. You once saw into my soul and proclaimed that my veins were flowing with the blood of Melchizedek and Moses. You said the words of the Scroll of Knowledge were written in your mind. The Aeons told you that I was the person to whom you were to reveal all your secrets."

My performance as a sorceress had come back to haunt me. I'd told those lies hoping to gain an ally. Instead, I'd created a monster.

I pulled away the pieces of helmet from Apollus' face. Blood trickled from his hair and down his cheeks. My heart tightened. My soul clouded with grief. The maniac had killed him!

Saturninus persisted. "Am I still the man who is to inherit the crown of the Standing One? Or have your Aeons, Kirk and Picard, given you new instructions?"

I turned on Saturninus, my teeth bared. "Get out of here! Leave me alone!" I wrapped my arms around Apollus' head.

Saturninus gawked at me openmouthed. He started shaking. I couldn't tell if it was anger or fear. "What are you saying? Your words couldn't have been lies. The angel confirmed them."

I could hardly hear him through my sobs. "Go away," I repeated, my spirit broken. "I don't want anything to—"

My tears stopped cold. Apollus moved!

Unexpectedly he drew a deep gasping breath. He was alive!

"Apollus!" I cried. "Apollus, can you hear me?"

He let out a low moan.

"Get your water pouch!" I commanded Saturninus. "He's waking up!"

Saturninus didn't budge. He hovered there like a specter. Finally, I looked into his eyes. They were black and burning. His hand reached down for the club and chain connected to the studded iron ball. He was going to finish the job!

I sprang. His fingers had already seized the club. I grabbed the ball. The studs were blunted. This made it easier to grip. Before Saturninus could wrench it away, I lunged forward and smashed it into his forehead.

Saturninus fell backwards, motionless. I went back to Apollus.

"Apollus, can you understand me?"

He opened his eyes. He tried to say something.

"Yes?" I asked. "What is it?"

Nothing came out. He couldn't speak.

"You have to get up," I said desperately. "You have to walk. We're in danger. Can you stand?"

I tried to help him. Oh, what a pair we were! I was all scratched up and bleeding. He was delirious and fading fast.

Saturninus moved again. Boy, knocking someone out was a lot easier in the movies. I grabbed some thongs from a pouch on Apollus' belt. I wrapped one around Saturninus' wrist. Then I pulled his other arm behind his back and wound them together. I tied about six knots, then I tied his ankles. I finished just as he become coherent enough to resist.

"Meagan," he said drunkenly. "Let me loose."

I ignored him and pulled Apollus to a sitting position. Blood continued trickling down his face. I had to stop that bleeding. I looked at his eyes. One pupil was twice as large as the other. This wasn't good. I started to panic. What should I do?!

He tried to lie back down.

"No!" I cried, propping him up again. "Don't go back to sleep."

If he had a concussion, falling asleep could kill him. I had to keep him conscious. I tried to sound soothing. "You can't sleep yet. We have to get you home. Doesn't that sound nice? Home. You can sleep in your own bed."

I unfastened the bulky armor from around his chest and set it aside.

"Now come on," I pleaded. "Stand up. Please stand up."

I closed my eyes and said a prayer. Somehow we had to get out of here. I placed Apollus' arm around my neck and tried again to lift him. Thank heaven! He stood on his own feet.

"Meagan, untie me!" shouted Saturninus. "Meagan!"

I reached down and grabbed Saturninus' water pouch. Apollus had one, too, but I wanted as much water as I could carry. Apollus' knees started to buckle. We nearly went down. He was so heavy. How could I do this? My cuts and scratches were stinging with sweat. We stumbled forward. Somehow Apollus stayed on his feet. Saturninus continued shouting, but his voice faded as we slipped into the trees.

Every step felt like an impossible feat. Apollus' eyes remained virtually shut. He was walking in his sleep. I don't know how I held him up. It was a miracle. Some miracles turn water into wine. Others restore sight to the blind. Mine was keeping a young Roman walking.

Periodically I could see the army camp in the valley. It was only about four miles distant. Four miles sounded astronomical. We'd be lucky to make it four more yards. I was sure the woods between here and the camp were crawling with Simon's men. We had to find a place to hide—and quickly. With every step I was sure one of Simon's henchmen would appear. His army of followers had grown. He'd apparently recruited some local peasants and villagers for today's attack.

To the west I could see a ridge and a dark hole, partially hidden by foliage. A cave? Oh, please be a cave.

Apollus tried to sit down again.

"Not yet!" I insisted. "Just a little farther. You have to hang on a little longer."

It wasn't much of a cave. More like a shallow depression, but it would have to do. To reach it we endured a terribly awkward climb over jagged boulders. Apollus collapsed ten yards short of our shelter. We fell to the ground. He was completely unconscious. I started to cry.

"Don't do this!" I wept. "We're so close!"

My determination started boiling. This was not going to happen. I experienced an eruption of strength and hoisted him to his feet. He was still as limp as a rag doll. I leaned him against a boulder.

"Stand!" I commanded, my tears flowing. His eyes fluttered open. He looked straight at me. I swear he was totally incoherent, but somehow as I carried him along, his legs started to walk.

"That's it," I said. "That's it."

Only fifteen feet to go. Just fifteen more feet.

"Come on, Apollus. You can do it!"

At last we arrived. The cave was only six feet high and ten feet deep. There were empty bird nests and lots of droppings. But there was also shade and a smooth bed of sand. I got Apollus in as far as I could. He went totally limp again, collapsing onto the sand. I heaved for oxygen. My strength was spent. I thanked God. We'd done it! By God's miracle, we'd done it.

I knew the Lord had been supporting me almost as much as He was supporting Apollus. The thorns had left deep cuts everywhere on my body. If someone had decided to follow a trail of blood, I'm sure they would have found it.

I washed the blood off Apollus' face and tried to give him a drink. He drank some. The rest trickled into the sand. One eye was still dilated. The blood had come from a single gash near his crown, caused by the edge of the helmet. There was a large area around the gash that looked hideously dark and swollen. I didn't want to touch it, fearing it might have been fractured. I still had no idea if he was going to survive. Even if he lived, would there be permanent brain damage?

I tried to rouse him. "Apollus? Apollus, just open your eyes. Just once. Then you can go back to sleep."

I had to make sure he wasn't slipping into a coma. Suddenly he pushed away my hands in annoyance. This, I felt, was a very good sign.

The cave sat a little above the trees. I could see out onto the rolling hills of Samaria. I could even see the blue Mediterranean in the far distance. The army camp was still visible on the right. How soon, I wondered, before Apollus' father sent a search party? Apollus needed a doctor. Even that quack back at the fort could treat him better than I could. Maybe some of the horsemen had escaped. Commander Severillus might come with every soldier in the garrison. But would it be enough?

I could see what looked like a large city to the north, about eight or ten miles. More Romans might have been stationed there. Today's ambush would surely be considered an uprising. The people of Samaria would pay a high price. It didn't seem right. Simon Magus was responsible for this. He alone should have to bear the responsibility. That's the opinion I intended to give to Apollus' father. That is, if I lived long enough to tell it.

The cuts on my body stung horribly. I rewashed the ones that hurt most. Then I curled up beside Apollus. I knew I couldn't rest long. I had to wake up Apollus every few minutes. If he was going to live, I had to keep up this routine the entire day.

He soon learned that all he needed to do was open his eyes, then I would leave him alone. I did my best to keep him full of liquids. I held his hand and spoke to him, telling all about my life in the twenty-first century, the gossip in my neighborhood, and the plots of several of my favorite films, including While You Were Sleeping and Heaven Can Wait.

As the sky darkened, there was very little change in his appearance. Now and then he would start moaning in pain. I continued my vigil of sleeping ten or fifteen minutes and waking Apollus throughout the night. It was hard to sleep anyway with all the pain and the gnawing hunger. I looked down at the army camp. It seemed to me there were more lanterns burning than usual, as if the place was on alert. Still, I had no idea what actions they were taking.

Toward morning I slept for about an hour and a half. When I awakened, Apollus was rambling.

"Common room . . . he's in the common room . . . news . . . be strong . . . be strong. . . ."

I leaned over him, lightly nudging his shoulder. "Apollus? Can you hear me?"

His eyes fluttered open. He looked much better. The pupils were the same size. He looked at me dazedly and said, "Albia's friend?"

"No," I said. "I'm not your sister's friend. I'm Meagan. Do you remember? Meagan."

He shook his head. "Can't . . ."

"Yes? Can't what?"

". . . tell you how sorry . . . about Albia . . ."

He closed his eyes and started to weep. I tried to comfort him by holding his hand and lightly touching his forehead. I gave him more water. He drank much better than yesterday. Afterwards, he fell asleep again.

I realized I couldn't wait any longer. I had to get help. We needed food, nourishment. I watched the army camp for several minutes. The thick trees prevented me from seeing much of the road outside the gate, but it did seem like there was a lot of activity— horses and foot soldiers coming and going. A search might have been taking place on the mountain at this very moment. If I could flag down a Roman horseman, we might be saved. I dreaded to leave Apollus alone, but I had no choice.

I took his dagger and left the cave, crawling back over the boulders and down to the trees. Many of my cuts opened up again and started bleeding. I tried to ignore it. I traveled along the hillside through the thick woods, working my way back toward the trail where we had been ambushed. The woods were quiet except for the *songs of birds. I gripped the dagger firmly. I was prepared to use it, too. I knew if I was captured, Apollus would die. If not from his wound, from thirst and hunger.*

A few minutes later I found the trail. I kept to the woods until I neared the place of the ambush. I braced myself for the sight of twenty dead bodies. Instead, all I found were the carcasses of horses. There were about a dozen of them. The bodies of the Roman soldiers had all been hauled away. Obviously the Romans had already been here, probably sometime yesterday afternoon.

I heard a voice and dropped to the ground. I pressed closely to the stiffened carcass of one of the horses.

"What did they leave?" the voice asked.

"Just the horses," someone answered. "We got the armor and weapons."

"They'll be back. Make your sweep quickly. We'll meet at the ruins."

I didn't dare breath. It was Menander's voice. I didn't recognize the second one. They were still up here. Why hadn't the Romans scoured the mountain and flushed them out?

"What about the girl?" asked the second voice.

"The Standing One says she's still around," said Menander. "She's not alone. Stay on your toes. He has promised that she will come to us."

The voices started moving away. I didn't move. Didn't even budge. A few minutes later I heard rustling on the other side of the carcass. I gripped the dagger, my hand shaking. After another minute, the feet moved on. I lay there for half an hour, perfectly frozen, breathing in slow, even breaths.

I continued reeling at Menander's words. Simon knew we were still up here. How could he be so sure? There was only one answer: he was having the fort watched. Obviously that was where we'd try to go. I realized I'd never make it to the fort. Simon's men would do anything to stop me, even seizing me within sight of the gate. What was I going to do? We needed food! Was that Simon's plan? To starve

us out? Menander had said, "He has promised she will come to us."
Did they think I'd become so desperate for food and water that I'd
have no other choice?

That wasn't going to happen. Somehow I had to signal the fort.
I had to find food. There had to be—

My eyes landed on the travel bags tied to the dead horse. I
recalled that Apollus had said we might have a picnic on the moun-
tain. I reached for the travel bag and cut open the leather straps.

Small bundles of cloth fell out. I unwrapped one. It was a chunk
of bread! A cheese sandwich! There were also fruits and almonds. I
saw other travel bags on other horses. I removed the first one and
stuffed it with every morsel of food I could find, keeping one eye
sharply peeled on the woods. Most of bags were already empty, but I
found enough bread and nuts and raisins to last us at least two days.

Swiftly, I made my way back to the cave. There were no other
voices, no other signs of a living soul. If there were spies and lookouts
on the mountain, they must have been near the bottom.

When I arrived back at the cave, Apollus stirred and opened
his eyes.

"Look," I said. "I have food. Are you hungry?"

He continued to look at me without replying.

"How do you feel?" I asked.

He groaned and shut his eyes.

"Can you eat something? You have to eat. You haven't eaten
anything since yesterday morning. Here."

I put a sandwich up to his lips. He turned away.

"You don't like sandwiches? All right. How about some raisins?"

I poked one inside his mouth before he could protest. His tongue
started working on it. His teeth bit down. I think he ate it only
because he didn't have the strength to spit it out. I got in about a
half dozen raisins that way, and even a small chunk of cheese before
he put up his hand to let me know he'd had enough. That's okay, I
thought. I'd give him an hour. Then I'd start again.

I continued my routine of prayer and dressing his wound and rambling on and on about nonsensical things from my life in the modern century. I told him all about my father's attack on my mother when I was five years old and about a car accident with my mother when I was seven. At one point his eyes were fully open. He seemed to be listening intently. I wasn't worried. If he tried to ask me later about cars and movies and songs on the radio, I could always tell him he'd been hallucinating.

Toward midday he did some rambling of his own. Something about swimming in a river and sneaking out with his friends to spy on the bathhouses. There were more tears, too, as he cried out the names of his two brothers as well as his mother and sister.

I continued to watch the Roman fort. Horses kept coming and going. The place was still on alert. Why hadn't Brutus launched an all-out attack on the mountain? Something must have altered his opinion about where the enemy had scattered. Maybe a false report from one of Simon's spies. That made sense. Simon would have wanted to keep this mountain to himself. It was still imperative for Simon to meet up with Harry if he ever arrived with the Scroll of Knowledge. That appointment was scheduled for the day after tomorrow. If he didn't have me or Jesse to negotiate an exchange, I felt sure Harry would be killed the instant he made an appearance. He'd certainly be killed anyway if Simon thought he didn't have the scroll.

The afternoon lengthened. I lay down for a nap. My stomach was full. I should have been able to relax. But my anxiety was inconsolable. If Harry arrived today or tomorrow, he'd be walking right into a trap. I was comforted at least to know that little Jesse was in capable hands.

"Please, Father," I prayed with all my soul. "I'll do anything—anything if you'll make Apollus well and protect Harry. Just let me know. Let me know . . ."

I finally managed to sleep. I lost track of time. When I awakened, the light had changed dramatically. It was late afternoon. I gasped and sat up straight. My heart stopped when I realized that Apollus wasn't beside me. Then I saw him. He was standing near the opening of the cave, pressing his temple. He turned and looked at me.

"You're up!" I said with surprise and delight.

"Mmmm," he answered.

"How are you feeling?"

"Headache," he said groggily. "How long . . . ?"

"We've been here for two days."

His eyes widened with surprise. I was afraid he might faint. He leaned against the cave wall. I went to him and offered my arm for support.

"What do you remember?" I asked.

He considered the question carefully. "Bits and pieces."

"Do you know who you are?"

"Who I am? Of course. Apollus Brutus Severillus, First Centurion of the Neopolis Garrison of the Fifth Legion of Rome."

I sighed with relief. He didn't have amnesia.

"Do you remember what happened?"

He became less self-assured. "I remember . . . thorns."

"That's right," I said. "We jumped into a thorn bush to escape. We were attacked on the trail. Do you remember that?"

He thought hard. "Bits and pieces." He pinched his eyes tightly. "I have to get back. Back to my post."

"You can't," I informed him. "The Sons of the Elect are watching. You're still not strong enough."

"I have to reach my father."

"It's impossible. Especially while it's light."

He looked at the sun. Finally he took a long, hard look at me. "How about you? How do you feel?"

"Better," I said. "Still sore. Do you remember who I am now?"

He studied my face. "I know your name is Meagan. But I'm not sure . . . I really don't know why you're here with me."

I frowned. I guess I'd hoped I might have made a stronger impression. It occurred to me that I could tell him anything.

"Maybe we're in love," I said. "Maybe I'm your fiancée and you brought me up here for a romantic picnic."

He huffed. "Not likely."

I felt insulted. He didn't even give it two seconds' consideration. "Do you remember when you said . . . when you told me I was beautiful?"

He gazed at me again. I became self-conscious. I knew I was covered with scratches.

"Like the face of a dove," he remembered.

I smiled. "Very good. You remember all the important things anyway."

He pressed his temple again. I got a damp rag and placed it gently against his gash. He took the rag and pressed it harder.

"I have to get back," he said again. "I have to report what happened. My men! *Milius and Cato! Scribonus!"*

It was all coming back very fast now. He became dizzy. I caught him and braced him up.

"You're not going anywhere yet," I said. "Not until dark. Here. Lie down again."

"Yes," he said. "For a moment. Then I have to go. I have to save my men."

"There's nothing you can do for them now," I said sympathetically. "You need to take care of yourself."

He lay back down and closed his eyes. Another wave of pain erupted in his head. It must have been excruciating. He nearly squeezed all the blood out of my hand. Moments later the pain passed. He opened his eyes and stared at me.

"You saved my life, didn't you?"

"Well," I said modestly. "Not as surely as you saved mine."

"Umm," he said, as if that was probably true.

I pulled in my chin. "Don't be so sure. How do you know who saved who?"

"*I remember . . . I remember this whole trip was to try to find . . .*"

"*My brother,*" I finished.

"*Yes, your brother. Did we find him?*"

"*No. Not yet.*"

"*That man,*" he said. "*The one we left tied up back there. Was he the one who walloped me?*"

"*Yes.*"

"*How did I subdue him?*"

"*Uh, that wasn't you.*"

"*You* did *that to him?*"

"*That's right. If I hadn't, he'd have given you another wallop to finish you off.*"

He pondered this, then he said, "*Hm.*"

"*Hm? That's all you can say is 'hm'? How about, 'Good one, Meagan! You sure showed him!'? Or how about, 'Thank you'?*"

"*Thank you,*" he said finally.

"*Don't mention it,*" I said curtly.

"*I really am grateful,*" he said more sincerely. "*Thank you. Thank you for everything you've done.*"

That was more like it. "*You're welcome. Same to you.*"

Apollus fell asleep again. As I looked into his face, I felt a tear of relief trickle down my cheek. I thanked my Heavenly Father. Apollus was going to be all right.

He slept another hour. When he opened his eyes the sun was going down. He looked much stronger, though he still complained of a headache. His memory for the most part had completely returned.

"*I'm going back,*" he said, tying his sword around his waist.

"*Shouldn't we wait until it's a little darker?*"

"*No,*" he said. "*That gives them the advantage. Assassins love the dark. And you're staying here.*"

"*What?!*"

"*That's right. I can move much faster without you. Besides, the risk is too great. You'll be safer here. There's plenty of food. Go spar-*"

ingly on the water. I'll return with an entire cohort of cavalry before noon tomorrow. I'll have my father enlist the garrison at Sebaste."

"But—"

"I'll hear no further arguments. My word is final."

I started steaming. A blow to the brain obviously hadn't lessened his arrogance.

He became more gentle. "Please. I know what I'm doing. Trust me."

I tried to be rational. Maybe he was right. If enough men attacked us at once, there was little he could do to protect me. If his strength had indeed returned, there was no doubt he could move much faster. Perhaps my presence only endangered his life all the more.

"Be careful," I said finally.

I had such a pleading in my voice that he actually hesitated and looked into my eyes. He stepped closer. My heart skipped a beat. Was he actually going to kiss me? Was there a romantic side to this Roman brute after all? He leaned in. I closed my eyes and puckered my lips.

The kiss landed—right on my forehead.

"Whatever you do," he said, "don't leave this cave. I'll be back before noon. I promise."

As I watched him skirt the boulders and enter the trees at the base of the ridge, a dark tremor passed through me. He didn't look steady on his feet at all. How would he fare against an opponent who was fully alert and agile? I couldn't think about that. It drained me of all sensibility. Nothing could defeat my Roman.

My Roman. I was such an idiot. I had to face reality. Even if we survived, a heartbreaking good-bye was inevitable. What hope was there for a first-century Roman soldier and twenty-first-century woman? Zip. This fantasy definitely needed a quick and lethal dose of reality.

But oh, how my heart ached as he disappeared into the trees. I had it bad. No question about it. It might take more than reality to kill this fantasy. I felt like such a loser. Hadn't I learned my lesson with Harry? With my luck Apollus would probably marry Harry's sister Steffanie. Then we'd all be one big happy brother-and-sister family. And yet I knew that even if I never saw him again, a part of me would always belong to him.

I hardly slept at all that night. I was terrified out of my mind. The darkness was thick and foreboding. Every shadow seemed to be a living thing—breathing, lurking. I was sure that one of them would turn out to be Simon Magus, approaching as calmly and venomously as he had that night near Jericho. He knew I was here. I had no doubt of it. Just like that night when I swore I saw him by the market stalls. He was lurking out there somewhere, waiting for the right moment to move in.

The night was unnaturally still. Nothing moved on the mountainside. I kept watching the army camp in the valley. There were still twice as many lanterns burning. I kept waiting for some sign that Apollus had returned. Maybe I'd see a score of torches ignited as five hundred horses thundered up the slopes. But there was no change. The same lights continued to burn throughout the night.

At last, dawn started to break. The first beams of sunlight stretched across the Samaritan plain. Still there was no sign of an approaching army. The morning trudged on. The day grew hotter. My nerves grew more and more frazzled. Midday came and went. Apollus had not kept his promise.

At last I drew the grim conclusion: Apollus hadn't made it. My eyes filled with tears. I saw the image of his body lying dead in the woods between here and Neopolis. I started to sob. I tried to suppress my fears. I couldn't give up. There was still hope. Just a few more hours. I could wait a few more hours.

The afternoon drifted on. The Roman army never came.

I started to wonder, what if Simon and his followers had left the mountain? What if they'd been forced to move on to some other location? What if I was totally wasting my time?

No. It didn't make sense. Simon wouldn't have left. And yet . . .

How could I wait here another night? I'd made Apollus a promise. But he'd failed to arrive. Maybe he was hurt and wounded.

Maybe he needed help. I couldn't sit here any longer. My water was gone. I was going absolutely stir-crazy. I had to take action.

Tomorrow Harry would arrive. I was sure of it. Either that or he was already here. I'd never really found out. What if Simon had already confronted him? What if he was just a single mile away, passing time in a cave just like this one? Why should we both just wait in our holes like frightened rabbits? Maybe he was out of water, too. I had to find out. I had to reach the summit and see for myself.

I emerged from the cave and stood among the boulders. The summit didn't look very far. I imagined I could be there in half an hour. I started to climb. Sweat seeped back into my healing wounds. They began to sting all over again.

As I neared the top, I saw all the signs of some other great conflict that had taken place. Many trees were burned. Broken lances and arrows littered the earth There were rusted Roman helmets and discarded shields. Finally, there were skeletons and the ashes of mass graves. I guessed it was two, maybe three years ago.

As I reached the final spur of the hill just below the wide, rounded summit, I stood to catch my breath. A light, cooling breeze was coming off the ocean. I basked in it for a moment and gazed out at the Samaritan plains. Something unusual caught my eye. I squinted to try to determine exactly what it was. Looking toward the larger city about eight or ten miles to the north, I could see that something was raising an enormous cloud of dust. My heart did a somersault. I knew the cause of that cloud. It was an army. A large army. It was coming in this direction.

I could hardly draw a breath. Did this mean that Apollus had succeeded? Did this mean he was on his way? It seemed too much to hope. The army might have easily come without his help. I turned quickly back toward the summit. I desperately wanted to call out Harry's name. If he was here, I had to find him fast. The place looked completely deserted. I decided if I couldn't find him in ten minutes, I'd try to make my way back down to the fort at Neopolis. I had to find out what had happened to Apollus.

I continued toward the summit as fast as I could. At last the ruins of a great building came into view. Brutus had mentioned that the Samaritans considered Mount Gerizim a kind of Mount Olympus. Apparently they'd once had a temple here to prove it. Just before I reached the crumbling walls, I halted in my tracks. Menander had said something about Simon's men gathering at some ruins. My stomach coiled with dread. I started to hear human voices. I was totally exposed! I swiftly moved to a cubbyhole in one of the walls, slipped inside, and curled up into a ball.

My heart was racing. I realized I'd made a monumental mistake. I should have stayed exactly where I was. I recalled Menander's words. He'd plainly stated that I would come to them. I'd done exactly as Simon had predicted.

No, I told myself. I hadn't been caught yet. I could still run. I'd go back to the cave. Come what may, this was where I'd said I would wait. There was no more time to search for Harry. I had to leave now!

A shadow fell across the cubbyhole.

"It's all right, Meagan," said a dreadful, wheezing voice. "You can come out now. We've been expecting you."

CHAPTER EIGHTEEN

We arrived at the little village close to dusk, our faces dusty and our feet sore and swollen. We'd been walking all hours of daylight for the past two days, stopping only briefly to eat or drink. Even this stop was meant to be brief, just a moment to refill our canteens and water pouches at the village spring. It was the same spring that Gid and I had visited during our journey to Jerusalem. The stray dogs were still lying around the cement enclosure, greeting us with vicious snarls. We drove them away with stones.

We hadn't been there a minute when a familiar face met our eyes—a woman with a scar on the bridge of her nose. She and her two young girls looked far better dressed and fed than when we'd first met them a week ago. She recognized us immediately, particularly Gidgiddonihah.

"Please," she insisted. "Take shelter under my roof tonight. I have hot food. There's much to spare. Very much to spare."

She smiled gratefully, acknowledging that we were the reason for her abundance. Gid's gift of the two jewels from his sword may have saved her life. It was enough that it had earned us a roof and a hot meal. And a lifelong friend.

During dinner Garth sat in the middle of the floor of the humble peasant hut surrounded by all the scrolls. I was aston- ished at how well he'd recovered from his hunger and ill treat-

ment at Jerusalem. Despite two grueling days of travel, he still
had the energy to read portions of every manuscript, except for
the Scroll of Knowledge, by the light of a small oil lamp.

"It's a veritable treasure trove of sacred scripture," he
declared. He went down the line. "This one is the Epistle of
James. This is another Epistle of James that we've never even
heard of. This one is Paul's Epistle to the Hebrews. Here's a
letter from Saint Jude. This is the Book of Isaiah, the Book of
Ezekiel, the Book of Daniel. Here's a new and unknown letter
from Saint Peter outlining the organization of the Church. And
this one—it's the testimony of Saint Mark," he read an inscription on the outside—"*Written for the Greeks from Alexandria
for a blessing to the world.*" Garth turned to me. "Couple this
with your Scroll of Matthew and we may have the only copies
of half of the gospels in the entire New Testament."

I sat there in awe. So many precious books. Some that had
never made it to the Bible. If I was looking for an answer as to
why we'd endured those terrible events at Jerusalem, maybe all
the reason I needed was sitting right before us.

"In the coming weeks the Romans will burn the Upper City
to the ground," Garth explained. "There were at least two three-
story buildings near the foundation of James' house. Even
protected inside that niche, the heat from a fallen wall might
have ignited or damaged them all."

"But we've still got the same old problem," I sighed. "How
do we get the scrolls to the Seven Churches in Asia? How do we
get them into the hands of the Apostle John?"

The question hung in the air only a moment.

"*I'll* take them to Asia," Symeon declared. "I've given the
matter much prayer and solemn thought. I no longer feel I
should return to Pella. At least, not yet. The danger is too great
that Thebuthis and the elders would reject the scrolls and cast
them into the fire. After we know Meagan and Jesse are in safe

hands, I'll sail to Ephesus with my daughter and hire scribes who will copy every word. Only then, if God is willing, will I return to Pella and offer them the holy manuscripts."

Mary embraced her father proudly. The Bishop of Pella had come a long way, I thought. His spirit had soared to the clouds. He'd given up everything he'd once been to do what was right. I think the Savior, his cousin, would have been pleased.

I went to sleep that night under a dark cloud of anxiety. I tried to get rid of it with prayer, but this one didn't go away so easily. Tomorrow was the day. Before the sun set again, I'd have my final meeting with Simon Magus. I'd done everything Simon had asked. I'd obtained the Scroll of Knowledge. Maybe the scroll really was all he wanted. Perhaps I could save Meagan and Jesse, and be on the road home as early as the day after tomorrow. I desperately needed to know what to do. If every other scroll from James' house was authentic and true, it seemed unlikely that the Scroll of Knowledge was anything less. I prayed for an answer with all my heart. I prayed a long time. Heaven was silent. Finally, I couldn't hold my eyes open any longer.

The following morning we embarked on the last leg of our journey toward Mount Gerizim. I kept praying to know what to do with the scroll, throughout the morning and past midday, hoping an answer would reveal itself at any moment. It never did. I was starting to get the terrible feeling that it was totally up to me. I feared that if any answer was going to come, it wouldn't be until the last possible second. By then it might be too late to save us all.

"That's it," Symeon announced, pointing toward a small, rounded mountain in the distance. "That's Gerizim."

I'd seen that mountain before. It had loomed in the distance the night Gid had made the sheath for his sword. My blood started pumping. My teeth began nervously grinding. We followed the road another hour, the mountain looming larger and larger.

"We should leave the highway," Garth suggested. "We'll approach through the woods. It's the best way I can think to avoid an ambush."

"Good idea," said Gid. "But if Simon Magus is planning an ambush, we won't be able to avoid it forever."

We took to the forest. It made the going much slower, but it made us all less nervous. The woods thickened as we neared the base of the mountain. I looked around for a place where Symeon and Mary might hole up. There was no reason to put them and all the other scrolls at risk. Besides, even if something terrible happened, Symeon might still make his journey to Asia.

Suddenly Gid held up his arm. He listened hard. Seconds later I could hear it, too.

Chopping.

Someone was cutting down trees. We turned west. No sense having a run-in with any local woodcutters. But to the west the sounds of chopping only increased. It seemed to be happening all along the base of the mountain. We crept a little closer. Finally, we reached the crest of a hill and saw the entire scene. The woodcutters were Romans. Dozens of soldiers were felling trees and dragging them off to the side. We looked at each other in confusion.

"More lumber for the siege at Jerusalem?" I asked.

"Awfully strange way to harvest it," said Gid.

The only trees they cut were the ones right along the base. I'd learned something about woodcutting with my dad's cousin Reuben in Montana. If I hadn't known any better, I'd have sworn they were making a firebreak.

"We'll try around the other side," said Garth.

"What if the same thing is going on over there?" asked Mary.

"If the Romans have surrounded this entire mountain," said Garth, "whoever's up there must have made them very angry."

Someone yelled behind us. "You there! What are you doing?"

We turned. In the shadow of the forest stood twenty to thirty soldiers, their swords drawn and bows loaded.

"Don't move," threatened a stern-faced man with gray hair at his temples. "None of you!"

I closed my eyes in futility. *Not again*, I cried in my heart. Gid left his sword in its sheath. We stood with our arms where the soldiers could clearly see them. As they closed in, their gazes were intense.

"Do you think they're with them?" one soldier asked another.

"That one is for sure." The man with gray temples indicated Gidgiddonihah.

"With who?" I asked.

"Shut up!" snapped the Roman. "You have ten seconds to explain yourselves. If you can't, we have orders to execute armed peasants on sight."

I looked into the man's eyes. He was itching to do it. They wanted to slaughter us all then and there.

"We're looking for a girl," I said urgently. "Her name is Meagan. She's with a young boy named Jesse. They're prisoners of a man named Simon Magus. His followers are called the Sons of the Elect—"

I'd said more than I had to. Meagan's name made them look at one another with surprise.

"This Meagan," said the soldier. "Is she your sister?"

My sister. It was true enough considering the future relationship of our parents.

"Yes," I said. "Do you know her? Do you know where she is?"

He indicated Gid and the others. "Who are they?"

"My uncle and friends. They're helping me." I wasn't sure what all they knew, but I was determined to keep talking to calm them down. "Meagan and Jesse were kidnapped. We've just come from Jerusalem to bargain for their lives."

Weapons started to be lowered. My heart sank back into the cavity of my chest.

"Come with me," the soldier with gray temples directed.

Twenty minutes later we were escorted toward an enclosure of tents just below the western slope. Trees were being cut around Gerizim's entire perimeter. From what we could gather from the soldiers, Simon Magus, the Sons of the Elect, and a group of local peasants had taken refuge on top of the mountain. They were blamed for attacking and killing a number of Romans three days before. Garrisons from as far away as the towns of Sebaste and Antipatris had been called in to squash the problem. When Symeon asked why they were cutting all the trees, the soldier smirked and replied, "After tonight, these woods won't be hiding any more rebels."

A runner had been sent ahead to announce us. Before we reached the center tent, a man whose hair was perfectly silver came out to greet us. He walked with a slight stoop, as if his back was giving him some trouble. Behind him emerged a much younger man. There was evidence of a nasty-looking gash on his head, scabbed over. I thought it should have been wrapped in a bandage. Obviously he didn't agree.

I noticed other men with officers' insignia, and several hundred cavalrymen camped in the woods about. The silver-haired man eagerly approached, his bright blue eyes full of concern.

"Are you Harry?" he asked.

"Yes," I said with surprise.

"I'm Commander Severillus of Neopolis. This is Commander Andronicus of Antipatris and Commander Scipio of Sebaste. And this is my son, Apollus, First Centurion of Neopolis."

The young man nodded, along with the others.

"This is my Uncle Garth," I said, "and my companions— Gidgiddonihah, Symeon, and his daughter, Mary."

"Daughter?"

I blushed. The word had just come out. I hadn't thought about the significance of Mary's disguise for days.

Symeon nervously tried to explain. "We cut her hair for fear of bandits."

Severillus looked Mary up and down. He smiled and grunted. "If you've just come from Jerusalem, I think you might have had more reasons than just bandits. Fifty thousand war-weary legionaries might have been reason enough."

I sighed with relief. He understood the disguise perfectly. I liked this Roman commander already.

"We've heard all about you," Severillus continued, "and your nasty business with the rebel leader, Simon Magus."

"Where's Meagan?" I asked.

The commander deferred the question to his son.

"She's up there with them," said Apollus gloomily. "Three days ago we were on our way to the top with a patrol of twenty men when we were attacked. Actually, we were up there looking for you."

I was dumbfounded. I couldn't help but wonder how Meagan got hooked up with these Romans in the first place.

"Where is Jesse?" I asked.

Severillus answered. "Until this morning your slave was healing in my infirmary. He had an arrow wound to the hand. I guess he felt he'd recovered quite enough. I was told an hour ago that the boy had disappeared."

"Where would he have gone?" asked Mary.

The commander shrugged. "He was a slave. There's no telling."

I looked toward the mountain. "He's gone up there. He's gone to try to rescue her."

"I was just about to head up there myself with two hundred cavalry," said Apollus. "I postponed the endeavor when I heard you'd arrived."

I raised my eyebrows in astonishment. "You were going up there to rescue Meagan?"

The young Roman looked somewhat embarrassed. I could tell the commanders from Sebaste and Antipatris weren't entirely supportive of this mission. "She's a citizen of the Empire," Apollus declared. His jawline relaxed as he added, "And she saved my life."

My eyes widened. Apparently a lot had happened while we were in Jerusalem. It was also clear that Meagan was up to her old tricks. There had to be a law against masquerading as a Roman. Did her claim that I was her brother make me an accessory?

Apollus continued. "She nursed me back to health after the ambush. For two days we hid in a cave on the north slope. As soon as I was strong enough, I went for help. Two men attacked me as I was crossing the woods to reach the fort. I killed them both, but my wound left me lightheaded. I'm afraid I fell unconscious for several hours. I had told Meagan to stay in the cave and promised to return for her by midday. Unfortunately, it was evening when I finally arrived with fifty men. She was already gone. She must have gotten anxious. Or else the rebels had found her. We crept as close to the summit as we dared. Simon Magus has a good hundred and fifty men up there. Most of them are hot-headed Samaritan farmers. Our two hundred cavalrymen should make quick work of them."

"Did you see Meagan?" I asked.

"No," Apollus confessed. "But they're holding someone in a pit inside the ruins of the old temple. It has to be her."

"If you ride up that mountain with two hundred men," said Gidgiddonihah, "you're liable to get that girl killed."

All eyes turned on Gid.

"Really," said Apollus severely. "And who are you?"

Gid looked into the eyes of the haughty young Roman without answering.

"He's a general," said Garth. "In his land he was a commander of the armies."

"And what land is this?" asked Andronicus, the commander from Antipatris.

"Zarahemla of the Nephites," said Gid.

"Zara-what?" asked Apollus.

"It's a land across the oceans," I cut in.

"Never heard of it," said Apollus.

"I'd like to hear his opinion," said Severillus. "Wherever he comes from, he carries himself like a warrior."

Gid explained. "If you show up with two hundred men against an army of a hundred and fifty, these hot-blooded farmers might just risk a battle. Especially if they're flushed with the success of some previous confrontation."

"I'm hoping there won't be a battle," said Apollus. "I'm hoping when they see us, they'll be willing to negotiate for her release."

"You might get them to negotiate if you had a thousand men," said Gid. "Not two hundred."

"We can't spare a thousand men," said Scipio, the commander from Sebaste. "At least not before morning. Until then we need every spare footman to set flame to the mountain."

"You're going to burn the mountain?" I asked with alarm.

Severillus nodded. "As soon as the sun touches the edge of the hills, our men will ignite every tree and bush as far up the slopes as we can reach. By morning this mountain will be as bald as any of Magus' disciples. Gerizim with its crumbling shrine has caused us enough grief. It's only been two years since Cerealis and the Fifth Legion slaughtered eleven thousand rebels on its slopes. We intend to make certain that its forests are never a haven for insurgents and criminals again."

"The sun will touch those hills in just a few hours," said Garth. "What did you intend to do if your son wasn't back?"

"We've already thought of that," said Apollus. He pointed toward a narrow ridge of rocks along the southwest side. "We'll make our retreat down that corridor. Most of the horses should make it. With any luck we won't lose a single man or beast."

"This is crazy," I declared. "There's no reason to risk the lives of anyone. I have exactly what Simon wants. If I just give it to him, he'll release Meagan without any bloodshed."

"Is it a religious document?" asked Severillus.

I stopped cold. Meagan had told them far more than I'd anticipated. Symeon and Garth were all staring at me in surprise. I wasn't turning back now. I'd made my decision. I was bringing the Scroll of Knowledge.

"Yes," I told Severillus. "A religious document."

"You believe if you just hand him this scroll, he'll release Meagan at the same moment?" asked Apollus.

"That's what we agreed," I said.

"What is this document?" asked Scipio. "Is it worth money?"

"I don't know," I said tentatively. "We haven't read it. The scroll is sealed."

"Perhaps we should have a look at it," said Andronicus. "I know people in Rome who'll pay good money for religious arti-facts. They're particularly partial to writings from the East."

I started to cringe.

Severillus stepped in. "No. If breaking those seals means that this young girl's life will be put at risk, we'll leave it as it is. What does it matter? When Simon surrenders, we can just take it back."

Obviously Severillus didn't know how slippery Simon could be. Still, the idea that Simon's men might be in custody before morning comforted me a little.

"All right," said Apollus finally. "We'll try it your way. You can take your scroll to the summit. I'll go with you. My horsemen will follow us halfway up the trail to a point where I can signal them. If they release Meagan as easily you say, I'll withhold my terms of surrender until she's in our custody. But if things go awry, I intend to take matters into my own hands. Agreed?"

We all agreed with a nod. The last two commanders merely shrugged.

"I've never really liked this escapade from the beginning," said Scipio. "It all derring-do anyway. We have them surrounded. I see no reason to risk two hundred good men and horses for one Sicilian, even if she is as beautiful as the young Apollus has described."

Apollus reddened. I scrunched my forehead. *Sicilian?*

Andronicus slapped his fellow commander on the back. "You've grown too stodgy at your cushy post in Sebaste, Scipio. The war is over. The rebellion is all but crushed. Many of our men will be retiring by year's end. Let them have this last bit of bravado to tell their grandchildren. Go, Apollus. Rescue your damsel."

* * *

Apollus gave us ten minutes to prepare. Garth and Gidgiddonihah would go with us. Mary and Symeon would remain behind with the other scrolls and our supplies. Garth and I had a moment by ourselves as we laid our things in a corner of Commander Severillus' tent. I emptied everything out of my travel sack except for the Scroll of Knowledge. Then I paused and held it in my hands. Garth was watching. I looked at him for reassurance.

"What should I do, Uncle Garth?" I asked. "I could give them another scroll. The Book of Isaiah. Surely there are other copies of Isaiah in existence. Even the Book of Mormon has—"

Garth shook his head. "Do you really want to take such a chance with Meagan's life?"

I sighed deeply. "But what if it really is the most sacred knowledge that Jesus ever taught? After tonight it might be lost to the world forever."

"I don't think so, Harry," said Garth thoughtfully. "Remember, you and I live in the dispensation of the fullness of times. If the saints are ready for such knowledge, the Lord can call forth a prophet whenever He chooses. I know the value of ancient texts. I've devoted much of my life to preserving and studying them. I'm sickened to think that *any* testimony might be lost. But if the information is truly meant to come to light, the Lord will provide a way. He'll fill in all the gaps that we scholars have been unable to discover for ourselves."

"But Simon thinks this scroll will give him great power. What if it's true? What if it disrupts the whole fabric of time and space and—?"

Garth chuckled. He put his arm on my shoulder. "There's one thing I know for sure, my nephew. If that scroll is really from God, it could never benefit an unrighteous soul. That's not how God's power works. At best, it could only curse them further. Even the righteous can't possess God's power. We just borrow it from time to time, through the priesthood, through our faith and obedience. Satan's power is a cheap imitation, running on short-life batteries. Time or space could never be disrupted for long. God is at the helm. He always will be."

I smiled. Garth had repeated the theme of this entire journey. But few people could say it better than my Uncle Garth.

"Let's go," I said to him. "We have a mountain to climb."

CHAPTER NINETEEN

They'd kept me imprisoned in the bottom of a pit during the hottest part of the day. The pit was actually part of a network of cellars that had once been part of the old temple. My hands had been bound in front. The knot was underneath so I couldn't get at it with my teeth.

They were all here—Simon, Cerinthus, Menander, and the rest of the Sons of the Elect, as well as several of the women, including Helga the Horrible, who'd once tried to give me a bath by grinding off the top layer of my skin. Along with them were about a hundred Samaritan peasants and villagers, mostly young men, seduced by Simon's promises of glory and revenge against the Romans. Most of their armor and weapons, I felt sure, had been stripped from the bodies and remains left behind after the last battle on Mount Gerizim several years earlier. They were a ragtag crew, but they acted like they could take on the entire Roman army by themselves.

To my surprise, Saturninus was also among them. He must have put his plans of founding his own religion on hold. He looked at me with utter contempt, but also with sadness, as if I'd broken his heart. I got the heebie-jeebies whenever he looked down at me, gloating.

That morning Simon himself had leaned over the pit. The feeling I got looking up at his cancer-eaten face, long gray hair, and white robe was far worse than the heebie-jeebies. It was mortal dread, though I fought hard not to show it. He tried to offer me some ripe figs, which I refused, especially since they'd been sitting in his sweaty, cancerous hand.

"Suit yourself," he said, eating a small bite for himself. "I've come to tell you that Harry is coming. I've seen him in vision. He'll be here late this afternoon. He's bringing the Scroll of Knowledge, just as I desired."

I couldn't imagine how it was possible, but Simon spoke with such conviction that I couldn't help but believe it. I remained curled up in the bottom of the pit and replied, "Then I'll bet you're a real happy camper."

He laughed once, more of a snort. "I also came to tell you that Jesse will soon be here as well."

I looked at Simon. "Jesse?"

"Yes. He's coming on his own accord, much like yourself, just as I have willed. So you see? All your efforts and troubles to free yourself from my grasp were for naught. Everything will be precisely as it was."

"Except that I'll bet your old house has a big "This Property Is Condemned" *sign sittin' out front, doesn't it?"*

Simon simmered a little, then he smiled and raised his arms. "This is my home. My real home. This mountain—the most sacred place on earth. Here Abraham was deceived by the Creator to sacrifice Isaac until his hand was stayed by the Unknown God. This place is blessed for all time."

"You think Abraham brought Isaac here? *Don't you mean a place farther south?"*

"Another fabrication of the Jews," said Simon coolly. "This is the true mountain of the Lord. The place of sacrifice. This is where all pure covenants with the Lord are made and kept. Including the covenant I made with you."

"What covenant is that?"

"To sacrifice the boy, of course. News has come from Jerusalem. The temple of Judah is destroyed. Your dark prophecy has come true. The boy's blood must be shed as a means of purging your soul."

I started to tremble. Jesse hadn't even been recaptured and yet I was terrified for his life. "You can't do that," I said. "You made a promise to Harry. You promised if he brought you the scroll, you'd let us both go."

Simon considered this. "Yes, I did, didn't I? Unfortunately, I can't go against the One Supreme Power. In the end, he decides all our final fates, now doesn't he?"

I didn't reply. Frankly, I didn't know what he was talking about, but my heart shriveled. Simon left me alone again to endure the oppressive heat. As the hours progressed, the Samaritans became more and more anxious.

"The Romans have surrounded the mountain!" I heard them ranting. "They're felling the trees! They're going to set it on fire!"

Menander scolded them. "Stop fretting. Don't you know that Simon wields the power of the Nameless God? He can squelch any fire with the breath of his lips. This is hallowed ground. From here the Sons of the Elect are invincible. Have no fear. Whatever may happen, your souls have been saved."

A short time later, the dreaded moment arrived. I heard Jesse's defiant voice. They'd caught him! I sank down in despair.

"Bring her here!" I heard Simon cry.

Saturninus and Cerinthus suddenly appeared over me.

"Give us your hands," said Cerinthus with a greasy smile. "The Standing One has something for you to witness."

I raised up my bound hands. I had to see Jesse. I had to see his face. They hoisted me out. The Sons of the Elect and all of the Samaritans were gathered around the remains of an altar at the front of the temple ruins. There was a wall of stone behind the altar. Tied to the front of the wall with his hands hoisted high was young Jesse. His right hand was still bandaged from the wound he'd received from Simon's archer. Except for being in such an uncomfortable position, he looked basically unharmed.

His face flashed excitement when he saw me. I was brought to stand directly in front of the altar. Jesse and I looked at each other *with pain. We'd endured so much. The tragedy that it should all end so fruitlessly right back where we started was almost too much to bear.*

The Sons of the Elect looked hungry for blood. The Samaritan peasants looked bewildered. They were still stewing about the army of Romans preparing to ignite the mountain. I noticed that the women were off to the left, brewing something over a large fire. It smelled horrid, like flowers and honey mixed with ammonia. To the north, in the branches of a large tree, I saw a man overlooking the whole gathering. It was the red-bearded archer with close-set eyes. Why, I wondered, would he be positioned up there?

Simon glided effortlessly to the front of the gathering. He stopped behind the altar, directly between Jesse and me. Then he climbed up on the altar stone.

"Sons of Light!" he shouted. "Today is our day of victory! Everything I have prophesied has come to pass. Can anyone deny the miracles? Our captives have returned of their own accord. The Scroll of Most Sacred Knowledge is on its way up the mountain at this very hour. The Sons of Darkness encircle us on all sides. Does anyone fear?"

A resounding "No!" rose up from the Sons of the Elect. I shivered with apprehension.

"The Romans cannot have any power over us. Our souls are already reaching out to the Immortal God. We need only the secret knowledge to consummate our final triumph. The victory will then be ours for all eternity. No demon of earth or hell may take it from us. And yet . . ." Simon climbed down from the altar and slipped his hands smoothly inside the folds of his robe. ". . . there is evil among us. Evil of the most vile and wicked sort. Until this evil is rooted out and destroyed, there can be no redemption for any of us. No unclean thing can dwell in the presence of the Great and Unknown God. As long as this evil is allowed to flourish and breathe, we are all unclean by association. Therefore, it becomes my solemn responsibility as the one who stands in God's image to crush its existence for all eons of time."

Simon's hands emerged from inside the folds of his robe. My heart stopped. Oh, my gosh! *He had a* snake! *There was a pale white snake about four feet long with pink eyes and a diamond-shaped head. I cringed in terror. The Sons of the Elect looked enraptured. The peasants gasped and stepped back. I tried to wrench myself free so I could run. Saturninus and Cerinthus held me firmly. I wanted to shrink. I hated snakes. Oh, I hated snakes. I hated them, hated them, with every crawling, squirming cell in my body.*

Simon wasn't even holding its head or hindering its movements in any way. It just rolled freely in his hands, its eyes alert and its red tongue flicking. It opened its mouth and struck lightning fast at the air. A few of the peasants shrieked and fell backwards. I was shaking violently. Where had it come from? I didn't want to know. Like the serpents of Pharaoh's magicians, it was sorcery for sure. I didn't doubt in the least that the creature's bite was lethal.

Simon took a step toward Jesse.

"Simon, no!" *I screeched.* "What do you want! I'll do anything! Please don't! Please!*"*

Simon didn't even falter. He continued moving slowly toward Jesse. I broke down in sobs, fighting to break free. I almost escaped. Two more of Simon's men moved in to help hold me. Jesse did not panic. He stood as rigid as a statue. Simon moved the snake right under his nose. It lingered there, flicking its tongue. I heard it hiss. It was ready to strike! *Jesse didn't budge a muscle. He held his breath and pinched his eyes shut. A tear squeezed out.*

But the snake did not strike.

Simon seemed satisfied. He pulled the snake back and turned to face the crowd. Then he looked at me! *The sorcerer's eyebrows were raised high. Slowly, he moved the creature toward my face.* Please, Heavenly Father! *I prayed.* If I have to die, I'll die any other way! Not this way, God! Not this way!

My eyes shut tightly. I felt the creature's head move through my hair. Its tongue flicked my ear. My mind started spinning out of control. I tried to faint. I wanted to faint! Some force kept me conscious. Simon pulled it back. When I dared to open my eyes again, the sorcerer looked gleeful, like a sadistic child. He moved the snake to the left, in front of Saturninus.

And then the serpent struck.

Saturninus released a terrible gurgling sound as the snake's fangs sank deep into his jugular. He let go of my shoulder and tried to pull the snake away. He clawed at it with his hands, spinning in a circle. At last the snake dropped to the ground, slithering into a crack between the stones. Saturninus fell against the altar. He hung there, gaping back at Simon, his face frozen in ultimate shock. Simon glared back with revulsion. I watched Saturninus' face turn white and then purple. He started convulsing. I turned away in horror, listening to his shrieks of agony.

"Thus is the fate of all who seek to betray the Aeons and their servants!" raged Simon. "Fade back into the abyss, Saturninus of Samaria. Fade away. Fade away."

Saturninus' shrieks grew quieter, then went silent. When I looked again, his body was behind the altar. There was no movement in his legs. The Second Elect was dead.

I closed my eyes again and prayed for strength. I felt my shoulders released as they let me go. Cerinthus, Menander, and all the other Sons of the Elect fell to their knees before Simon. Steadily, perhaps out of pure terror, the peasants of Samaria began to kneel as well. I took advantage of my freedom and rushed to Jesse. I touched his face with my bound hands and pressed close to his side.

Simon had his arms outstretched, basking in his followers' adoration.

"Now," said Simon, "the moment has arrived. We must all make way for the Sons of Darkness who bring with them the Words of Light."

I caught my breath. I looked down the pathway leading to the edge of the western slope of Gerizim. Three people were approaching from the trees. Tears sprang from my eyes. I knew them all! One was Gid—I could never pronounce his full name—the Nephite we *found injured in the tunnel. The other was Garth!* Harry's Uncle Garth! *Was it possible? And the last one I'd have known anywhere. My champion, my friend, and my brother, Harrison Hawkins. My soul exulted with gladness.*

But how could I feel joy? The nightmare had reached its blackest moment. Here we were, about to be reunited in the face of the grimmest gathering ever combined. The crowd parted for their arrival. The three men looked stunned by the way that Simon seemed to have been expecting them. They approached slowly and cautiously. Harry was in the middle. He held a leather satchel. Protruding from the top was a scroll. Unlike the Scroll of Matthew, it had a large clay-colored seal near the edge. Was it really the Scroll of Knowledge? I would never have believed it. He'd really done it. He'd really gone to Jerusalem. How was it possible? I would never have thought in a hundred years he could ever succeed. But here he was. He'd done it for Jesse. He'd done it for me.

CHAPTER TWENTY

We stopped abruptly twenty yards from the circle of ruins where Meagan and Jesse were being held. I looked at my friends who I hadn't seen in ten days. Tears came to my eyes. They looked battered and bruised, but they were *alive*.

Simon stood in the center of the crowd, just waiting, his arms folded, as if he'd foreseen this exact moment. But I'd come as far as I was willing to come.

"Simon!" I called out. "I've brought what you wanted. I have it here. Now let them go."

Simon moved directly in front of the stone altar. "Bring it here, Harry Hawkins. Put it in my hands."

"First let them go. As soon as you cut them loose, I'll set it on the ground. I've done as you asked. Now let us leave in peace."

"Unacceptable," Simon snapped.

He let the word ring in the air. My flesh went cold. What was I going to do? Shout, "No deal!" turn around, and walk off? That might be the precise moment Simon started cutting throats. If his followers all charged us at once, we didn't stand much of a chance anyway.

"How do I know that it's really what you say it is?" Simon asked. "I'm afraid I can't release your friends until it's sitting in my fingers. Not until I've read its words and confirmed that it is the Scroll of Knowledge."

"It's a trap," Gid said in a low voice.

I sighed, exasperated. "What are we supposed to do?"

"Tell him about Apollus," said Garth.

My eyes widened in dismay. Apollus was our wild card. He'd crept up to the summit by a different path. I'd seen the flash of his shadow in the trees to our left. If we told them about Apollus, we had no cards left.

"Garth is right," said Gid. "Tell Simon we have a man with an arrow trained right at his heart. Let Apollus hear it too. Tell Simon he can break the seals and read the scroll as long as he likes, but he has to stay in the open. When he's satisfied, tell him to let Meagan and Jesse go."

I shook my head. "You don't understand. The threat of an arrow wouldn't even *faze* Simon."

Gid let this sink in, then he turned to me, deflated. "It's all we have, Harry. Unless you have another suggestion."

I had none. Bristling with frustration, I told Simon our terms. I said it loud enough for Apollus to hear. Simon lapped it up. He liked the terms. He liked them far too much.

"Let your bowman train his arrow wherever he likes," said Simon. "Now bring me the scroll."

"Stay here," I told Garth and Gid. "No reason for all of us to go in."

"If you go in, we all go in." Gidgiddonihah pulled his gladiator sword out of its sheath.

"Tell your friend to leave his sword!" snapped Simon. "If your unseen companion is as proficient as you believe, what need do you have of other weapons?"

I watched the vein throbbing in Gid's neck. His nostrils were flaring. He tossed his sword to the dirt. This had become almost farcical. Simon had us exactly where he wanted us. All we had left, if things went wrong, was to hope that Apollus could signal his men. He'd have to run two hundred yards to reach a place where they could see him. Even if he made it, what were the chances that any of us would be alive when the cavalry got here?

The sun had nearly reached the edge of the hills. From the perspective of the men at the base of the mountain, it might have already touched down. Any minute the Romans would start their fires. I figured there were at least fifteen hundred soldiers at the base of Gerizim. If every one of them had a torch and moved from tree to tree, this place would go up like a haystack. In a matters of hours, it would become a barren, smoldering mound. Man, I wanted to be off this mountain before the fireworks started! It didn't appear that this was even a remote possibility.

We walked in. Simon waited patiently, gloating from head to foot.

"Harry!" said Meagan. "Simon has his own archer. In those trees!"

I looked where Meagan was pointing. There he was. Our old friend from Qumran. While Apollus had an arrow aimed at Simon, Simon's archer had an arrow aimed right at me. Could this scene become any more grim?

Simon put out his hand. "The scroll," he demanded.

I reached into my shoulder sack and pulled it out. I shuddered with regret as I placed it into Simon's scabby hand. *That's it*, I thought. *The deed is done.* What was left to keep us alive?

Simon's hands were shaking with delight as he squeezed the scroll firmly in his grip. He held it high over his head.

"Feast your eyes on earth's highest knowledge!" he shouted. "Our work is all but finished! The secrets are ours! Now we will all pass by the Aeons who stand as sentinels at the gates of eternity and gain our golden inheritance in spite of earth and hell!"

The cheering had nearly reached a frenzy. Everywhere Simon's men were crying tears of unrestrained joy. My nerves were set on edge. The spirit was darker than I'd ever felt it before. Simon's followers began swarming all around. There was no way Apollus could have gotten a clear shot.

"Let them go, Simon!" I commanded. "You have what you wanted. Now let us all go."

"Harry, how could you ask such a thing?!" crooned Simon. "Don't you realize what is about to happen? As soon as I read these words, I will know everything that must be known to grant exaltation to whomever I choose. There will be nothing left for us on this corrupt, material earth. I'm inviting you to join us! Despite your ignorance! Despite your impurity!"

I started trembling. I was beginning to understand. The horror welled up in my throat. No *wonder* Simon had brought his followers up here. No wonder they didn't fear the Romans. They never intended to fight any battles. They never intended to face the fires that would soon sweep over Gerizim like a flood. Like Jamestown, like Waco, like those weirdos in California who wanted to ride the comet—*they intended to take their own lives!*

"Let us go, Simon!" I shouted. "You gave us your word!"

"My word is to the Immortal God!" he declared. "Bind them!"

The crowd turned on us like a pack of wolves.

"*Apollus!*" shouted Gidgiddonihah.

Gid had saved a dagger. He drew it from his belt. He knew that this would make him the archer's prime target. He spun behind the man named Cleobius. Cleobius was struck directly in the chest. At that same moment I watched the archer himself rear back in agony. He fell from the tree. Apollus had directed his first arrow at *him*.

"Get the bowman!" Simon commanded. "*Slay him!*"

"Apollus, run!" shouted Meagan.

Fifty men, including Menander, took off in the direction of the woods where Apollus' arrow had originated. Gid tried to get at Simon. If nothing else, he wanted to be sure that the twisted leader of the Sons of the Elect never lived to read that scroll. But the delay as he dodged the arrow was just enough for Simon's men to pounce on him from all directions. Simon slipped through to the outside of the crowd. Gid fought like a lion, but there were too many of them. The butt end of a lance caught him on the jaw.

Garth had been thrown down, his hands hoisted behind his back. I was seized from behind. They had my legs as well and wrestled me to the ground. I felt the rope as it was cinched around my wrist. I wrenched out a cry of despair.

Looking south I saw Apollus bolt from the trees. He'd killed two men with his arrows, but there were dozens more. He ran pell-mell toward the slope to signal his horsemen. Arrows were being fired at him. I watched him leap into a ravine and disappear. Menander and the Samaritan soldiers plunged into the ravine after him.

My mind sank into oblivion as I was dragged over to kneel with the others along the wall, like trophies on a bookshelf. I smelled smoke. The Romans had already started the fires. At the same time I smelled a terrible odor from a boiling iron pot about thirty feet to our left. It was like nothing I'd ever smelled before. One of the women near the pot—a husky woman with a gaping underbite—was laying out a set of eight wooden goblets. *It's the poison*, I told myself. This was how Simon intended to help his followers receive their "golden inheritance."

The Sons of the Elect looked resigned, even hypnotized. The peasants looked nervous and frightened. They hadn't quite understood their final fate until now. But they believed in Simon. They'd seen his magic. They were willing to do whatever he asked.

I looked at my companions. Gid was shaking off the blow from the lance. He and Garth fought against the ropes. Meagan held onto Jesse. Simon had cracked two of the seals on the scroll. His fingers were working on the last.

"We're almost ready, my children," said Simon. "Rejoice! Prepare your minds for our painless journey to the seat of bliss and oneness. We'll begin with our captives. Then you shall see. Even the impure will feel no pain, unlike Saturninus, whose soul has been annihilated. Only myself and Cerinthus the Divine will remain to very last. When we join you in your journey, we will possess the sacred keys."

Gidgiddonihah was looking at me fiercely. I couldn't figure it out. Was he angry at me? Then it struck me like a bolt of lightning.

The blade!

A week ago in the hills of Judea, Gid had given me a broken blade. He'd taken it from the bandits who'd attacked Symeon and Mary. *Find a place for this*, he'd said. *A hidden blade could save your life.* That very night I'd sewed it into the hem of my cloak. The cloak was so heavy and scratchy that I'd nearly forgotten. Now I felt behind my back until my fingers discovered the stiff piece of metal. I'd wrapped it in a piece of leather. The blade was only three inches long—barely long enough to get a grip. I found the tip and tried to work it through. At that instant Menander and the Samaritans came scrambling back into the ruins, running at full tilt.

"They're coming!" Menander shouted. "Hundreds of horsemen! They'll be here in minutes!"

Tears sprang from Meagan's eyes. "Apollus made it," she whispered.

Urgency gripped the hearts of Simon's followers.

"Fill the goblets!" called out the man named Cerinthus the Divine.

The women fulfilled the command.

"Bring the first goblet here!" said Simon.

Gid looked at me in desperation. Garth glanced at my hands, then glanced away quickly. I worked the tip through the cloth and slid the blade into my palm. I started cutting. I sliced my finger! The blade was just so small.

The woman with the underbite brought the first goblet filled with hot poison and handed it to Cerinthus. Cerinthus walked it toward Simon. Other goblets were filled. Smoke was drifting up from the base of the mountain on all sides. The fires were spreading. Simon took the cup from Cerinthus.

I dropped the blade! It fumbled right out of my fingers! The cord was only half severed. Gidgiddonihah went white. I couldn't reach down to grab it. Simon and Menander were standing right over me!

Simon held up the goblet for all to see. "By this sweet nectar we bid farewell to this wicked world and unite our hearts with prophets and kings. Bow your heads and let us pray."

Heads bowed and eyes closed. This was my chance. I bent down. Garth leaned against me to keep me from falling over. My fingers found the blade.

"O Father of Life and Light!" Simon prayed. "Father of all that is! Father of that wicked Creator who sentenced us all to our term of mortal misery! Father whose name will never be known while we dwell in the flesh! We give thanks to thee for the sacred knowledge that is now ours. We thank thee that we may all escape this cycle of death and embrace thee among the clouds. Make our journey sweet, dear Father! Into thy hands we commend our spirits!"

"Amen!" cried the congregation with tears of ecstasy.

"*Wait!*" cried Meagan. "Don't do this thing! Simon is a liar! He's a deceiver! This is suicide! He's fooled every one of you! He's a demon! You can't let him make you do this!"

"Is it more honorable to die by a Roman sword?" asked Menander.

That squelched all arguments. Meagan fell silent. In the distance we could hear thundering hooves as the horsemen neared the summit. Goblets were distributed through the crowd. All they needed was Simon's cue.

Simon looked into my eyes. He floated the steaming goblet close to my lips. Several men stood nearby in case I offered resistance.

"Sip it slowly, Harry Hawkins," Simon advised. "It only takes a few drops."

At that instant the cord that bound my hands snapped.

CHAPTER TWENTY-ONE

I screamed as Simon pushed the cup against Harry's lips. Suddenly Harry's arms exploded from behind his back. His fist knocked the cup out of Simon's hands. The steaming liquid flew right into the face of Menander. The First Elect of the Unknown God screeched in agony and brought his hands to his eyes. I was sure some had splashed into his mouth.

Harry lunged at Simon. The sorcerer fell backwards. At the same moment Gidgiddonihah fell over and grabbed something shiny on the ground. Cerinthus and two other men stepped forward to seize Harry. Garth sprang off his knees. With his hands still tied behind his back, he barreled into Cerinthus' stomach.

"Meagan, pull me down!" shouted Jesse.

I reached up and slipped the rope off the hook above Jesse's head. Harry was fighting four men at once. Others were trying to get into the fray.

Simon staggered to his feet. "Let them all die by the sword!" he shouted.

Garth was on the ground. Another Son of the Elect held a sword over his head. But Gid's hands were free! Before the sword came down, Gid seized the man's arm and wrenched it backwards. Jesse threw himself into the back of a man preparing to attack Gid with a club.

I raised my eyes and looked to the south. The summit of the mountain suddenly erupted with thundering horses and fiery red capes. *Leading the charge was Apollus—my wonderful Apollus!—his sword held high, raising a war whoop at the top of his lungs. The horsemen surged over the lip of the hill, seemingly coming out of a misty fog as smoke continued to engulf the mountain.*

The men of Simon Magus were thrown into confusion. Gid had managed to get his hands on a sword. That effectively ended any ambitions they had of attacking those of us near the altar. The few takers were cut down in a heartbeat. I saw many of Simon's followers drinking from the goblets. It was their last hope for the peaceful, unviolent death Simon had promised. And yet the death looked anything but unviolent. Menander's writhing and vomiting appeared far worse than the torment endured by Saturninus.

The horsemen began to fall on the crowd. Some of Simon's men tried to flee to the woods. Most didn't even make it out of the confines of the temple ruins.

Suddenly a bony white hand clamped over my face. I tried to gasp or scream but the hand was too strong. I'd been standing at wall's edge. Within seconds I was dragged behind it and into the woods. Simon Magus had one arm looped through my bound hands while the other continued to cover my mouth. Inside his robe I saw the Scroll of Knowledge.

I was shocked at his strength. How could he be so strong? He was eighty or ninety and rotting with cancer! Yet he dragged me easily down the trail of the northern slope. Had anyone seen him take me? It had happened so fast!

"Come along, Meagan," said Simon. "Let's find a quiet place. You're my security, my dear. I must have time to study the sacred words."

I couldn't breathe! He'd sealed my mouth and nose under his scabby hand. I started to panic and thrash. I smashed his face with my hands. He grunted and let go. I fell to the ground and began sliding down the trail—sliding right between two burning trees! Below us half the mountain was already raging in flames. I coughed and choked in the smoke. Simon pursued me, his arms reaching and eyes blazing.

* * *

The Roman horsemen rode back and forth across the summit, cutting down anyone who tried to escape. Most of the Samaritans and Sons of the Elect died by their own hand, passing the goblets quickly as the Romans infiltrated their ranks. Apollus was the first one to ride into the hysterical mass. A spirited Samaritan leaped into the air and dragged him off his horse. Just as he was about to put a knife in Apollus' belly, Gidgiddonihah's sword struck him down. Apollus got to his feet and nodded to Gid in thanks.

I was freeing Garth from his bonds when Jesse yelled, "Where's Meagan?"

I turned and looked back toward the wall behind the altar. She wasn't there! Where had she gone? She'd been standing there only seconds ago. Apollus heard Jesse and immediately reacted. His eyes searched all directions.

Garth was looking too—but for someone else. "What happened to Simon?"

I rushed around the wall. Apollus remounted his horse. He rode to the edge of the summit with several other horsemen and peered down the slope. The trees were too thick and obscured by smoke. Daylight was also fading fast.

"Search those woods!" Apollus ordered his men. "Search all the woods on every side!"

One of the horsemen, an officer of equal rank with Apollus, protested. "The fire is climbing too fast, Apollus. We need to ride down that southwest corridor. We need to get our men and horses off this mountain."

"*No!*" Apollus blustered. "We need to find the girl!"

* * *

The burning forest surrounded us in all directions. I continued to scramble downhill to escape Simon's grasp. At last I hit against the base of a tree whose branches overhead were being consumed by the flames. Simon gripped my bangs.

"Get up!" he raged. "Get up or I'll drag you by the hair! Tell me where it is!"

"What?" I shrieked.

"I know you never left this mountain after our ambush. Where were you hiding? Was it a cave?"

I nodded, my mind swimming in terror.

"Where is it?!"

"Please—" I begged.

He tightened his grip on my hair and shook me. "Where is it!"

Sobbing, I pointed down the mountain and across a field of boulders. He started to drag me across the rocks.

"Simon, stop!" a voice shouted above us.

I looked back up the hill. Apollus was perched on the ledge directly over us, sitting atop his horse. The horse threw its head anxiously, reacting to the fire on both sides. Harry, Garth, and Gid were coming down the hill behind him through the only strip of forest not yet aflame. Simon pulled a small curved dagger out of his robe and held it against my throat. The blade was hot. I cried out in anguish.

"Go away!" Simon ranted. "You're all fools! All I wanted was to read the Scroll of Knowledge in peace! You can't save her! You can't even save yourselves! You hear me? You can't even save yourselves!"

At that instant the strip of forest surrounding Apollus and the others exploded into flames. It happened spontaneously! The men threw their arms over their heads as burning branches and leaves rained down. Apollus' horse reared, and Apollus was thrown to the ground. The horse bounded through the fire, back toward the summit.

Simon took a step backward, as if he was still determined to reach the cave. Out of the corner of my eye, I saw something move behind us. I bent my neck in time to see Jesse! Young Jesse was standing on top of a boulder, his arms raised high over his head. In his hands was a rock the size of a car battery. Before Simon could look, Jesse flung the rock with all his might. It hit Simon directly in the back. He was knocked forward. The impact took me with him. I screamed as we toppled to the base of the boulders. The Scroll of Knowledge flew out of Simon's robe, unraveling. I came to a hard stop against a rock while Simon flipped right over the top of me. He crashed into the thick of a burning bush. The branches seemed to suck him in. Almost instantly his white robe burst into flames.

Harry leaped down from the ledge, scrambling to reach me.

"Meagan!" he cried. "Are you all right?"

His voice echoed. My head was spinning. I saw four different images of Harry's face. I also saw the gruesome specter of Simon Magus rising from the flaming bush behind Harry. The fire had engulfed him from head to foot. His long white hair was singed away and the skin of his arms and face were covered with blisters. His mouth was stretched wide in a silent scream. He tried to lunge. The flaming bush wouldn't let him go. He staggered and tripped back, his body overwhelmed by fire. At last his cancerous form seemed to melt into a charred and blackened mass. Simon the Sorcerer, the man who claimed to have already been resurrected, was finally and certainly dead.

The next thing I knew, Jesse, Garth, and Gid were all around me. Harry was leaning over my face, glowing with relief. Where was Apollus? Just then, with his beautiful, blustering arrogance, Apollus pushed his way through the middle of everyone else, wrapping his arms around my body and lifting me into the air as easily as a butterfly.

We were far from out of danger, but I felt as safe as I'd ever felt. All of the strongest, bravest, most wonderful men I'd ever known were surrounding me on all sides.

* * *

"Which way?" I yelled above the roar of the flames.

"Right back where we came from," shouted Apollus. "Straight up the mountain! It's the only way!"

Apollus began climbing with Meagan in his arms. I turned and saw Garth gathering up the Scroll of Knowledge. It had hit the rocks and unraveled like a king's carpet. The end of it was inches from the fire. It looked undamaged, but there was no time to roll it back up. He stuffed it inside his shirt. When he was finished, I took his arm. We quickly climbed to catch Gidgiddonihah, Apollus, and Jesse. The six of us stormed our way up the mountain between the burning trees and falling branches. It was almost as if the flames on both sides were blowing out away from us, as if a thin channel through the fire had opened up, offering us safe passage until we reached the security of the unburning forest near the summit.

We reached the top and coughed the smoke out of our lungs. Without a moment to spare, we started down the rocky corridor on the southwest slope. About a quarter of the way down, we were met by thirty Roman horsemen that Apollus had commanded to wait. They'd nearly given up hope and left without us. Perhaps it was their fear of telling Apollus' father that they'd left his only son that kept them waiting so long. We rode the rest of the way down the mountain on horseback, each of us doubling up with a Roman cavalryman. As soon as we'd crossed the firebreak at the bottom of the mountain, we dismounted and joined the rest of the two hundred horsemen gathered about. I turned back and looked up the mountain.

Night had fallen. The flames were engulfing the summit. Mount Gerizim looked like a volcano with streams of lava flowing down all sides. Jesse came and sat beside me. I put my arm around his shoulder. The wound on his injured hand looked like it had opened up again. It was bleeding beneath the bandages.

"You'd better have that looked at as soon as you can," I said.

"It doesn't even hurt," said Jesse.

"I'll bet," I said, nudging his shoulder with the affection of a big brother.

All of us sat basking in the mountain's glow. Meagan sat comfortably with Apollus' arms around her. I smiled. She seemed to have gotten over her crush on me in a hurry.

Garth was sitting on my opposite side. He'd pulled the Scroll of Knowledge out of his shirt and was carefully rolling it back up the way we'd first found it. I studied Garth's wise and gentle face. Something about him seemed to have profoundly changed. He had a look of deep satisfaction. I knew the cause. Garth had read a portion of the scroll. How could he not have read it? It had been opened right before his eyes.

He noticed me staring and returned a broad smile. He knew that I knew.

"'*The Words of Most Sacred Knowledge*,'" said Garth, repeating the title on the Greek inscription on the outside of the scroll.

"Is it really what it says?" I asked. "Is it the mysteries of the universe?"

"Oh, yes," said Garth. "And much more. The most sacred knowledge that any of us might ever possess. But Simon was wrong to believe it would ever get him into heaven. He was horribly, bitterly mistaken if he thought it would give him some kind of ultimate power. As for all those poor souls who followed him—theirs is the most tragic story of all. They gave him all their faith, all their energy. It was the same old deception: men wanting to know secrets that other men can never know, lusting for powers that no one else can possess. Men like Simon feed on that kind of pride."

"But what does the scroll say?" I asked.

"Everything you were told is true, Harry. This is what the resurrected Savior taught his apostles for forty days before His ascension into heaven. It's also the information that Joseph Smith taught repeatedly and relentlessly to his modern apostles in the months before the martyrdom. But these are not secrets. Not to people of righteousness. Soon, you'll be able to hear these words too, Harry. As can any other endowed member of the Church."

I furrowed my brow. "You mean . . . the temple?"

Garth nodded. "That's all it is. Actually, it's quite a lot, isn't it? It's *everything*! The most sacred blessings that our Father in Heaven can bestow. It's all here, contained in these words. No secrets or formulas. Not complex rites, or recipes for splitting the atom, or distances to Kolob. The simple, sacred covenants of eternal life. The ordinances of the temple. That's what Simon wanted so badly. But he could have never had it. Not if he'd read these words a million times. He chose to pursue a different course long ago. We'll reseal the scroll as soon as we can. Then we'll give it to Symeon to take to John. It won't be long before God has no people on the earth who will hear these words. But it's for John to decide what to do with it now."

Garth finished rolling up the scroll and carefully tucked it back inside his shirt. I sat back and marveled. I laughed at myself a little as well, thinking back on that night when I imagined that the Scroll of Knowledge might help me to harness the powers of the Galaxy Room or cure every disease and affliction that had ever beset the world. I'd been thinking way past the mark. I felt ridiculous and even a little foolish.

Then I thought about it a little longer, and something about it all didn't seem so funny after all. Was I really so far beyond the mark? I thought again about the basics of the gospel of Jesus Christ: faith and hope, charity and love. If the knowledge contained in that scroll really did provide God's most powerful tools to magnify those things, maybe it really did contain the secrets of mastering the powers of the universe.

The hour was late. We mounted several horses and prepared to depart. With the fires of Mount Gerizim lighting the trail before us, Apollus and his cavalrymen brought us to his father's fort outside the village of Neopolis. There we were reunited with Symeon and Mary in a sea of tears and gratitude to our Father in Heaven.

It was time to think about the future. A future that was finally bright and glowing with promise.

Tomorrow we would make our plans to go home.

CHAPTER TWENTY-TWO

I might have slept for a week. We all deserved a few days' rest to heal from our wounds and bruises. But something more powerful was driving us now—the thought of being reunited with our families. The idea renewed my energy in a way I would have never dreamed possible.

But there was still one thing to do before Meagan, Garth, Gid, and I began the long journey home. We were determined to help Mary and Symeon reach the seaport at Ceasarea where they could take the scrolls and safely board a ship bound for Ephesus. Symeon, Mary, and little Jesse were still Jews in a land that was very hostile to them. Commander Severillus of Neopolis had to write a special recommendation so they could travel without fear of harassment. All the seaports for hundreds of miles were flooded with captives from the war, mostly Jews and Samaritans, waiting to being shipped off to destinations across the Roman empire. There was a real possibility that if our Jewish companions showed up in Ceasarea without special papers and a Roman escort, they could be rounded up by the local authorities.

It was decided after a short discussion—mostly because of Mary's insistence—that Jesse would join them in their journey to the Seven Churches. In essence, he would become Symeon's adopted son, an idea that filled the old man with beaming pride since he'd never had a son of his own. Jesse was also thrilled. Frankly, he had few options left.

Apollus was given leave to accompany us to Ceasarea, much to the delight and relief of Meagan who was not looking forward to saying good-bye. The day after we reached the fort at Neopolis she nervously filled me in on the awkward situation she'd created for herself—and for me.

"We're Roman citizens from Sicily," she explained.

"We are?"

"That's right. Provo, Sicily. You and I are brother and sister. Our father is a wealthy sea merchant named Romeo Travolta—"

"Romeo Tra—? That's the best name you could come up with?"

"Let me finish. We were kidnapped in Ceasarea by Simon Magus. Actually from here everything is pretty much how it happened. Oh, one other thing. Our family owns a lot of slaves, Jesse being one of them."

"How do we explain him going with Symeon to Ephesus?"

"Already covered it," said Meagan. "I told Apollus that I was giving him his manumission in gratitude for his saving my life. I'm setting him free."

"You're good."

"Thank you."

"But you have to stop telling stories, Meagan. They're gonna get us into a lot of trouble one day."

"This is the last one. Cross my heart. We just have to pull off this charade another few days. Then we'll have Apollus and all the other Romans out of our lives for good."

She frowned. No matter what she said, I could tell she wasn't looking forward to that moment at all.

"What are you gonna tell Apollus when it's time to say good-bye?" I asked. "I think he likes you. So does his father. Folks around here get married pretty young. Chances are, if he thinks you're going to Sicily, one day he'll come looking for you."

"I'll just give him a fake phone number," shrugged Meagan. "Girls do that all the time, right?" Meagan tried to grin, but she couldn't hide the pain.

"It won't be easy, will it?" I observed.

She sighed miserably. "Oh, Harry. I've really done it to myself this time. It's going to be the most awful moment of my life." She looked back at me. "How will it be for you when you say good-bye to Mary?"

I stared off into space. "She's a wonderful girl. Strong, beautiful . . ." I felt a stab of grief. "Ah, this is ridiculous! We're not even old enough to date. We'll forget about them. And they'll forget about us."

"I've seen the way she looks at you, Harry. I think she really hopes you'll change your mind and sail with her to Ephesus."

The stab went in deeper. I swallowed it down. "We have to let them go, Meagan. There's no other choice."

Her eyes filled with tears. I tried to comfort her with a hug. This was the hardest part of traveling to other worlds and times. You knew when you said good-bye, it was probably forever.

Two days later we reached the bustling seaport of Ceasarea. For the first time in this entire journey, my feet weren't sore and swollen. Apollus had arranged for us to take horses from the camp stables.

We went down to the docks to find a ship for Mary and Symeon. It was getting late in the season for shipping on the Mediterranean. There were no ships going to Ephesus until spring. The best we could do was buy passage to Athens on a vessel leaving the following morning. Symeon was confident he could hire another ship there to take him the short journey across the Aegean Sea. To pay for the trip, Gidgiddonihah sold the red ruby from the hilt of his gladiator sword. It bought tickets for all three passengers, with enough left over to buy all the supplies we would need to reach the cavern near the fortress of Masada. Gid was eager to keep the rest of the jewels handy in case we needed to bribe any Roman patrols along the way.

The moment of departure arrived the following morning. It began with a fond farewell to Jesse. I gave him a strong embrace.

"Brothers forever?" I asked.

"Brothers forever," he replied.

The moment was particularly difficult for Meagan. She and Jesse had been through so much. That small boy practically worshipped the ground Meagan walked on. Not only because he thought she was a prophetess. I think the nine-year-old had had a secret crush on her the entire time.

"I'm never going to see you again, am I?" Jesse choked out as they embraced.

"Don't say that," insisted Meagan, tears streaming down her face. "We *will.* Remember my powers," she winked. "Just imagine that I can see you wherever you are, Jesse. Whatever you do. One day I expect to see a strong young man, a beautiful wife, and lots of kids, living far away from here."

"Yes," said Jesse. That's all he could say.

Symeon could hardly speak either for all the emotions swelling in his throat.

"Take care of those scrolls," I said to him. "You have no idea what they'll mean one day to billions of people."

"I'll guard them with my life," he said. "And I'll never forget you, Harry of Germania."

Next came the most difficult moment of all. Mary had said very little all morning.

"I don't understand, Harry," she said finally. "I don't understand why you can't come to Ephesus. It's not far. I only need to see that my father settles safely with the saints. You could travel home right after."

I didn't know what to say. She had only a vague picture of where we were really from. It didn't seem to change my feelings about her. Something inside me seriously considered her offer. *Sail to Ephesus*, a voice resounded.

It just wasn't possible. We held each other a long time. And then a strange feeling set in, an impression that I *would* see her again in some strange place and time. I shrugged it off, but as I watched her ship row away from the dock, the feeling wouldn't go away. She stood on the deck with her eyes glued to mine. I didn't turn away until the ship was a tiny speck on the horizon.

Before we left the dock, Apollus asked Meagan, "When will you and your brother sail back to Sicily?"

"Soon," said Meagan awkwardly. "A few days."

"I see," said Apollus. "Perhaps I should wait until then."

"No," she said with difficulty. "You have to get back. Your father will be anxious for your return."

"My father's orders were to remain with you until I was certain you were safe. I've never disobeyed my commanding officer. I'd receive thirty stripes."

"I'm safe enough," said Meagan. "I shouldn't ask you to stay any longer."

"Just the same," said Apollus. "I'll stay until your ship departs."

I started to become concerned. Meagan had a dog-loyal fan on her hands. I feared we weren't going to get out of town without Apollus finding out that Meagan wasn't really who she claimed to be.

But Meagan, in her smoothest fashion, conjured a solution.

"Actually," she said. "We might not take a ship. We might just travel overland to Egypt. That's where my father is stationed at this time of year. We might as well travel home on one of *his* ships. Don't you think?"

Apollus frowned. Traveling to Egypt probably *was* pushing his father's orders a bit far. There really was nothing to keep him from returning to his post at Neopolis.

Meagan's face filled with distress. She'd succeeded in her objective far better than she'd intended. She opened her mouth as if to say something else. I think she was actually tempted to ask him to help us reach the cavern. A Roman escort would surely have been helpful. I stiffened. If Meagan asked, Apollus would immediately suspect everything she'd said. The repercussions for all of us could be disastrous.

To my relief, she closed her mouth and said instead, "But if you wanted to stay until tomorrow morning, I'd be very grateful."

"Yes," said Apollus, looking into her eyes. "That much would be appropriate."

We put up that night in one of the several inns along the waterfront. Ceasarea was a new and clean-looking city. Apollus called it the Roman pearl of the East. I was glad to have one more night of rest, but I was still eager to be on our way. The streets were filled with soldiers and slaves and people of every rough-and-tumble sort that you might expect in an ancient seaport.

Our room was on the second story. There was a balcony overlooking the cool, dark waters of the Mediterranean. I might have thought it was a modern hotel smack dab in the center of a Middle-eastern paradise, except for the smells of camels and sweat, and the bustling sounds of the first-century world.

I leaned over the railing that night, basking in the glow of the orange-crimson sunset and listening to the soothing rhythm of the surf breaking against a stone wall several hundred feet offshore. Gidgiddonihah joined me at the balcony. We smiled at each other, thinking to ourselves how far we had come.

"What will you do, Gid?" I asked him candidly. "Will you go back to Zarahemla?"

"That's my home," he said. "Where else should I go?"

"It may not be the home you knew. Thirty-six years may have passed. There may be no one left who even knows who you are."

"It will still be my home. Where else would you suggest?"

"You could always . . . come to my world," I said.

He shook his head regretfully. "I'd only be a stranger in your world. Just as I'm a stranger here. I long for the clear skies and green mountains of Zarahemla. I'm getting older, Harry. I think my warrior days are nearly over. It's time that I found another good woman and raised a family in the world I know."

I smiled sorrowfully. I knew he was right. And yet I would have loved to have shown the Nephite warrior life in the twenty-first century. I decided not to count out such possibilities quite yet. Home was still a far distance away. Anything could still happen.

A part of me felt strangely regretful, almost as if I'd left something undone in the world of 70 A.D. I never had reached a stronghold of the Church. I never had felt the security of being among the saints. I almost wished I could have known how the Church had kept the light of faith burning in such darkening times. But I dismissed such thoughts. For now nothing in my mind burned stronger than my desire to go home.

I closed my eyes and thought of my family. I missed them so much. A long journey still lay ahead. But tonight I had the company of my best friends in the world and the glow of a Mediterranean sunset.

Whatever awaited, I knew with God's help, I could always come off the conqueror in any adventure.

EPILOGUE

My name is Jim Hawkins.

My son, Harry, is fifteen years old. He's been missing now for nearly six months. It's a fact I can't escape. But it's a fact that I refuse any longer to fear.

The Spirit has whispered comfort to a father's weary heart. I know that all my desires and hopes, faith, and prayers will come to pass. All in the Lord's due time.

For now I glory in the blessings that are already mine. My daughter, Melody, is much stronger. Her treatments are complete. She looks healthy and beautiful. I fully believe she is on her way to a full and remarkable recovery. But most comforting of all, she has Marcos, her one and true love.

As for my son, I'm certain that I will see him again. In fact, I've seen the day. I've seen it as clearly as any vision. The details may be obscured by the sheer brightness of the event. But I know it will happen. And I know it will be happen soon enough.

Harry, my boy, if somehow you can hear a father's quiet whisperings through the fabric of time and space, then hear this: Everything will be all right. How do I know this? Because I'm your father. You're a part of me. It's a connection that can never be severed.

And because . . . I love you.

ABOUT THE AUTHOR

CHRIS HEIMERDINGER'S FIRST NOVEL, *TENNIS Shoes Among the Nephites*, first appeared in August of 1989. With the twelfth installment, *Drums of Desolation*, the Tennis Shoes Adventure series has sold over a million and half copies on book and audio. Chris is the author of the novel *Passage to Zarahemla* and producer/director of the feature film of the same name, as well as its book sequel, *Escape from Zarahemla*, which are now officially part of the Tennis Shoes "universe." He is also the producer/songwriter on the album *Whispered Visions*. With *Drums of Desolation*, Chris presents the twentieth novel of his writing career—a creative span of more than a quarter century.

He is married to Emily and has eleven children, the youngest being Hunter Helaman, who is pictured here. Chris lives with his family in Providence, Utah.